REDWORLD

Redworld is published by
Capstone Young Readers, A Capstone Imprint
1710 Roe Crest Drive
North Mankato, Minnesota 56003
www.mycapstone.com

Library of Congress Cataloging-in-Publication Data
Names: Collins, A. L. (Ai Lynn), 1964– author. | Tikulin, Tomislav, illustrator.
Title: Redworld : year one / by A.L. Collins ; illustrated by Tomislav Tikulin.
Description: North Mankato, Minnesota : Capstone Young Readers, [2018] | Series: Redworld |
Summary: Twelve-year-old Belle Song finds it hard to adapt when she and her
   parents move to Mars and begin farming, but soon new friends introduce her to
   all the red planet has to offer.
Identifiers: LCCN 2017025503 (print) | LCCN 2017039147 (ebook) |
   ISBN 9781623709877 (reflowable epub) | ISBN 9781623709860 (paperback)
Subjects: | CYAC: Life on other planets—Fiction. | Moving, Household—Fiction. |
   Farm life—Fiction. | Toleration—Fiction. | Friendship—Fiction. | Mars—Fiction. | Science fiction.
Classification: LCC PZ7.1.C6447 (ebook) | LCC PZ7.1.C6447 Red 2018 (print) | DDC [Fic]—dc23
LC record available at https://lccn.loc.gov/2017025503

Previously published as four library-bound editions:
Homestead: A New Life on Mars – ISBN 978-1-4965-4819-1
Raiders: Water Thieves of Mars – ISBN 978-1-4965-4820-7
Tharsis City: The Wonder of Mars – ISBN 978-1-4965-4821-4
Legacy: Relics of Mars – ISBN 978-1-4965-4822-1

Editor: Aaron J. Sautter
Designer: Ted Williams
Production: Kathy McColley

I'd like to thank everyone who's had a hand in making this book a reality, especially to Aaron, my
editor. This book was truly a collaboration. A huge shoutout to my Back Row Ninjas and to the
Grou. You are the reason I dare to write. Sonnie, your patience and generosity have allowed me
to pursue this dream. Bekah, Niki, and Laura – you are my inspiration. To my four pups, who sit
around me at my computer and listen attentively as I read aloud to them every day – good dogs!
And finally, I'd like to dedicate this book to all children who, like me, dream of what lies among
the stars. — A.L. Collins

Printed and bound in Canada.
010789S18

REDWORLD

YEAR ONE

BY A.L. COLLINS

ILLUSTRATED BY TOMISLAV TIKULIN

Capstone Young Readers
a capstone imprint

MT. OLYMPUS
(RESERVOIR)

MT. ASCREUS

MT. PAVONIS

MT. ARSIA

SIRENUM ROAD

BARREN
LANDS

CITIES

ROADS

MOUNTAINS

FOREST

DESALINATION
PLANTS

FARMS

ABANDONED
FARMS

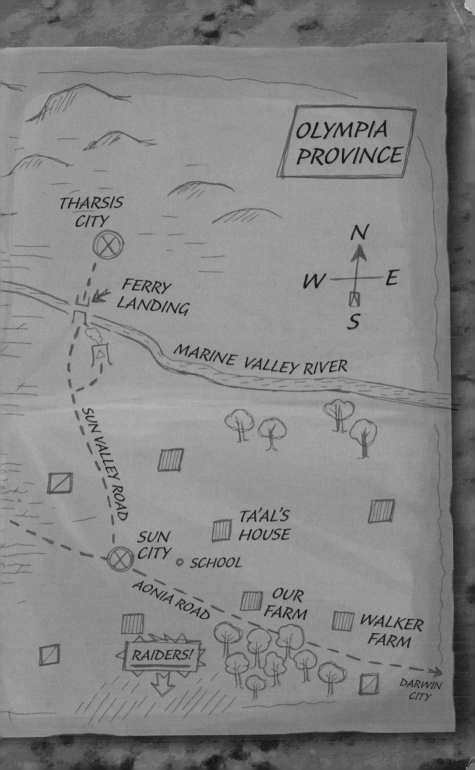

Belle Song
Twelve-year-old Belle can be headstrong and stubborn. Her curiosity and sense of adventure often get her into trouble. Still, she has a good heart and is passionate about fairness. She is fiercely loyal to her friends.

Yun and Zara Song
Belle's parents sometimes seem really strict. But Yun has a great sense of humor, which Belle both loves and is embarrassed by. Zara has a generous heart, which has taught Belle not to judge others too quickly.

Melody
Melody is an old model 3X Personal Home Helper android. She was given to Belle by her grandmother before she passed away. Melody is Belle's best friend and protector, and she enjoys telling bad jokes to seem more human.

MAIN INHABITANTS

Lucas Walker
Lucas is Belle's neighbor and classmate. He is part Sulux and part human. Meeting new people is not easy for him. But once he knows someone, his adventurous side emerges. He is full of ideas, which sometimes gets him and his friends into trouble.

Ta'al
Ta'al and her family are Nabian, an ancient alien race from another star system. Born and raised on Mars, Ta'al is intelligent and curious. She enjoys exploring and adventure and quickly becomes Belle's closest friend on Mars.

Raider
Raider is a hybrid wolf-dog. These animals were bred to be tame pets, but some of them became wild. After Raider is rescued by Belle, he becomes a faithful and protective companion.

It is the year 2335. Life on Earth is very difficult. Natural resources like trees, water, and oil are nearly gone. Many animal species have become extinct, and air pollution is causing widespread disease across the planet. More than 50 years ago, intelligent androids rose up to overthrow their human creators. After the Robot Rebellion, many Terrans, people from Earth, were suspicious of advanced technology. They chose to return to a simpler, more basic lifestyle. Only a few families kept their outdated, less-advanced androids to help them with work and family.

Many people have traveled to the Moon to begin a new life on Lunar Colony. But it's overcrowded and has limited space and resources. So now many families are choosing to move to Mars instead. With the help of two alien races — the Sulux and the Nabians — the red planet was transformed to support life. Terraforming the red planet has taken nearly 200 years.

Mars has much more to offer those searching for a new beginning. Opportunities for work can be found in the planet's largest cities or in the areas set aside as farmland. For those willing to face Mars' unpredictable weather, dangerous water raiders, and other unexpected surprises, adventure awaits them on . . .

REDWORLD

PART ONE:
A NEW LIFE

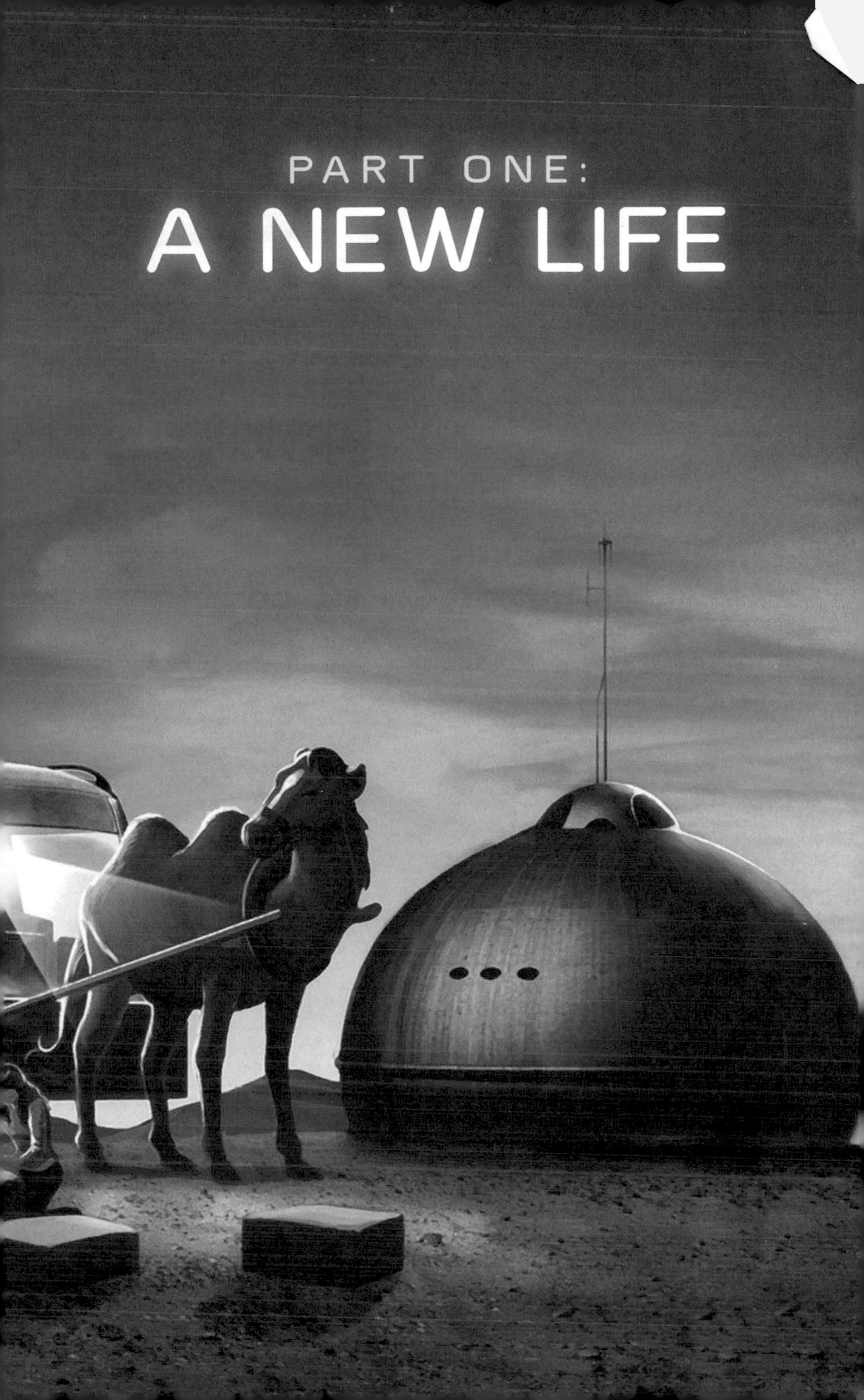

Hoping to begin a new and better life, the Song family has cashed in their savings and moved to Mars. But as soon as they arrive, they learn that their new jobs with the Belt Asteroid Mining Corporation, or BAMCorp, have been eliminated by the company.

What will they do now? They can't return to Earth, where nothing but hardship awaits them. Their only option is to find a way to build a new life for themselves here on this strange new world . . .

CHAPTER 1
STUCK ON MARS

"So we came all the way to this planet for nothing?"

Belle couldn't believe their bad luck. The Song family had sold all of their belongings and flown to Mars to start a new life. Her parents had been so excited about their new jobs with BAMCorp . . . and now those jobs were gone.

"Made redundant." Whatever that meant. Those were the actual words used by the company's representative.

"What do we do now?" Belle's mom, Zara, pressed her hands to her temples in frustration.

"BAMCorp gave us a week's stay in a hotel here in Utopia. They'll pay for the return trip too. Bah!" Her dad, Yun, exhaled loudly. "Some comfort that is!"

"I believe you are using sarcasm," Melody, Belle's android companion and best friend, chimed in. "Would a joke help to make you feel better?"

Belle nudged her. Melody often said the wrong thing at the wrong time in her quest to be more human. Secretly, Belle was happy that they'd be heading back to Earth. She'd never wanted to move in the first place.

"Let's go to the hotel, then," Belle said. She was careful not to sound too cheerful.

Zara sighed. She pulled her long hair back into a ponytail and put on her brave smile.

"The hotel can wait," she said. "On the way here, I saw a lively marketplace. Why don't we do some exploring first?"

Outside the corporation's big, black gates, the Song family was attacked by hot, red dust. Belle sneezed uncontrollably. Melody's white body became a dusty rust color in a matter of seconds.

The red dust was everywhere. People kicked it into the air as they walked. Transports created giant dust clouds with their wheels. Low flying shuttles whipped up even more. There was so much dust that the sky looked brown and rusty. And there wasn't a single tree to be seen. This was why Earth people rarely moved to Mars.

"Isabelle Song! Keep up," Zara called. "We don't want to lose you in this crowd."

"Coming." Belle rolled her eyes. She hated when her parents used her full name.

The market was crowded. Row upon row of makeshift stalls were crammed together. The fabric roofs flapped in the breeze as vendors shouted to people passing by.

"Finest meal worm flour this side of Mars!"

"Most tender meat you'll ever taste!"

"Scarves of all colors — buy two, get one free!"

People filled the alleys, making bargains and shouting at each other. Melody shuffled along next to Belle. Zara stopped at one stall and bought scarves for herself and Belle to wrap around their heads. Melody got one too. Belle tied it around her android's neck joint to help keep the dust out.

"You look just like a Martian girl," Zara said. But Belle didn't want to be a Martian girl. She was Terran and couldn't wait to head back to Earth.

The scarf did help Belle to breathe better though. She relaxed enough to enjoy checking out the merchants' stalls.

She was struck by all the smells — roasted meats mixed with flowery perfumes. It made her stomach grumble and her nose tickle at the same time. Walking through the alleys, she was drawn to a store that sold antique books.

"Journals . . . these are rare back on Earth," Zara said, picking up a soft, brown, leather-bound book. On the front cover was an engraved image of the first human ship ever to land on Mars. "No one writes on paper anymore."

"It is not real paper, Zara," Melody corrected. "Even on Earth, there are not enough trees left to make the original product. This is 3D-printed, imitation paper."

Zara smiled at the android. Belle thought the journal was fantastic, especially the spaceship on the cover.

"Can I use my allowance credits to buy this?" she asked.

"Do you know what a journal is?"

Belle laughed. "Of course I do, Mom. I record log entries through Melody all the time."

"It's quite different using paper and pen. Writing and drawing on paper is an ancient art form," Zara said. "But if you promise to give writing a try, you may purchase it."

Belle bargained the price down until the seller's face turned a bright red. She even got him to throw in a pencil for free. After she pressed her finger to his datapad to pay, she realized that they had lost sight of her dad. Melody extended her neck to stretch her head up about a meter higher in the air. This was one android ability that Belle sometimes wished she had. It was very useful for finding people and things. Everything Melody could see was projected onto the screen on her torso, so Belle could search for her dad too. Within seconds, they located him.

Melody led Belle and her mom past several vendor stands, squeezing past clusters of people until they reached the middle of the market. Yun was leaning up against a stall, talking to a woman who was wrapped up in so many scarves that all Belle could see were her eyes.

Yun greeted his family with a huge grin. It was the first time Belle had seen him smile since they'd landed on Mars.

"I've found the solution to our problems," he said, spreading his arms open wide. "We're going to be farmers!"

It took several seconds for the news to sink in. Belle had just been looking forward to going back to Earth and telling her friends about her vacation on the red planet. This was a whole different story.

"That's wonderful!" Zara said. "Farming's been in my family for generations. Up until my parents' time, that is, when they moved to the city."

So Mom is excited too? Belle thought worriedly.

"Farms are located on the other side of Mars," Yun explained. "There's a lot of land to be had. The possibilities are endless."

"The region is called Olympia, after the big volcano," the woman at the stall said. "Locals call it the Wild West."

"It'll be a grand adventure," Yun said. "It's just the thing we Songs need."

Belle looked at her dad, then at her mom. Zara was looking at Yun like he was her hero. Melody was busy scanning the woman in the scarves. Nobody could see how ridiculous this idea was.

Nobody but Belle.

Earth Date: March 13, 2335
Mars Day 1, summer

We're going to be farmers?

Let me tell you a secret. No one in the Song family can even keep a cactus alive for more than a week. On Earth, we lived in a city apartment on the 25th floor! Dad has never even mowed a lawn. Mom is allergic to cats! We don't know the first thing about growing crops or taking care of animals.

How are we going to survive here as farmers?

CHAPTER 2
JOURNEY TOWARD
A NEW LIFE

"Three tickets to Darwin!" Yun waved the tickets in the air as he walked into their hotel room the next morning.

"Darwin?" Belle said, stretching out in her comfy bed. "I thought Tharsis City was the capital of the Olympia region."

"Darwin is the second largest city in Olympia," Yun pointed to the map printed on the back of the ticket. "They say it's about half the size of the capital. And it's in the south, where we're headed."

"We'll stop in Darwin to pick up supplies," Zara added. "Then we head out to Sun City, where our farm is."

"That's too many cities to keep track of," Belle grumbled.

Her dad laughed. "We're new here. By the end of summer, it'll all be as familiar as home."

Belle's heart sank. Mars would never be home. She half-hoped this crazy plan would fail so they could head back to Earth. That would be embarrassing, but it was better than starving to death in the middle of nowhere.

"The transport departs in one hour," Melody said with a squeak. Her joints were squeaking from all the dust.

They checked out of the BAMCorp hotel and headed toward the other side of town. Belle hiked her pack higher up on her back and followed her parents. It took a lot of effort to get used to the lower gravity on Mars. Each footstep took her higher off the ground than she wanted, so she had to adjust her pace.

The heat added to Belle's grumpiness. Her scarves were glued to her face with sweat. When she'd finally peeled the last scarf off, she was standing in the middle of the noisy Utopia Transit Station.

Belle gaped at the cavernous building. Giant pillars held up the corrugated roof. Shuttles of all sizes lined up on one side of the station like huge hibernating animals. On the other side were the land vehicles — some resembled regular Earth buses, and others looked like flying boats.

"Those are hover buses," Melody explained. "They are faster and more comfortable than the wheeled ones."

"Come on." Yun jogged toward what looked like a gigantic life raft crossed with a catamaran. It had windows all along its sides, and three pairs of propellers attached to engines on top. Smaller land transports rumbled onto the craft and disappeared into its midsection. Meanwhile, long lines of people waited to enter through one of two ramps. "That's our shuttle."

Belle and Melody were the last passengers to climb the ramp. As Belle stepped into the main cabin, she was hit by the stench of sweaty bodies. She quickly re-wrapped her soggy scarves over her mouth and nose, and then squeezed onto the last available bench with her parents.

"Androids belong in the next compartment." A man in uniform pointed at Melody. "Strap yourself to a wall port."

As the shuttle ramp clanked and wheezed itself closed, the engines began to rumble. The air around Belle grew warm and stale. She felt dizzy.

"I think I'm going to be sick," she said.

A large woman who sat at the end of their row looked alarmed. "First time on a shuttle?" she asked.

Belle nodded.

The woman slapped her thighs and snorted. Belle could smell her onion breath. It made her gag. The woman rose out of her seat.

"Sit down!" yelled the uniformed man.

"Keep yer britches on!" she yelled back. "I'm trying to prevent an incident here."

The woman scooted past three other passengers, and signaled to Belle's family to stand up. Was she kicking them off the flight?

Belle opened her mouth to protest, but then the woman waved the Songs over toward her seat by the window.

"Can't have this young one up-chucking on us all, can we?" she said with a grin. One of her teeth was black, which made her look like she had a gap in her mouth. "Come along, newbies. The view will make yer forget the sickness."

Sitting by the open window did help the dizziness. The gentle breeze lulled her into a much needed nap.

Hours later, Belle was awoken by her dad nudging her.

"Look, Belle. You've got the best view of the land below."

The shuttle had long left the Utopian plains behind. They were now flying low over the outer lands. Yun leaned over her, craning to see out the window.

"That's the three Terras below."

"The three terrors?" Belle asked.

He laughed. "No, *Terras*. It's the way people once referred to regions on Mars. These days they're known by their modern names — Araba, Saba, and Meridian."

"I've never heard those names." Belle had studied maps of Mars on the flight from Earth. But these names were unfamiliar.

"That's probably because no one can live in these three regions," Yun said. "Look carefully, you might spot the old terraforming machines. No one knows why terraforming didn't work here."

The red planet had been transformed about two hundred years earlier. Before the terraforming machines did their work, Mars didn't have enough air or water to support human life.

Belle stared at the dry reddish brown land below her. "It's nothing but desert."

"You can't see it, but right now we're flying over an underground river that starts in the mountains and ends at Lake Hellan. It's actually the deepest crater on Mars."

"Cool! But how do farmers grow anything here?"

"There!" Yun pointed ahead. "That's how!"

Suddenly the red dusty land transformed into spaces of brilliant greens and blues. Even the sky seemed to change color, and there were clouds.

"You see that big river?" Yun said. "The underground one rises to meet it. That's the Marine Valley River. Several smaller rivers join it at different points to the west."

"It's beautiful," Belle said. "And so blue!"

"Yes, but it's also very salty water," Zara added. "That's why you'll see huge buildings alongside the rivers. We can't drink salt water, so those desalination plants purify it for us."

Yun then pointed to three large mountains in the distance. "Those are extinct volcanoes," he said. "They're used now as reservoirs to hold the planet's most precious resource — purified water. And those giant buildings are the desalination plants."

"There's a bigger mountain even farther out," Zara said. "Can you see it?"

Belle squinted through the low clouds. She could only make out a large shadow looming behind the three closer volcanoes.

"That's Mount Olympus," Yun said. "It's the biggest volcano, not just on Mars, but in the entire Solar System!"

"I guess that's why they named this part of Mars Olympia, huh, Dad?"

"You're absolutely right, Belle."

A loud voice crackled through the shuttle speakers, announcing that they were about to land in Darwin. The shuttle bumped and jostled as it descended and dropped onto the landing pad with a sharp thud. Every passenger let out a loud sigh.

"Let's go find our new farm!" Yun said. He and Zara hurried off the shuttle.

Belle waited for Melody, her only friend on this strange new world. Together, they stepped onto the soil of Olympia.

Earth Date: March 14, 2335
Mars Day 2, summer, evening

This has been the longest day of my life. When I woke up two days ago, we were going to live in Utopia and my parents were going to work for BAMCorp. All the photos Dad showed me made it seem that life on Mars would be great. Even the company's hotel was fantastic.

But here we are in the middle of nowhere — Darwin, Olympia. Sure, the flight over was interesting. I've never seen such big volcanoes so close together. I admit, the landscape is amazing. One moment it looks like desert, the next, it looks like Earth.

But Darwin is a poor and dusty version of Utopia. It's so backward. There are no tall buildings or aircars like at home. It reminds me of an ancient western town in those old cowboy movies Dad likes to watch.

Dad says it's too late to go on to Sun City, where our new farm is. So he got us a motel room for the night. It's nothing like the BAMCorp hotel from last night. The video-wall doesn't even have Earth programming. I'm stuck watching some boring documentary about whether humans or aliens came to Mars first. Who cares?

CHAPTER 3

HOMEWARD BOUND

Morning in Darwin dawned bright and hot. The heat rose from the ground and beat down from above at the same time. Belle felt like she was part of a heat sandwich.

She held on to Melody's hard fingers as they followed Yun and Zara out of the motel and into the streets of Darwin. The noise of transport craft and shouting voices gave Belle a headache.

Yun led the family to a large store. The sign outside read Guntar's Emporium. Once inside, Belle felt better. It was cooler and quieter in here. She wandered through the aisles, looking at all the pretty things in the "luxury items" section. There were beautifully decorated plates and lacy fabric that she didn't dare to touch. In another section she marveled at ancient books that were made out of actual paper. She pulled one gently off the shelf, slid to the floor, and began to read.

● ● ● ●

"It is time to go," Melody interrupted. Belle blinked up at her android. "You have been sitting here for two hours."

How had so much time passed without her realizing it? She reluctantly replaced the book back on the shelf and followed Melody outside.

There, in front of the store, were her parents, loading up an old, rusted wagon.

"What's this old thing?" Belle blurted.

Yun wiped his forehead with his sleeve. "It's all we could afford. At least it moves."

"It is a Mark II hover-wagon," Melody said, lifting a large package into the back. "I know several jokes about this model."

"It's big enough for us all to camp in," Zara said, ignoring Melody's offer.

"Sure, if it doesn't break down on the way." Belle stared at the clunky hover-wagon. With its landing gear lowered, and its side panels removed, it looked like a cross between an old camper in a junkyard, and an ancient wagon from her history texts. She didn't want to know what jokes Melody could tell about it. "Will it get off the ground?"

"With Loki's help, it will," Yun said.

Belle walked around to the front of the wagon. There, harnessed to the wagon was the most enormous creature she'd ever seen.

"It's a horsel," Zara said, smacking her hands on her pants. "A horse and camel hybrid. They can go for days without water and can outrun a dust storm, or so they say."

Belle stood back from the animal. Loki was twice the size of an Earth horse. He stared at her with his gentle, brown eyes. Belle took a step closer. She reached out her hand and stroked his nose. It was soft, warm, and fuzzy.

"Hi there," she said timidly. She hadn't had much exposure to real animals. But from her virtual games, she knew they liked to be stroked and talked to.

Loki lowered his head and huffed loudly. Belle jumped back.

Yun laughed. "He's just saying hello."

Belle decided she would get to know Loki later. She helped her parents load supplies into the wagon instead.

When everything was packed, Belle sat in one of the seats in the rear of the wagon. Melody strapped her in, and then did the same for herself. Yun and Zara sat up front, on a bench seat that had the steering controls.

While Zara programmed the guidance system, Yun charged up the engine and retracted the landing gear. The wagon rose several feet in the air. Then pointing Loki west, the Song family left the town of Darwin behind them.

With Loki's size and the gravity difference, they traveled at a surprising speed. Most of the time, if Loki kept his pace steady, the wagon moved smoothly. Unfortunately, Loki was not always steady. The old wagon often leaned left and right as the horsel avoided rocks or stumbled over potholes.

From where Belle sat, her parents looked tiny, compared to the giant creature they were guiding. Even with shoulder straps holding them in their seats, they still gripped the bench with all their might. As Loki tried to find his stride, the Song family was bounced and jostled about. Belle hung on to Melody till her fingers were sore. Nobody spoke or moved as they left the outer limits of Darwin.

As they traveled west toward Sun City, where their farm was, they passed open field after open field.

"These are some of the earliest colonized farms," Melody explained. "Many of them grow versions of Earth crops that require the least amount of water."

Once past the farms, the land around them alternated between yellow grasslands and dusty desertlike plains. After a while, Loki picked up speed, which stabilized the wagon. The wind began to blow stronger. It was a refreshing change from the stifling heat of the town.

Melody turned up her volume so that Belle could hear her over the wind whistling past them. "Terraforming has made this land usable, but there are not enough farmers signing up for land. A lot of people prefer to work in asteroid mining."

Melody pointed out interesting geological formations as they went along. Meanwhile, Belle fought the growling in her stomach. Soon she decided to unstrap herself and stood up. It was easier to balance now.

"I'm hungry," she said. "I'm going to get snacks."

"I should do that for you," Melody said.

"No, that's okay. I need to move around." Belle held onto the android's shoulders as she squinted at the scene around them. Everything was a blur because of how fast Loki was going. Belle held her breath in amazement.

"Please be careful," warned Melody.

Belle climbed over some packages stacked up in front of her. She found her pack and pulled out the snack bars she'd brought with her from Earth. She also grabbed a scarf for herself and one for Melody. The wind was getting chillier with each passing mile. Then she carefully climbed back over the packages, holding the scarves in one hand and her precious snacks in the other.

But just as she reached the edge of her seat, Loki faltered and the wagon tilted. Belle was jolted off her feet for a second. Shoving the snack bars between her teeth, she reached for Melody's outstretched hand. But then the wagon dipped suddenly, jolting Belle again. She yelped out loud, and her snack bars fell out of her mouth. Without thinking, she reached out to snatch them back. But the wagon jerked a third time, and Belle lost her balance.

She fell through the opening in the side of the wagon and floated in the air for the longest second of her life. Then, *THUMP!* Her backside hit the ground and she went rolling — over and over. She didn't notice any pain at first. She only wanted to stop rolling. She couldn't even scream because air was forced out of her lungs with each bump.

In the distance, she heard Melody's voice calling for the wagon to stop. More yelling followed, then she heard the pounding of hooves and a deep grunting-neighing sound. She finally stopped rolling, but she couldn't move. She inhaled dirt, which made her cough . . . causing her to inhale even more dirt. Her lungs ached, and her heart raced. Tears blinded her. She soon felt every pebble under her stabbing at her face and bare arms. Slowly, her scraped skin started to burn. Then her bones began to throb. She found her breath and let out a terrible scream.

Mars Day 3, Summer, 2335, evening
Somewhere on the plains outside of Darwin

I fell out of the hover-wagon! Stars, did it hurt!
Mom and Dad patched me up with the med-kit
we just bought. Nothing broken, according to the
handheld scanner. Could've fooled me. Ooh, the pain!
Now my arms and legs are blue and green, and all
scratched up. It's hard to hold this pencil. Mom said
it was a miracle I didn't hit my head. Dad didn't say
a word the whole time. Mom put some weird cream
on my wounds. She said it was Martian medicine.
It smells strange — like flowers that have died in a
vase. At least I don't hurt so much now . . .

Ugh . . . the smell of the cream just made me throw
up. And now, even the air outside smells awful —
like damp laundry. We got caught in a dust storm,
so we've stopped for the night to rest. We parked our
wagon in front of a small cave. Loki gets to sleep in
there while we camp in our wagon. Outside, it sounds
as if a million cows are on a stampede, but it's only
the wind and the sand. I hope we don't get trapped in
here like we used to back home during a snowstorm.

This is NOT a great way to start a new life!

CHAPTER 4
THE SHACK

The dust storm lasted all night, but when morning came, everything was very quiet. So quiet, that for a moment Belle thought she had lost her hearing. Looking out the wagon window, she saw that the land was a yellowish brown, as if some giant had laid its blanket on the ground. Everything as far as she could see was covered in sand-colored dust.

Belle's body ached and her skin itched. She tried to get out of her cot, but it hurt too much to move.

"Oh, no you don't. You're going to stay put for the rest of the journey," her mom insisted.

Belle stared at the wagon ceiling while her family cleaned off the wagon and fed and harnessed Loki. She felt the wagon rise and then jerk forward as they began to move again. Yun had replaced the wagon's side panels, and Belle wished she could see more than the small clouds passing by through the small windows. Instead, for the next few hours she listened to Melody tell the most awful jokes about horses and camels.

The journey to their farm took them through the southernmost area of Olympia. It was cooler here than in Darwin, so Zara insisted that Belle wrap herself in several blankets.

Melody showed Belle various holo-maps of the region. She told Belle how the seasons on Mars lasted much longer than on Earth. Right now they were in the middle of the summer season, which was why it was so hot. Later on, they played several games of 3D chess. Finally, Belle grew tired and drifted off to sleep.

● ● ● ●

She was woken by Loki's grunting. The wagon had stopped, and Belle was all alone. She couldn't hear or see her parents. Even Melody was gone. Belle pushed herself up and winced.

"Mom! Dad!" she cried, but no one answered her. She took several deep breaths and called out again. "Melody!"

"We're here," Zara said, poking her head in through the back door. "We're at our farm." She didn't sound very excited.

"What's wrong?" Belle asked, trying to get onto her feet.

"Wait for Melody to come help you," Zara said. She bit her lower lip. "It's not quite what we were expecting."

Belle felt a tinge of pleasure when she heard that. *Maybe now we can finally go back home*, she thought.

Melody helped Belle climb out of the wagon. It was the middle of the night, and the air was cold. The only light came from the millions of stars above and one of Mars' moons, Phobos. Melody's wide-beamed headlamp lit up the ground immediately in front of them. Belle shivered and rubbed her arms. After the heat of the cities, she wasn't used to how cool it was at night. The ground beneath her feet was covered in pebbles, and they crunched with each step. In the distance, Belle saw shapes — trees, perhaps. And there were two barnlike buildings, all dark gray and shadowy.

Right in front of Belle was a smaller building. Melody shone her light in that direction. When the beam landed on their new home, Belle groaned. The house was a run-down shack. The roof was crooked and leaned to one side. Several window shutters were bent out of place, one hung unsteadily on a hinge. The place looked like it hadn't been lived in for a hundred years.

Yun had settled Loki in the smaller barn just beyond the house and was returning to unload the wagon. He flashed Belle a smile that looked like a grimace.

"It'll look better in the morning," he said. He was trying so hard to make her believe they had made the right decision.

"I'm sure it will," she said. She didn't say what she really felt — that her dad had made a big mistake by dragging them out here.

"Maybe we should spend the night in the wagon," Zara suggested. "We'll unpack in the morning."

That night, it took Belle a long time to fall asleep. She wondered just how much worse things had to get before her parents finally gave up.

● ● ● ●

When she woke up again, the sunlight was streaming through the open window beside her. She rubbed her eyes and sat up, surprised that her body didn't hurt so much anymore. That horrid-smelling Martian medicine really worked after all.

Belle got out her journal and began to write out her thoughts about their new home. As she wrote, she heard voices outside. But the voices didn't belong to her parents.

Peering out of the wagon's window, she saw a woman and a boy talking to Yun and Zara. The woman was taller than her dad. Her long, copper-colored hair was tied in a ponytail that fell to her thighs. She also had rough, purplish skin. The boy beside her had similar purple skin as well.

Aliens!

Mars Day 5, Summer, 2335, morning

The sunlight is so bright it woke me up. All is quiet inside the wagon. Perfect for journal writing. I don't ache so much anymore. It doesn't even hurt to write. Not like last night. Ow! I never want to feel that kind of pain again.

My parents and Melody must be moving things into our new home — which is awful! Our "homestead" (as Dad calls it) is old and run down. I don't think anyone has lived here in years. Mom doesn't like it either, but she won't say anything to Dad. Still, I can tell she feels like I do. Dad, I'm not sure... I don't think he's as excited as he appears. I think they secretly wish their engineering jobs with BAMCorp had worked out.

I don't believe it — my parents are talking to two aliens!

CHAPTER 5
STRANGE VISITORS

Belle had never met an alien — they weren't allowed to visit Earth. But she'd heard there were many aliens on the offworld colonies, like Lunar Colony, and here on Mars. And here were two aliens, talking to her parents!

Belle's mind was filled with questions as she walked toward the visitors. She wondered what planet they were from and how long their journey to Mars was. She wanted to know everything about them.

But the questions stuck in her throat. She was an alien too, in a way. True, most Martians were human, but Belle was born and raised on Earth. That made her as much an alien here as the purple people now laughing with her parents like old friends. How would *she* feel if they shot question after question at her on their very first meeting? She decided the questions could wait.

"I'm so sorry," she heard the lady say. "We really had no idea this farm was taken. We often drop by for a rest when we're out on our walks. But we're so happy you're here now. This farm has badly needed a *korDar* — a family."

"We're just so thrilled to meet a neighbor," Zara replied. She looked back at the shack. "Even though we're not quite ready to be good hosts."

Yun waved Belle over. "This is our daughter, Isabelle."

"It's *Belle*!" she corrected. She hated it when her parents used her full name. It sounded so formal.

The woman nudged the boy. He was about Belle's age, and looked very much like a human. But when Belle looked closer, she saw that he had arm and neck ridges like his mother. His skin was a lighter color purple though. Belle tried not to stare.

"I'm Lucas," he mumbled, looking at his feet.

What an odd boy!

"And I'm Myra Walker," his mother said. Her purple skin shone in the sunlight, highlighting flecks of gold on her ridges and the sides of her face. She shook Belle's hand with such warmth, Belle liked her instantly.

"You're so shiny," Belle blurted, wide-eyed and staring. *Oh dear, did she just say that out loud?*

"Belle!" Both her parents gasped in unison.

"That's not very polite," Zara chided. "Please apologize."

"I'm sorry." Belle could feel her face burning with embarrassment.

Lucas scowled at her, but Myra laughed. "It's okay," she said. "You've probably never met a Sulux before."

"Sulux?"

"People from Suluxa," Lucas said. He looked annoyed at having to explain. Belle felt like such an idiot.

"My family has lived on Mars for a hundred cycles," Myra said. "I'm actually half Sulux and half human. Lucas is one quarter Sulux. But my ancestors are from the planet Suluxa. It's the fifth planet in a nearby binary system. That means it has two suns. They arrived here around the same time Terrans colonized Mars."

"Sulux technology is what helped terraform Mars." Lucas said.

"What's a cycle?" Belle asked.

Lucas rolled his eyes. "You don't know? A cycle is one revolution around the sun. Duh."

"Now it's your turn to apologize," Myra said to her son. Then turning to Belle, she added, "A hundred cycles on Mars is about 190 Earth years."

"Oh, I didn't know," Belle said, staring at her feet. She hated sounding like a fool. "I mean . . . I knew about the revolutions. I just didn't know what it was called."

Myra put her hand on Belle's shoulder. "No worries, child," she said. "You'll soon get used to your new life on Mars. This world is so rich and full of new discoveries."

"Like Water Raiders!" Lucas' eyes lit up.

"What are those?" Belle said. They didn't sound like fun.

Myra scowled and waved her son away. "That's not something you should worry about right now. My husband, Padraig, is at our homestead. He can fill you in on that topic. We live a little to the southeast of here. You likely passed by our farm on your way here."

She pointed in the direction they'd come last night. Belle saw nothing but yellowed grassland and clusters of enormous trees stretching up to the sky.

"We couldn't see much on the way in; it was too dark. We relied completely on the guidance computer," Yun said, scratching his head. "Plus, I'm afraid our home doesn't look any more livable in the daylight than it did last night."

Myra laughed. It was a great sound — like a flock of happy birds twittering. "Oh, that's not your real house. We call it the front porch. It has no security. Anyone, like us, can just walk in. But come with me. Let me show you how we live on Mars."

The entire Song family let out a sigh of relief. Even Melody seemed to perk up as they followed Myra back toward the house. She led them into the shack. Inside, there was a single table and two chairs in the middle of a large and very dusty room. At the other end was another door. This one was heavier and more solid than the front door. To the side of the door was a small wooden flap. Myra lifted it, revealing a computer panel hidden behind it. She turned to Yun.

"Do you have your security key code?" she asked. "It should be on your title papers."

Yun pulled out his datapad and pulled up the relevant page. He entered the endless string of numbers and letters into the computer panel. The panel lit up, flickered red several times, and finally settled on a bright green glow.

"Now, each of you stand here, one at a time," Myra said, gesturing to a spot in front of the computer panel. "Let the computer scan you so your house will recognize you."

"It's just like back home on Earth," Belle said.

"Mars isn't behind Earth in any way, you know," Lucas said sulkily. "In fact, we're definitely ahead in environmental tech and terraforming knowledge."

Myra shushed him.

"What?" Lucas looked up at his mom. "Terrans who are new to Mars always expect us to be more backward. I was just explaining the truth."

Myra sighed and nodded.

"That's not what I meant," Belle spoke through gritted teeth as the computer took her image. She didn't really like this boy. Maybe he didn't like the idea of Terrans moving to Mars.

Once the scanning was complete, they each had to say their name and a few key words so the computer would recognize their voices. Finally, the computer displayed "Welcome Home, Song Family" on the entrance panel. Then the door clicked open.

Myra led them through the door and down a set of stairs. With each step, a light came on, illuminating their way. It was cold, and the air smelled stale. But Belle soon heard the heater turn on. She could feel the air warming up as they reached the bottom of the stairs. Myra waved her hand in a wide circle.

"Welcome to your real home," she said. "It's a little dusty, but I think you'll agree it's quite pleasant. The building above is really just a false front, to make it seem more like a home on Earth. It's a human thing, I suppose."

They were greeted by a white-walled kitchen filled with equipment that, by Earth standards, was seriously old. There was a refrigerator, a food hydrator, and a microwave oven.

"All faucets are equipped with water purifiers too," Myra said. "The house has all the conveniences you could ask for."

"I can learn to use these," Belle heard Zara whisper to Yun.

There was also a small dining table, a living area, three small bedrooms, and two tiny bathrooms. One bathroom held a water shower, while the other was equipped with a sonic shower.

"Mars law prohibits more than one water shower per week," Melody informed everyone. "Water is even more precious on Mars than on Earth."

Myra and Lucas eyed Melody suspiciously, as she spoke. *They don't like her*, thought Belle. *I wonder why?*

"We can handle that." Yun sounded cheerful. "On Earth, we had very strict restrictions on water usage too."

Belle could tell his smile was fake. She knew he hated sonic showers. He always said it didn't feel like he was any cleaner just because some fancy vibrations removed surface dirt and old skin.

Belle leaned against a wall as she took in the idea of living underground. There were no windows. It felt like they would be living in a box. Then her hand rubbed against the wall behind her. It came to life — displaying the view of their homestead outside. She stared at the wall. It was just as if she were looking out a window at the stone path that led to the shack above. Beyond that, she saw the yellowish-green pasture and the two barns. She even saw Loki's head peeking out of his stall.

"It's a viewscreen?" she gasped.

"Yeah. It's really cool." Lucas' eyes lit up. For a second, he actually smiled. "You can program any of the walls to display what's outside in real time. Or you can see other locations on Mars, or Lunar Colony, or even Earth."

"This way you don't feel so claustrophobic," Myra said. "Mars' weather makes it hard to live above ground much of the time."

"We Martians don't have a problem with living underground," Lucas added. "But I've noticed Terrans hate the idea."

"Only at first," Myra said. She nudged her son. "And in the non-winter months, it can be quite pleasant to spend the day *deng yav* — upstairs."

"When there are no dust storms," Lucas grumbled.

"Does it ever snow?" Belle guessed Lucas would laugh at her for asking, but she didn't care.

"Only in winter, which lasts one hundred and fifty Sols," Myra said. "Winters here are often severe. We rarely leave the house, so it's important to stock up."

"Sols?"

Myra looked pleased to answer Belle's questions. "I see you're a curious person, Belle. That's a good quality to have. A sol is one day on Mars. It is thirty-seven minutes longer than a day on Earth."

Belle caught the smirk on Lucas' lips. She really didn't like him.

Sol 98/Summer, Cycle 105
(Myra said that's how to write the date here on Mars.)

Myra Walker is so genuine and nice. Her son, Lucas, is something else. I get the feeling he doesn't like new people. I was hoping we wouldn't have to see each other much after today, but stars, was I wrong!

The Walkers are our closest neighbors. Before they left today, Myra invited us to their home, so Mom and Dad could learn about farming from her husband. I'm quite relieved that someone will be showing us what we'll need to do to survive here.

But then Myra dropped the bombshell! She said that since I was still in the sixth grade, Lucas and I would be in the same class. The parents all thought that was great news. But Lucas didn't look too thrilled. I know I wasn't either. Hopefully, the class will be big enough that we won't have to talk much. Otherwise, I'll never get away from this grumpy, sarcastic boy.

PS — Things to remember:
1 Mars cycle = 687 days = 1.9 Earth years
My age on Mars = 12/1.9 = 6.32 Mars cycles
8 Sols = 1 week on Mars

CHAPTER 6

VISITING THE NEIGHBORS

"What a perfect day for a walk to our new neighbors," Zara said. It was a bright and sunny morning. Low, puffy clouds floated on a gentle breeze.

It made Belle feel homesick for Earth.

"Walk?" Belle looked around. "How far is it to the Walkers' farm? Why can't we take Loki and the wagon?" She couldn't tell where their own farm ended and the next one began.

"It's only a few kilometers. We'll take our time and explore a little," Yun said.

In the daylight, the Songs' farm looked a lot more pleasant. Large clumps of bushy trees dotted their property as far as the eye could see. Crossing in front of their farm gate was a dirt road that seemed to stretch on forever.

"This is Aonia Road. It links all farms in the area," Melody said, projecting a holo-map of the area. "It joins the route to Darwin to the southeast and runs to Sun City to the northwest."

Melody was always full of useful information like that. If nothing else, Belle could spend the day listening to Melody's fun facts about Mars. But then Yun told Melody that she had to stay behind and watch their house. The android shut the gate and headed back to their house. Belle huffed.

"You saw how Myra and Lucas reacted to her when they were here," Yun said. "The Robot Rebellion didn't happen on Mars, but news travels. They might not be comfortable with robots acting like they're part of the family."

Belle huffed again. The rebellion ended almost fifty years ago. Were people really still afraid of androids?

"You know," Zara said. "If we didn't have Melody, we might be terrified of androids too. Let's get to know our Martian friends first, before introducing her, okay?"

Belle didn't answer. Anybody could see that Melody was special. She wasn't going to try and take over the planet or anything. She was Belle's best friend.

"Myra told me that Sun City is where the marketplace is," Zara said, changing the subject. "You love markets, don't you, Belle?"

Belle shrugged. She knew her mom was trying to lift the mood. But Belle didn't want to like Mars, and she missed having Melody around. Her mom sighed quietly.

The road they walked along separated two distinct biomes. On one side was plot after plot of flat grassland. Some of it was fenced in by wooden posts with laser crossbeams in between. Yun pointed out where the Song farm ended and the Walkers' began. Belle was surprised at how big their land was and worried at the same time. What would they do with all of this land?

On the other side of the road was a lush green forest that seemed to go on forever. Tall trees rose high into the sky. At the top, they stretched out their branches like arms, touching their neighbors. Their leaves wove together to shadow the forest in almost complete darkness.

"Trees were vital for terraforming Mars," Yun said, looking back at Belle, who stared with curiosity at the forest. "Strips of forestland like this were planted to help purify the air, and to prepare the soil for eventual farming. A hundred cycles ago, much of our farmland was forest too."

"I thought that removing the Earth's forests was what helped to destroy the air," Belle said.

"You're right," Yun said. "That's why some forests on Mars will be permanent."

"Like this one?"

"I don't know. But I'm sure you could ask your new teacher when you start school."

Belle didn't want to think about school. She hated the idea of being the new kid. She dragged her feet as she followed her parents. They were holding hands and chatting, far too happily for Belle.

The Walker farm was almost exactly like the Song farm, except for the unusual crops growing in the fields. Belle couldn't make out what they were. Behind the fields were the corrals, where several animals grazed. Belle spotted three horsels that looked even bigger than Loki. Next to them were a bunch of creatures that resembled sheep, but Belle couldn't be sure. A handful of huge alpacas grazed near a giant barn. One of the alpacas bounded over to greet them.

"Wow!" Yun cried. "I've never seen an animal jump that high."

The sight of this huge animal leaping high off the ground was so amusing, Belle forgot for a moment that she was in a bad mood. She laughed and ran over to the waiting alpaca. With each step, she pushed against the ground a little harder. The land beneath her felt like a trampoline. She soared higher and higher with each leap.

"Look at me!" she cried.

"It's the gravity difference." Yun laughed, leaping next to her.

Belle was breathless when she reached the corral post. She'd been so busy missing Earth that she didn't think how fun it might be to explore a different planet. She and Yun petted the alpaca for a while, before Zara called them over to the Walker house.

As the Songs walked up the driveway, they saw a small building similar to the one on their own farm. The Walkers had obviously done theirs up to look more livable, but it still had a shack-like appearance. Belle wondered if that was on purpose. Maybe it was meant to act like camouflage. If so, who were they trying to fool?

Padraig Walker ran up to the house as soon as he saw the Songs. He was a funny man with curly gold hair and a sunburnt face. He waved and shook hands as if he couldn't be happier to meet another person.

"Call me Paddy," he said with a catchy laugh.

Myra and Lucas soon joined the group. Within seconds, the parents were all chatting like old friends. Belle and Lucas stood staring at each other in silence.

Myra and Paddy began showing the Song family their farm.

"Alpacas are one of the few Terran animals that haven't struggled to adapt to life on Mars," Myra said, pointing out their herd. "Except that they seem to grow bigger with each generation."

"What's wrong with your sheep?" Belle said.

Lucas snorted.

"They're shoats," Myra said. "A hybrid cross of sheep and goats. Scientists cloned the first shoats to adapt to Mars. Since then they've become a natural farm animal here. They're our own version of livestock. Aren't they cute?"

Belle didn't think so.

"So you only have two dozen alpacas?" Yun asked as they passed the grazing animals. "How is that enough to survive?"

"The authorities are very serious about limiting livestock," Paddy said. "Mars' ecosystem is much more sensitive than Earth's. They outlawed cattle because the methane gas they produced damaged the atmosphere. Alpacas are the new cows."

"The large numbers of cattle on Earth helped to ruin its atmosphere." Lucas had his hands on his hips, and spoke as if he knew everything. Belle couldn't stand him.

"Now, Lucas," his dad warned. "You know we learned from the mistakes of the past. So now we have a better life here. Livestock numbers are purposely kept low. Only a few farms are allowed to have animals. You're lucky the De Sousa family retired. Otherwise, you wouldn't have received a livestock license. We live mostly on turken fowl and shoat. Alpacas are farmed for their milk and wool. Their meat is a rare luxury."

Paddy pointed out the crops he was growing — millet, beans, and a hybrid squash-zucchini.

"These require less water than traditional crops. Water is our most treasured resource." Paddy led the Songs to an area behind their house. "That's why we spend so much money and energy on securing our water tanks."

"Where is the tank?" Belle asked, looking around. All she could see was the Walkers' large backyard.

"You're standing on it," Paddy said proudly.

"So it's underground? Why do you keep the tank hidden?" Zara asked.

"Raiders," Lucas whispered with a wicked gleam in his eyes.

"Raiders are never funny," Myra scolded her son. "And I don't like you scaring our new friends."

Paddy crouched to the ground and lifted a patch of earth. Hidden underneath was a computer panel similar to the one that opened Belle's house door.

"Water Raiders," he said. "They often try to steal our water. They're organized and ruthless. That's why it's vital to secure our tanks like this. Replacing the water is expensive. It can break a farmer's livelihood."

Belle felt a shiver go through her body. "What do these Raiders look like?"

The Walkers shook their heads in unison.

"We don't need to think about that now," Paddy said, replacing the patch of grass covering the computer panel. He put his arm around Yun. "Let me show you how you can secure yours."

Myra slipped her arm into Zara's. "No more unpleasant talk. Let me show you our barn." She put on a smile, one that Belle could tell was forced. Belle wanted to hear more about Water Raiders, but she went along with Myra. Lucas dragged his feet behind them.

The barn was a high-ceilinged, double-story building. It smelled like rotting vegetables. The floor was covered with brown and tan wood shavings. On the ground level were pens that held the funniest two-legged creatures Belle had ever seen.

"What are they?" She crouched down to look through the netting to get a better look. They had tails like turkeys. Their faces were a strange mix of turkeys and chickens — and they stank.

"You've never seen a turken?" Lucas said.

"They're a hybrid fowl," Myra said. "We're allowed to have more of these than alpacas, because they're smaller and don't pollute as much. They smell unpleasant, but they're quite delicious."

Belle whipped around with her eyes wide. "You mean that actually *eat* these?"

Myra laughed her bird laugh again. "That's the farming life. We have to eat what we grow. So we eat some of the turkens, and we sell others at the markets. They also provide us with eggs, which we sell too. Their feathers are made into household items, and we grind up their bones into feed for our mealworms. We don't waste a thing."

She led Belle and Zara to the second level of the barn. It was clean up here with no smell. There were long counters holding transparent tanks, each containing thousands of wriggling worms. Above each tank, a warming light lit the worms with a bluish tinge. Belle felt her skin crawl. She wanted to run outside, fast.

"Mealworms are the staple food of Mars," Myra said. "They're cheap to grow and very nutritious." She picked up a worm and showed it to Belle, who jumped back a few steps. "They can be ground into flour, fried, or baked. They're very useful and produce no pollution at all."

"They're environmentally friendly," Lucas said, appearing out of nowhere. He carried a box with him.

As Myra put the worm back, Belle noticed her hands.

"You have six fingers?" Belle asked in amazement.

Myra smiled. "A blessing of the Sulux."

As they left the barn, Lucas handed Belle the box he was carrying. Belle heard scratching sounds coming from within. She lifted the lid and gasped. Four tiny chicks stared at her. They smelled like old socks. Belle wasn't sure what to make of them.

"These are for you, Belle," Myra said with a big smile. "You can learn a lot when caring for other living creatures. Treat them with respect, and they will serve you well."

"Thank you," Belle said, trying not to gag at the chicks' smell. Her mom gave her a stern look, so she stuck a finger in the box, pretending to stroke them. She couldn't wait to get home and dump them in the barn. She had no intention of taking care of them. Her mom could do that.

"I feel overwhelmed," Zara said. "There's so much to learn about this life."

Myra put her hand on Zara's shoulder. "That's what neighbors are for. We're all here to help each other."

Walking back to the house, Belle held the box at arm's length, faking excitement about her new "pets". Lucas walked beside her, with a sneer on his lip the whole time.

"What?" Belle said, as he led them into their house.

"I didn't say anything," he said.

Belle felt he was mocking her. He probably thought she'd fail at farming life. She was afraid he might be right.

Sol 100/Summer, Cycle 105

I admit it. There are some things that I like about Mars. On a nice day like today, it feels a lot like Earth. I like the gravity too, because I can jump pretty high. My highest leap today was so high I could almost have landed on Dad's shoulders.

But I don't like it enough to want to stay here forever. I put those turkens into the big barn. They scratched me with their sharp claws. I have the marks to prove it. One of them even pecked me. That really hurt! They're not the sweet creatures Mom seems to think they are. They're evil and they hate me — just like Lucas.

I still can't believe I have to see him at school next week. I persuaded Mom to walk there with me on the first day, since it will be a new school on a whole new planet and everything. As for walking with Lucas after that? Maybe I'll suddenly take up cross country running — or cross country leaping — so he won't want to keep up with me, and I'll be rid of him.

CHAPTER 7

MELTDOWN

Life as a farmer was hard.

The turken chicks stank up the barn. They pooped everywhere and pecked at Belle whenever she tried to touch them. They scared her.

She made Melody help her clean the pen, since the android didn't mind being pecked. But when her parents found out they took Melody away to help Yun with the water tank repairs.

"Myra gave you those chicks to learn how to care for other living creatures," Zara said. "How will you learn if Melody does all the work?"

So every morning, Belle was left alone with her killer chicks. In the afternoons there were farm chores, most of which she did by herself too. She tended her mom's vegetable patch and helped her dad put up fence posts around the corrals. He made it her job to see that every fence post was properly placed. She also had to check the crisscrossing laser beams between the posts to make sure they functioned correctly. Then she cleaned the house and studied up on how to care for the new farm animals that her parents had applied for. But the worst chore of all had to be mucking out Loki's stall every day. Belle couldn't believe how much of a mess a horsel could make. After three days of this, she was tired and bored.

On the fourth day, her parents received their permits to grow crops and keep livestock.

"There's such a shortage of farmers," Yun said. "The authorities are practically giving these permits out as you land in Olympia."

A truck arrived two days later. It carried dozens of bags of seed, twenty-four alpacas, three dozen shoats, and a bunch of turken.

"I didn't think the animals would arrive this quickly," Zara said, examining the alpacas.

Belle approached a shoat. It rammed her legs with its hard head. From a distance these animals were almost cute. But up close, they could be scary.

For the next week, Belle rose with the sun and worked all day helping her parents around the farm. They fed and watered the animals twice a day. There was now even more mucking of pens and stalls for Belle to do. Yun programmed and reprogrammed the laser fences to the right intensity.

"Don't want to fry these animals before we learn how to care for them, do we?" Yun said. He laughed, ignoring Belle's sulky face.

Belle didn't think any of this was funny. Each day she longed to go back to Earth, back to her city life, and to going out to the holo-movies with her friends. But her parents wouldn't listen. They were too busy being happy about "going back to their roots" and "being the backbone of a new civilization." Someone forgot to tell them that Mars was not a new civilization — it was more than a hundred cycles old.

Then there was the food. Myra was wrong when she said mealworms were delicious. They were tough and chewy. Zara ground them into flour and made bread. Belle barely nibbled at it. She kept seeing the disgusting worm wriggling in Myra's six-fingered hand. It was a good thing the Walkers had given them some meat and eggs or Belle would've starved.

At dinnertime on the night before school, Belle was in a foul mood. She didn't want to start school. She'd had enough of her chicks, and she'd definitely had enough of being a farmer. Yun was telling stories about his trip into Sun City for supplies. Zara suggested names for their alpacas. But Belle felt more and more miserable. Her parents would never want to leave. She'd never see Earth again. She stared at the food on her plate, pushing the beans around with her fork.

"Aren't you eating?" Zara asked. Yun stopped talking and looked at Belle as if he hadn't noticed her lack of appetite until that moment.

"Not hungry," murmured Belle.

"Well, you need to keep up your energy," Yun said. "You've got school tomorrow. Now, eat."

"No." Belle smacked her fork onto her plate.

"Isabelle Song . . ." her mom warned.

"*What?*" Belle dared to glare at her mom, but only for a second.

"What has gotten into you?" Yun asked. "You were quite happy helping me with the animals today."

"I'm never happy," Belle said. "Not anymore."

"Oh boy," Yun said, leaning back in his chair. "Is this what we have to look forward to when you're a teenager?"

"*Really*, Yun?" Zara said.

Belle jumped out of her seat. "Dad! Stop it! Why can't you just listen to me?"

"Then tell us, what's wrong?" Zara asked.

"Nothing!" Belle got louder with each sentence. "You two just don't get it. You're acting like you've been farmers your whole lives, when you know nothing! In the meantime, I have no friends and no life! I hate Mars. I want to go back home!"

"I understand. It's been a big change for all of us," Yun said. "But I bet you'll make new friends when you go to school tomorrow."

"Not if they're anything like Lucas Walker. All he does is laugh at me." Belle shoved her plate off the table, spilling food and making a loud clang that echoed through their house. "He was right about one thing though — I hate living underground!"

She stormed up the stairs and knocked over a chair in the shack. She stomped hard on the front step, putting a hole into the wood. Cursing it, she ran.

And ran.

The sun lingered on the horizon, lighting the sky in blue first, blending upward into a fiery red-orange. As Belle ran, startled birds took flight, cawing noisily as they rose into the chilly evening air.

Belle's face and lungs stung as the cold whipped by her. She ran all the way to a big cluster of trees at the farthest end of their farm.

She leaned against a wide trunk, rubbing the stickiness of dried tears off her cheeks.

She slid down to the ground and lay her head against the rough tree bark, listening to her own breath and the silence around her. Earth didn't have this kind of silence. It was frightening, but also sort of comforting. Slowly, she drifted off, dreaming of her apartment back home, and her old friends, whose faces faded away one by one.

The sudden sound of grass rustling woke her.

"Who's there?" she called. The familiar squeak of her android's joints told her she was safe. "How did you find me?"

"I followed you," Melody said. "I was giving you some space, as humans like to say."

"Thanks," Belle said. It was nice to know that at least Melody understood her.

"I advise you to return to the house now. It is getting very cold."

Belle stood up and stretched. "I'm not ready to go back yet."

"How do trees get on the Internet?" Melody asked.

"What? I don't know. What do you mean?"

"They simply log on," Melody replied, waiting for Belle to laugh at her joke.

Belle shook her head. "You're going to have to work on your timing, Melody."

She looked up at the thick, low branches above her. They stretched outward like giant arms. "Let's climb."

Belle reached up and swung one leg over the first limb, and then the next.

"You should not go any higher," Melody said, when Belle had climbed up four thick limbs.

Melody hovered up and landed on the tree next to Belle. The limb was wide enough to hold them both. They sat there in silence. As they looked out over the Song farm, the sun sank below the horizon. The sky was filled with shades of red, orange, and purple. It was a spectacular sunset.

"It is a very pleasant farm," Melody said. "And in an ideal spot."

"You don't approve of my outburst," Belle stated.

"It has only been two weeks," Melody replied. "You begin a new chapter tomorrow. You should give this life a chance."

Belle was about to tell Melody she sounded a lot like her mom when she heard something.

"What was that?" It was a sound she'd never heard before.

They sat quietly and listened. Soon they heard it again.

"It sounds like a howl," Melody said.

"Shh!" Belle put her finger to her lips.

There was definitely a howling sound in the distance. Then something else howled back. Belle removed a pair of binoculars from Melody's central storage compartment. She focused them on the direction of the howls. But even with night-vision activated, she couldn't see anything.

"It's getting closer," Belle said in a loud whisper. "Are you carrying any of my Petripuffs?" Belle had created the small, handheld defensive weapons as a science project the year before. They could paralyze an enemy long enough to let someone escape.

"Your father forbade them on the journey here," Melody said. "He said they were too dangerous to carry."

"Really? Too dangerous for an alien planet, with strange alien animals lurking in the darkness?" Belle tried to swallow her anger. She had to focus on those howls.

"We should return home," Melody said.

Belle wrapped her arms around Melody's neck. The android hovered down to the ground in seconds. Melody activated her light beam and guided Belle home. With each kilometer, more howls seemed to join in — each time sounding closer.

Belle's heart was pounding when she dashed inside the shack. She slammed the flimsy door behind them.

"What *was* that?" she panted.

"According to my archives, that would be the night call of wolves," Melody responded.

The door to their underground home slid open. Her parents came rushing out.

"We were so worried!" Zara pulled Belle into a hug.

"You shouldn't be outside after dark," Yun said.

"Did you hear them?" Belle asked.

"Hear what?"

"Wolves!"

They stood very still for a long while, listening. There was nothing more than the occasional caw of an unknown bird outside.

Yun sighed. "There are no wolves on Mars. People here never cloned any predators, unless you count dogs. And they're tame."

"But I heard them! You have to believe me," Belle exclaimed. Her anger came flooding back.

"You have an overactive imagination, Belle," Yun said. Then he insisted that Belle head straight to bed. "You don't want to show up on your first day of school exhausted and cranky."

Sol 114/Summer, Cycle 105

Those were wolves I heard. I don't care that my parents don't believe me. I can't imagine hearing something that I've never heard before in my life! Whatever. I've got to start making more Petripuffs to protect myself. I've given Melody a list of ingredients to buy. I hope Dad doesn't notice my allowance shrinking.

I'm not looking forward to school tomorrow. Martian kids go to school from Spring to Fall because winters are too cold. Thank the stars we only go twice a week. The rest of our school work is done at home.

I'm sure I'll have a lot more to write about the school — just don't expect it to be good.

CHAPTER 8

AN UNUSUAL NEW FRIEND

The next morning was cold and misty when Belle crawled out of bed. She'd barely slept. She kept waiting for more wolves to howl to prove to her parents that she hadn't imagined it. But they never howled again, not once.

At breakfast, Belle wasn't in a good mood. She was mad at her parents and how they thought she'd made up the wolf stuff. But she knew that arguing wouldn't solve anything. So she decided that she just wouldn't talk at all.

Zara and Belle left the house early. They headed north, strolling through the fields and cutting across the back of their farm.

"I don't see Lucas," Zara said, breaking the silence.

Belle grunted.

"I wonder who else lives here? It would be nice to get to know more neighbors, don't you think?"

Belle bent down to pull a pebble out of her shoe. They walked on for a while longer.

"There!" Zara pointed ahead. "That's the school."

The low, box-like building stood alone in a vast empty area of grass and dust. It had smooth gray walls and barely any windows. Belle couldn't see a playground or a sports field anywhere. It was the saddest looking schoolhouse she'd ever seen.

Only when she squinted could she see the outline of a town beyond the building. She saw more low, boxy buildings with flapping canopies shading the alleyways between them.

That must be Sun City, Belle thought.

Zara turned to Belle. "Okay, I get that you're angry," she huffed. "But nothing ever got solved by sulking. If you want to be heard, you have to speak up."

Belle kicked at some pebbles at her feet.

"I know you're unhappy about moving here," Zara said, more gently. "But what did you expect us to do? We have no jobs with BAMCorp. And we can't force them to give us jobs, can we?"

"That's not it," Belle mumbled.

"So you hate being a farmer." Zara threw her hands up. "What would you like us to do instead? I'm open to any ideas."

Belle shrugged.

Zara sighed. "Well, when you think of something, let me know." She pointed to the building. "Do you think you could try to be polite to your teacher, at least?"

Belle gave her half a nod, and they walked on toward the school.

Sun City School occupied a corner of the gray block building. The building also housed a medical clinic, a library, and the community center. The school had children from kindergarten all the way through senior high school. Children from all the farms in the area came here for their education.

"Your class is in room number one," the principal, Ms. Yuko, said. She seemed nice, though Belle thought she smiled too much. "Please say your goodbyes now."

"Have a great day," Zara said. She opened her arms and Belle gave her a long hug that said "goodbye" and "I'm sorry" at the same time.

Ms. Yuko walked Belle down the long, narrow hallway. There were three doors on each side, all slightly open. Belle looked back to watch her mom leave the building. She missed her already. Then someone tapped her on the shoulder.

Belle turned around, and her mouth fell open. Here was a girl (at least, Belle *thought* it was a girl) who was definitely not human. Her shoulder-length black hair looked like it was made of plastic. She had a high, ridged forehead, where her nostrils were located. Her two large eyes seemed to glow gray and yellow. And her lips were a bright red, which made her smile surprisingly pretty. She lowered her head when Belle looked at her, and made a gesture with her hands, weaving them around like a dance.

"*Gyrvel* — Welcome. I'm your buddy for the day," she said, in a soft voice. "My name is Ta'al."

"Ta'al will show you around until you are comfortable," Ms. Yuko said. "Have a productive day."

She disappeared back into her office.

"Are you Sulux?" Belle asked as Ta'al led her down the hallway.

"Oh no!" Ta'al said. "I'm Nabian. The Sulux don't really —"

Before she could finish her sentence, someone ran past them, shoving Ta'al against the wall. Before he disappeared into the last room on the left, he turned back to look. It was Lucas Walker. He had a strange expression on his face as he looked at Ta'al and then at Belle.

"Hey!" Belle said. "Watch where you're going."

Ta'al straightened out her long tunic and continued to lead Belle to the room Lucas had just entered.

"Are you all right?" Belle asked. "That wasn't nice of him."

"It was just *ivusyxd* — an accident," Ta'al said. "This hallway is very narrow."

Belle wasn't so sure of that.

Ta'al introduced Belle to their teacher. She was a tall, dark-haired human with green-blue eyes ringed by a circle of red.

"Good morning Belle, I'm Ms. Polley," she said. "Welcome to our class."

The classroom was a lot smaller than at Belle's old school. There was one large table for four students in the middle of the room. Four other small desks were scattered about the room. A holo-screen computer lay in front of every seat. Screens along the walls alternated posters for all the different ages of students that occupied this room.

Lucas, two boys, and a girl sat around the large table. They were all human, except for Lucas. They were very tall for sixth graders, which made Belle feel like a kindergartner. They also had red ringed irises, just like their teacher. Was this a trait of Martian-born people?

"You will be our sixth student," Ms. Polley said.

A bell rang from somewhere outside. Ms. Polley clapped her hands, and everyone turned to look at her.

"This is Isabelle, our latest addition," she said. She dragged two individual desks together and added, "You and Ta'al will be table buddies this term. I'll rotate you all next term."

Lucas and his table friends moaned. They stuck two fingers on their foreheads in some kind of secret signal. Ta'al looked away and took her seat. Belle glared at Lucas.

The lessons that day focused mostly on agricultural topics. Belle learned about the latest methods for growing meat in a lab and the needs of cross-bred animals. The class also discussed advancements in plant modification and the advantages of micro-algae. She wondered when they'd be learning math, or her favorite subject — space science.

Through most of the classes, Ta'al was silent. As the other students raised their hands and asked questions or gave comments, Ta'al seemed content to sit quietly and listen. She only spoke when Belle asked her questions. Even the teacher left her alone.

At lunchtime, Ta'al led Belle to a small cafeteria shared by the middle school classes. They sat at their designated class table. Belle met Trina, the other girl in their class, who seemed nice. Pavish, Brill, and Lucas made up the rest of their table. They all spoke to Belle, asking her questions about her family and where she came from. Lucas even managed to ask her about the games she played. But no one spoke to Ta'al. It made Belle uncomfortable.

After lunch, the others invited Belle to join them outside. The weather was nice enough to be outdoors, and Martians took every chance they could to get some sunshine. They played a disc throwing game that Belle found too hard to keep up with. The Martian-born humans were taller and faster than her. She did her best but wasn't very good at the game. After watching for a few minutes, she wandered off by herself.

She spotted Ta'al sitting next to a tall tree stump. All its branches had been sawed off.

Belle sat down beside her. "Hi Ta'al. Why are you sitting by yourself? Don't you like the games we're playing?" she asked.

Ta'al closed the book on her datapad and looked toward the other students.

"I prefer to read," she said.

"I do too," Belle said with a big smile. She liked Ta'al, and she hoped they could be friends. "Tell me about your book."

Ta'al seemed happy to talk about the story she was reading. Belle told her about her own favorite books. Before long, the two girls were laughing like old friends. When the bell rang, it was time for class to resume.

"I have an exciting announcement," Ms. Polley said as they took their places. "The schools of Olympia are having a science fair, and we've been invited to compete."

At the words "science fair" Belle perked up. This was her kind of thing.

"I'm going to pair you up with a classmate, and you'll come up with a project to work on," Ms. Polley continued. "One winning pair from each grade will be chosen to represent our school in Tharsis City, the Martian capital of Olympia, next summer."

Belle's mind was whirling with ideas. She looked at Ta'al.

"I hope we can be partners," she whispered.

"*Teyqarro.*" Ta'al crossed her fingers.

"First, I'd like us to discuss what we've done in previous years," Ms. Polley said.

Belle was too busy coming up with ideas for projects to listen to her classmates. Besides, no one asked Ta'al about her ideas, so Belle almost didn't care. The others were polite enough to Belle, but she didn't understand why they ignored her new friend. She really hoped that Ta'al could be her partner. Together, they would come up with something amazing for the Fair. Belle was certain that the other kids would then want to be friends with them both.

"Isabelle," Ms. Polley called. Belle looked at her, realizing that she hadn't heard anything the teacher had said. "Tell us what you've done before."

Belle sat up straight. She loved talking about her science projects. She was an expert. "Well, my latest invention was a defensive weapon that I call Petripuffs. They're covered with gel and are shaped like a ball that fits in your hand. You throw them at an enemy. If the ball hits, the powdered ingredients inside puff out to paralyze the target for about thirty seconds. This gives the thrower the time needed to get away to safety."

Everyone gaped at Belle. Ms. Polley coughed into her hand.

"I see." She spoke slowly, as if Belle didn't understand English. "In Olympian towns, we try to confine our science projects to those with agricultural applications. Perhaps you may have grown a plant in varied environments? Or extracted the DNA of a fruit?"

"Sure," said Belle, puzzled by the way her teacher was speaking. "Back when I was in kindergarten."

"Hmm. I see." Ms. Polley walked around her desk and sat down. "I suppose you are new to our planet, so I can't expect you to be aware of . . . our priorities." She looked down at her computer screen. Looking back up, she seemed to have come up with an idea. "Since you live so close to Lucas, I think it would be best if you were paired with him for the Fair. What do you say to that?"

The expression on her teacher's face told Belle that she'd better say it was a great idea. But inside, Belle was horrified.

"As neighbors, you should be able to work together easily." Ms. Polley leaned back in her chair. "And Lucas is an experienced student. He can help guide you in how we do things."

Belle couldn't look at Lucas, or at Ta'al. This day turned out as badly as she'd expected — just when things had begun to look more hopeful.

Sol 115/Summer, Cycle 105

All we learn in school is farm stuff. It's all SO boring!

I met a really nice girl. Her name is Ta'al. She's Nabian, a different alien race from Lucas and Myra. The others in class treat her like she's weird, but I think she's pretty. And she's fun to talk to. I think we could be best friends. I don't understand why the others don't like her.

Our teacher is odd too. She wasn't impressed by my Petripuffs. Why not? They won the science fair last year.

I can't believe I've been partnered with Lucas for the science fair. Even worse — the projects all have to be related to FARMING!!! Ms. Polley said it's because we're from Sun City and farming is our "primary industry," whatever that means.

Aaaaaaaggghhh! It makes me want to scream! I really wanted to be partnered with Ta'al. She got Brill, and looked as horrified as I was. Poor girl.

At least Lucas seemed pleased to be my partner. He didn't stop talking all the way home. I was too busy thinking about Ta'al to hear what he said. We're meeting in the big barn tomorrow. I hope he's ready to hear my ideas.

CHAPTER 9

NIGHTMARE PROJECT

"I don't want to experiment with turken chicks!" Belle stomped her foot at Lucas, as he put his tools down on the barn floor. He had an entire wheelbarrow full of mesh wiring, wooden stakes, and aluminum panels.

"It's our best chance of winning the science fair," he said. It was the day after being paired with Lucas, and Belle felt that he didn't hear a word she'd said. She had lots of great ideas, but he kept shaking his head.

"Turken are very important for our economy. We'll definitely win if we can find a natural way to grow them bigger and faster."

He went on and on. Belle heard only one in three words. The chicks in her pen made so much noise, it made her squirm. She couldn't bear the thought of getting scratched again.

Lucas moved about the barn, setting up three separate pens. He hammered and cut, while Belle stood there and watched him. When he was finished, he opened his arms wide, like a presenter at a game show. "Here's the future — Super Chicks!" he said with a big smile. "They're all natural and more nutritious than ever before." He looked like he was expecting Belle to applaud.

She didn't.

"I don't really like chicks," she said.

"You don't have to like them to win the science fair," he said. "Now let's go look for bugs to feed one set of chicks."

"Bugs? There are bugs on Mars too?"

Lucas gave her a funny look. "Duh. They hitched a ride in the earliest bags of seed from Earth. They've been here ever since."

Belle cringed and gave up trying to protest. It didn't matter what she wanted. Lucas had already decided everything. What was the point of being his partner? He was a one-man show. She watched him lift rocks and scratch beneath tree trunks until he'd found dozens of insects. Her skin crawled each time he showed them to her.

On their way back to the barn, he grew quiet. Belle was about to finally tell him why she would rather do something else for their project. But then he turned and said, "You're not much of a partner, are you?"

Belle couldn't believe her ears.

"What? *You're* not much of a partner!" Her cheeks were burning with anger.

"I did everything here today." He crossed his arms. "Is this the way it's going to be for the whole project?"

"You didn't even ask me if I wanted to do this," Belle retorted.

"You're new here," Lucas responded defensively. "You don't know what sort of projects win. And I heard your parents say you've never been farmers before. I was trying to be helpful."

Belle didn't have a chance to defend herself. Lucas stormed back into the barn, refusing to look at her. He poured his insects into one of the pens and then placed two turken chicks inside. He was spreading the bugs around with a stick when Belle marched up to him.

"You're not being fair," she said. "We're supposed to be partners, but you've made all the decisions."

He didn't say anything. He wasn't even paying attention to her. Belle grit her teeth and grabbed him by one shoulder. She tried to swing him around, so he'd at least look at her. She had to make him listen because he was being so unfair.

But instead of swinging around, Lucas lost his balance and fell backward into the nearest pen. The posts holding it up fell over, which knocked down a second pen, and then the third. This terrified the larger turkens, which squawked and flapped their wings. One bird hopped onto Lucas' chest as he lay on the ground, while another flew straight at Belle's face. She screamed and turned her back on it, which scared it even more. It flapped and squawked again, scratching Belle's arms and back. It landed on her shoulders and started pecking at her head. Belle ran around the barn, flailing her arms, trying to get the bird to leave her alone.

Finally, the turken let go of Belle and fell to the floor with a plop. It clucked angrily and headed back to its original pen.

"Just look at what you did!" She turned on Lucas.

"What *I* did? *You* shoved *me.*"

"I did not," Belle shouted. "You've been nothing but a big bully."

Lucas stared hard at Belle, and then turned away from her. He got down on his hands and knees and gathered up the escaping bugs. He dumped them into a bucket nearby and then started to pick up the fallen posts.

Seeing Lucas' response, Belle realized that maybe she had taken things too far. "Careful not to cut yourself on those wires," she said softly.

"What do you care?" he snapped. "You didn't lift a finger to help me build this."

"I really didn't mean to ruin all your work." She could see now how her anger had caused all of this mess. "Let me help you fix it. Please? I'd like to help."

Lucas' glare softened. Belle could see by the look on his face that he was trying to decide if he could trust her.

"Fine," he said at last. "But let's do it tomorrow. It's getting late, and I have to get home for dinner."

● ● ● ●

All through dinner, Belle kept thinking about her terrible behavior. Lucas had actually been nice to her. He had done so much work for a project they would both get credit for, and she hadn't helped at all. On top of that, he was coming back to fix the damage she had caused.

"May I go back to the barn tonight?" she asked her parents. "I have some work to do on our science project."

Her parents beamed at her.

"I knew you'd like it here once you went to school and made friends," Yun said. "Would you like Melody to help you?"

Belle shook her head. "This is my responsibility. I should take care of it." She couldn't bring herself to confess that it was her mess to clean up. And the less her parents knew of her bad behavior that day, the better.

Sol 110/Summer, Cycle 105, night

It took hours of work, but I fixed all the broken pens. It was hard putting the fencing panels together the right way, but I figured it out. I even put the chicks in their respective new pens. I barely got scratched this time. I think they still hate me, but I'm getting better at handling them.

I'll check on them again in the morning before Lucas comes. I hope the one I pushed off me isn't hurt too badly. Lucas would never forgive me for that. What a stressful day!

Oh shooting stars! I forgot to lock the barn door!

CHAPTER 10
MARTIAN DANGER

Sneaking out of the house was hard. Every movement alerted the home computer system. As soon as Belle's feet touched her bedroom floor, the lights came on. As she headed to the door, every room she passed lit up. Luckily, her parents' door was shut tight.

"Where are you going?" Melody unlatched herself from her charging port and strolled over to her. "May I help you?"

Belle put her finger to her lips. She told Melody about the barn door. Melody insisted on coming with her. Together, they made their way out to the barn. The night air was freezing so Belle ran. Melody hovered along behind her. She stopped suddenly.

"Wait!" Melody said.

"What is it?"

Then Belle heard it. Something was making a shuffling sound inside the barn. There was a whimper and another sound she couldn't describe. She tiptoed to the barn door. It was open. Belle swallowed the lump in her throat.

"Something's inside," she whispered.

"Throw open the door when I say so," Melody said, as she positioned herself in front of Belle. "Now!"

Belle swung open the door. Melody turned on her light beam. Staring back at them were four shining eyes. And two sets of sharp, gleaming teeth!

Wolves!

There really were wolves here. Like the llamas, these were much bigger than wolves on Earth.

Belle froze. For the longest moment, the wolves stared at Melody and Belle. Belle stared back.

"Step to the side, very slowly," Melody said.

Belle obeyed, moving over to the side. As she did, she saw the entire picture. Around the wolves' mouths and at their feet was a pool of blood . . . and bloody feathers.

Her chicks!

"No!" Without thinking, Belle ran toward the pen.

"Stop!" yelled Melody.

Belle stopped. Her heart was racing, but not because she was afraid of the wolves. One of her chicks lay dead on the ground. And the pens were destroyed. Chicks were hiding everywhere, shivering and frozen in fear. Suddenly a fire seemed to light inside Belle's chest. She screamed at the wolves and waved her arms at them.

"How dare you! You ruined everything!"

One of the wolves tilted its head to the side, making it look almost tame. Then the other wolf took a step forward. Belle heard a low growl coming from its chest. Slowly, it bared its teeth at her.

Belle realized what was happening, and now she was scared. She wished she had some Petripuffs with her. But she hadn't been able to make any. She was still waiting for the ingredients to be delivered.

Melody placed herself between Belle and the wolves. Her lower cavity opened and a yellow and white stick emerged. It looked like an oversized two-pronged fork. Belle had never seen it before.

"What is that?" she asked, careful not to take her eyes off the wolves for a second.

"Your father thought we would need a livestock prod," Melody said. "This should scare them." She activated the device, and it crackled a flash of electricity into the air. Belle jumped. The wolves cowered.

Melody made a rumbling sound similar to the wolf's growl. She moved closer to the animals. They took a few steps back, lowering their heads.

"Shoo!" Melody shouted.

One wolf yelped, turned tail, and ran out the barn door. The other one bared its teeth even more, and snapped at the android. Melody took another step closer and repeated her order, only louder. The wolf lunged at her. Belle screamed just as the barn door swung open wide. Her parents stood in the doorway, the light of the night sky making them look like shadows.

"Get out!" Yun shouted. He moved toward the wolf. The animal crouched low on all fours as it saw the sonic blaster Yun was carrying. Belle heard the hum of the blaster as it began charging. Zara ran to Belle's side.

"What's Dad going to do?" Belle had never seen her dad with a weapon before.

"Hush," said her mom. Belle held on to her mother.

Yun fired a shot at the ground next to the wolf, and it yelped. Keeping its eyes on the blaster, the wolf slinked past Yun and ran away into the night.

Belle burst into tears. She couldn't tell if it was due to fear of the wolves, all of the damage done, or because of the dead chick.

"Wolves!" Zara said. "Oh my! They're so huge!"

"You were right, Belle," Yun said. "Are you hurt?"

"You shouldn't have come out alone," Zara said. "This isn't Earth, child. You can't keep going outside after dark. It's dangerous at night."

In between her tears and catching her breath, Belle told her parents how Melody had protected her. "I didn't even know Melody had an electric prod."

"I picked one up in Darwin, just in case," Yun said.

Belle hugged her android. "You saved my life."

"I was simply performing my primary function. You behave rather recklessly in dangerous situations."

Yun chuckled, rubbing his face. "It's a good thing I practiced using this blaster today. I didn't want to kill the wolf, but the gun sure scared it."

Belle was still shaking from the encounter. As she looked around, she became even more upset about the chick that died. The others around the barn looked all right, but they were too scared to come out of their hiding places.

"Lucas will never forgive me now."

Yun put his arm around Belle. "I'm sure he'll understand when we explain what happened."

Belle wasn't so sure about that. It was her carelessness that let the wolves into the barn in the first place. Yun picked up the remains of the turken chick and together they buried it out back.

"I'm sorry we didn't believe you about the wolves," he said. "We haven't been listening to you much, have we?"

"I'm sorry too." Belle hugged her dad. "I know I haven't been very helpful either."

They went back to the barn and Belle looked over all the damage. She couldn't let Lucas see this. "I want to fix this before I go to bed," she said.

"If we work together, it'll get fixed faster," Zara said.

Belle looked over the mess. It looked hopeless. If they couldn't fix this, Lucas might never speak to her again.

Sol 111/Summer, Cycle 105, almost morning

It's almost morning but I can't sleep. I'm exhausted but my eyes won't stay shut. I keep seeing those scary wolves' huge yellow eyes staring at me through the dark. And the sound of Dad's sonic blaster firing — my heart still hasn't stopped racing!

We worked all night to fix the pens. Mom and Dad were actually pretty cool about it. They didn't yell or scold me even once. The pens look OK now. I kind of miss that one chick that died. I can't stop seeing its bloody body. It was a nightmare. Dad said some nice things about it when we buried it. It made me cry, but I guess it was kind of silly at the same time.

What I'm worried about most is Lucas. When I see him later, he'll be so mad. What if he doesn't want to be my partner anymore? How will I get to compete in the Science Fair? After the way I've behaved, maybe I don't deserve to. Serves me right.

CHAPTER 11
HOME SWEET HOME

Lucas showed up a few hours later. He brought more supplies to fix the broken pens. Belle's stomach twisted painfully as she explained to him what had happened the night before. As he listened, his shoulders slumped and his face darkened. Belle was afraid to hear what he was going to say. This had been all her fault. She braced herself for yelling.

"*Iqnah!*" Lucas mumbled without translating the word. Belle didn't want to know what it meant. She waited for more. He dug his toe into the dirt. "I guess we have a lot of work to do today."

"I'm really sorry," she squeaked.

"Sulux have a saying — *Veth yln*. It's sort of like 'That's life.' Life here on Mars can be unpredictable. You didn't know about the wolves. How could you?"

Belle swallowed. She couldn't tell him she had heard the wolves once before.

"Why aren't you mad at me? I ruined everything."

He looked at her. "Why should I be? You didn't wreck everything on purpose, did you?"

"No, of course not," she responded.

"Well then, what's the point of being mad? It just wastes energy. And we need to use our energy to fix the project."

He headed for the barn. Belle held the door for him. She waited outside for a moment, holding her breath.

"It doesn't look so bad," he said. "You did a good job of fixing things up."

"My parents helped. So did Melody." The pens looked almost as if nothing had happened. Except for the missing chick.

"Melody?"

"She's my android," Belle said. "A Personal Home Helper, model 3X. She's great."

"I've seen it around, but I didn't know it was an intelligent robot. Aren't you afraid?" he asked.

"First, 'it' is a 'she'. Second, why should I be afraid?" she replied.

He put his supplies down. "Because of the Robot Rebellion back on Earth, and everything that happened back then."

"That's old news," Belle said. "And Melody is even older. She belonged to my grandmother. Her model type wasn't responsible for the fighting or the attempt to overthrow the government. Those rebel robots were highly advanced. Besides, they were all taken offline and dismantled. Melody is completely safe. She's helped take care of me and has been my friend since I was a baby."

He nodded. "Okay. If you say so."

Belle looked at him. She had to figure him out. Why was he being so nice to her?

"You didn't like me at first." The words just tumbled out. "And honestly, I wasn't sure I liked you either."

Why did she say that? Now, he'd be mad at her for sure. Sometimes she didn't think before she spoke, and it offended people. But Lucas just looked at the chicks searching for food in their pens and smiled shyly.

"I'm not very good with meeting new people. My mom says I'm an 'introvert', whatever that is. There is no Sulux word for it."

Belle started to say that it meant that he was shy. But she bit her tongue instead. She didn't want to come across as too much of a know-it-all, not when they were just beginning to get along.

"Honestly, a lot of Terrans move here, thinking life will be easy. They like to call it the 'simple life.' It's an insult, really. Farming on Mars is no picnic. I see how hard my parents work. They love it, but it's not easy. So sometimes I get mad with Terrans. Although, I see that your family is serious about making a go of it."

He pulled out a bag of seed and threw a handful into the pen. The chicks rushed toward it.

"I get that," Belle said quietly. She threw a handful of seed into the second pen.

He shrugged, not looking away from the chicks. "So, I guess I'm sorry for being so rude. You're not so bad, after all."

"Thanks," Belle said. "You're not so bad yourself." She paused. "Why don't you like Ta'al? She's not Terran."

Lucas exhaled loudly. Something in his body language told her that this was not something he wanted to talk about.

"We really should get to work," he said.

Belle nodded. She knew not to push him for an answer. They were becoming friends. She didn't want to ruin it now. She could wait until he was ready to talk.

The rest of the day, Belle did everything she could to be helpful. She didn't complain about how wriggly the chicks were, and she went out to dig for insects when Lucas asked her to. She did her best to ask lots of questions. Some of them seemed pretty dumb, but Lucas didn't seem to mind answering them.

All in all, it was a really good day.

In the evening, Lucas' and Belle's parents came to check on their project.

"We're so proud of how much work you two have done on your project," Yun said.

"You're bound to win at the fair," Paddy chuckled.

Paddy asked Belle to explain what they were doing, and surprisingly, she was able to answer some of his questions. Lucas helped with the rest.

Then Melody came to the barn, carrying a tray of drinks and food and a large blanket.

"Zara felt you might all like to have a picnic. It is an unusually warm evening, and the stars are particularly bright tonight."

As Melody led them outside, Lucas lagged behind. After she spread out the blanket for them to sit on, Belle brought her over to meet Lucas. He shook Melody's hand awkwardly, standing as far away from her as possible.

"He's a little afraid of androids," Belle whispered to Melody.

"Shall I tell him a few jokes?" Melody asked.

Melody stepped closer to Lucas, who froze in place.

"A duck walks into a pharmacy and says, 'Give me some chap stick. Feel free to put it on my bill.'"

Belle held her breath. Would Lucas always be afraid of Melody?

Lucas burst out laughing. "Ha! That's so bad."

Belle laughed too.

"Apparently, my work is done here," Melody said, as she returned to setting out the picnic dinner.

The two families settled around the blanket as Melody served everyone. Belle told the Walkers all about what had happened the night before.

"Melody actually protected me from the wolves," she said.

Lucas' eyes grew wide as he looked from Belle to Melody and back again. The purple rings around his brown eyes glowed in the starlight. Belle took a bite of turken leg, wiping the dripping juices from her chin. She enjoyed entertaining everyone with her story.

As the night went on, laughter and light from the moon Phobos filled the air. Belle smiled as she watched her parents and the Walkers exchanging stories and having fun. This was the first moment that Belle felt truly happy since moving to Mars. She was finally ready to call this strange red world her home.

Sol 112/Summer, Cycle 105

Tonight was pretty perfect. Lucas and I fixed our project, and then we had a fantastic picnic under the stars. Myra talked about the constellations. Paddy told us Martian fairy tales. Afterwards, Lucas showed me how to make a slingshot. Melody and I taught him about Petripuffs. We might just make him an android fan after all.

I think, even after everything that's happened, I might just start to like it here on Mars — maybe.

PART TWO:
RAIDERS!

Farming life on Mars can be very difficult. The weather is unpredictable, and growing hybrid crops and animals takes a lot of hard work. Most challenging of all is having enough freshwater. It is the most precious resource on the planet. Unfortunately, some people would rather steal water from others than buy it legally. These rough Water Raiders pose a serious threat to every farmer trying to make a living on Mars . . .

CHAPTER 12
SIGNS OF TROUBLE

"Fresh turken eggs, shoat milk, and cheese!" shouted Belle. The market at Sun City was especially crowded today. Belle was helping at her family's stall while her parents stocked up on supplies. All the farmers were getting ready for winter, buying everything they needed to keep them comfortable for the long, cold months ahead. Mars winters were harsh. Temperatures often plunged to 50 degrees below zero or more.

In four hours, Belle had sold all their produce. Only a few skeins of alpaca yarn were left on the table. Belle was proud that she'd helped her parents shear the alpacas on their farm. Then Zara had taught her how to spin the alpaca wool into yarn. Her mom had learned from her grandmother, who in turn had learned it from her grandmother. By market day, the Songs had a large collection of wool and yarn ready for sale.

"I suppose we can pack up now," Yun said as he returned with his own bundle of supplies. He seemed happy to see that sales had gone so well.

Zara dragged an enormous, colorful rug behind her. It was woven from shoat wool that had been dyed in various bright colors.

She exhaled and wiped her brow. "Please, let's go. I'm exhausted. I'll need help getting this rug onto the wagon. Your dad insisted on buying it."

"It will come in handy during the cold nights," Melody chimed in. With one heave, the android lifted the rug with her strong arms and threw it into the back of their hover-wagon. She scanned the contents of the wagon, checking the items off a list that was displayed on the screen on her torso.

"It looks as if we are all set for winter," she announced. Her eyes glowed pink. Melody was happy.

"Belle!"

Belle had one foot on the wagon's back step when she heard her name called. She turned around to see her friend Ta'al approaching.

"*Gyrvel*, my friend." Ta'al dipped her head and wove her hands in a dancelike gesture, the Nabian way of greeting others.

"Hi, Ta'al! Where were you yesterday?" Belle said. "You weren't at school."

Ta'al dabbed a handkerchief on her nostrils located on her ridged forehead. It had taken Belle awhile to get used to her alien friend's appearance. But in spite of her strange features, Belle thought Ta'al was beautiful. She especially liked Ta'al's large eyes that reflected the colors of her surroundings. Today, they were green and brownish orange, the colors of the marketplace.

"I caught a cold," Ta'al said. "I'm sad that I missed the end-of-year party. Was it good?"

Belle nodded. "But it wasn't any fun without you."

Ta'al laughed and prodded Belle's arm with her thick finger. "Silly girl," she said. "Now that I'm better, do you want to come over for *matekap* — a sleepover?"

Belle looked over at her parents, who had finished stacking their supplies in the wagon. They were busy checking that nothing was missing.

"That sounds like a lovely idea," Zara said, stepping out of the wagon and wiping her hands on her skirt. She smiled at Ta'al. "But I'd like to speak to your parents about it first, if you don't mind."

Ta'al pulled out a flat disc from somewhere under her many layers of clothing. She tapped on it several times, and then looked up. "They're on their way."

As they waited, Ta'al showed Belle her new communication device and how it worked using a code known only to Nabians.

Three large aliens, dressed like Ta'al in flowing layers of fabric, gracefully moved toward the Song family wagon. They walked as if their feet barely touched the ground.

Yun descended from the wagon as they approached.

"Who's this, then?" he said, with his usual grin.

"Nabians have three parents," Ta'al explained. "The human equivalent of my mother is So'ark."

The tallest of the three Nabians stepped forward, with both hands outstretched. She took Zara's hand in one and Yun's in the other. "I am pleased to know you," she said. "This is He'ern, my first *elixian*. The closest word in your language is *equal*."

"He'ern's function is much like that of a father to humans," Ta'al said.

He'ern greeted them all in the same way. Then he introduced Fa'erz, their third *elixian*.

"Without Fa'erz, I would not exist," Ta'al said. "To my knowledge, humans don't have an equivalent to the role Fa'erz plays in our family."

Belle had so many questions, but thought it best to keep them to herself. She didn't want to be rude. And she definitely wanted to do a sleepover. She hadn't had a sleepover since moving to Mars.

"We'll have so much fun," Ta'al whispered to Belle. "I have some new gadgets that I can't wait to show you."

Before Belle could ask about the gadgets, Lucas Walker came running up to them. He and Belle had become good friends in the last months, but for some unknown reason, he didn't like Ta'al. His parents, Myra and Paddy, followed closely behind Lucas.

"Come on, neighbor," Paddy said to Yun, chuckling. "Time to get going." But then he stopped very suddenly. He stared at the Nabians. "Having some trouble, Yun?"

"Not at all," Yun said, puzzled.

"Have you met Ta'al's parents?" Belle asked.

Lucas scowled at Ta'al, the same way he'd scowled at Belle when they'd first met. Back then he explained he'd been shy about meeting new people. But he'd known Ta'al longer than Belle. Yet, he never talked to Ta'al in school.

Belle didn't expect him to behave differently now. It was his parents' reaction that surprised her the most. Grown ups were supposed to have better manners. But Myra and Paddy ignored Ta'al's parents too!

For a long moment, no one spoke. The adults stared at the ground or the wagon. It was extremely awkward.

"We're ready to go as soon as you are, Paddy." Zara finally broke the silence. "It was so nice to meet you, So'ark. I hope we can set up a play date soon."

"Mom!" Belle cried. "I'm too old for *play dates*. It's a sleepover. A mat . . . a *matekap*. Why can't I go tonight?"

Zara gave Belle a stern look. "You can't go tonight. We have to get home and unload the wagon. We can talk about it later."

"It's okay Belle, we can plan for another time. Until then, we can work on your pronunciation." Ta'al smiled.

Ta'al's family bowed their heads and walked past the Song's wagon without another word. But Ta'al turned around to wave, and Belle waved back.

Myra Walker shook her head. As soon as Ta'al's family was out of sight she turned to Zara. "Are you sure you want Belle socializing with a Nabian?" she asked.

"Ta'al is my friend!" Belle was surprised at how loud her outburst was. She bit her lip.

Paddy put his arm around Yun. "It's just best not to," he said, speaking softly as if he were telling Yun a secret. "You know, for the safety of your family."

Yun nodded without speaking.

Paddy patted him on the back. "Good man," he said.

Belle was troubled during the ride home.

"Why don't the Walkers like Ta'al's family?" she asked her mom, who was programming knitting patterns into an old robot.

"I have found some historical archives," Melody said. "They might explain the tension between the Martians, the Sulux, and the Nabians."

"Tension?" Belle said. "But I remember reading that Sulux and Nabians came from the same planetary system."

"That is correct," Melody said.

"Yes, one system over from Earth's solar system," Zara added. "I remember you telling me that."

"So they were neighbors," Belle said. "Why would an alien species hate their neighbors?" Belle asked. "I'm an alien here too, since I was born on Earth. Does someone hate me for being Terran?"

"Of course not," Zara said. "We don't hate each other for where we're from. That's primitive."

"But that's what's happening here," Belle said. "I just want to know why."

"Perhaps some studying will help you discover the answers you seek," Melody said. Sometimes she sounded like an old professor. But this time she might be right.

Belle settled down to read the documents that appeared on Melody's chest display. She was quite absorbed in the history of Mars when she was jolted out of her seat.

"What was that?" she cried, regaining her balance.

Loki whinnied and stopped the hover-wagon. He sounded scared. Then Belle heard her dad yell. She peeked her head out by the front bench seat where Yun sat.

They were at their farm gate. Beyond it, Belle saw that all their animals were loose and running around. Alpacas and shoats roamed the front yard. Turkens pecked and scratched in Zara's little vegetable patch.

"Did we have a power outage?" Zara asked as she got down to open the gate.

"Maybe. But we have backup power," Yun said, guiding Loki through the gate.

As Melody began chasing the fowl back into the big barn, Belle ran to one of the corrals. "Some of the corral posts have been damaged," she said. "Could the alpacas have done that?"

Yun examined the posts. He was quiet for a long time. Suddenly he ran to the back of the house. Belle followed while Zara led Loki to the stables.

"Good. The water tank is safe," Yun said as Belle reached him. He scratched his head. "But it looks like someone made this mess on purpose."

"Who would do that?" Belle couldn't believe it. They were only gone for the day.

Sol 110/Autumn, Mars Cycle 105

Someone wrecked our fences and let the animals loose. Dad thinks it could be water raiders. I don't know who did it, but it was scary. I'm so glad we weren't home and that our security system held the intruders off. But why did they have to go and release all the animals?

I'm too scared to sleep. I did more research on the Nabians and Sulux instead. This is what I learned:

1. They're both from planets in the same binary solar system — that means they have two suns.
2. They both came to Earth for a first contact conference when the Terrans achieved interstellar flight.
3. Nabians are an ancient race. They're much older than the Sulux. They may even be related. But don't ever say that to them.
4. Nabians claim that they were on Mars long before Terrans. They resent the Sulux for sharing their terraforming technology.
5. Sulux think the Nabians are jealous of their friendship with Martian humans.

Basically, they've hated each other for years. And there's no convincing either side to be nice to the other. But I don't understand why humans should care. Why should we treat Nabians like they're the bad guys?

CHAPTER 13
HOME DEFENSES

The following evening, Belle sat quietly at the dining table, listening as her dad spoke to the Olympian authorities. It had taken him all day to reach them on the holo-vid. The authorities enforced the law for the entire region. They operated out of Tharsis City, Olympia's capital, on the other side of the Marine Valley River.

"If your tank is intact and nothing was stolen, there isn't much I can do." The holo-vid of the man's head floated above the dining table like an eerie balloon. He wasn't even looking at his camera.

The hologram also lit up Yun's face, making him look angry. "Then what am I supposed to do? The raiders are certain to return. I'm sure they were just testing our defenses."

"Like I said, there's nothing —"

"— you can do," Yun interrupted. "I got that. You might as well say I should put up a sign inviting them to just take my water."

The man finally looked up. He had circles under his eyes. Belle wondered if a lot of people complained to him every day. He slowly shook his head. "All I can say is, some communities have formed their own, sort of, watchdog groups. We don't condone violence. But banding together to keep the raiders out has worked before."

The man continued, "It helps to build morale too. I wouldn't worry too much. These raids usually don't last long. Raiders tend to get desperate right before winter sets in."

The screen fizzled out and the holo-vid faded back into the computer. Yun slammed his fists on the table, making Belle jump.

"I'm sorry, Belle," he said. "It's just so frustrating."

Belle put a hand on her dad's shoulder. "I think it's a good idea to have all the neighbors looking out for each other. I'd be happy to get Lucas and the other kids together to see what we can do."

Yun smiled at her. "You're very thoughtful. But please don't worry too much about it. This is an adult problem. Let the adults handle it."

Belle hated being told that she was too young to be helpful. Her parents didn't know how good her inventions were. She could help to protect their home just as well as they could.

"It's time for bed," Zara said.

"But it's barely sunset," Belle argued.

"You have to get up early for school tomorrow," Zara replied. "You don't want to keep Lucas waiting."

"Besides," her mom continued, "we need to give Dad some space to figure things out. Now, off to bed with you."

Belle knew this was an argument she couldn't win. So she and Melody headed to her room.

"I can't sleep this early," Belle whined to Melody.

"We could think up some new jokes," Melody said. "I will start. What did one ocean say to the other ocean?"

"I'm not in the mood for jokes," Belle snapped. Then she felt bad for being so rude. Melody was only trying to cheer her up. "What did the ocean say?" she asked.

"Nothing," Melody replied. "It just waved."

Belle rolled her eyes. That was bad. "No more. Please."

"Then perhaps you should work on your science project?" the android suggested. Belle and Lucas had been researching ways to grow turkens bigger and faster for their project. They were supposed to make their final presentation before the school year ended. The top two projects from the school would be chosen to present their findings at the Olympia Science Fair in Tharsis City the following summer.

Melody projected Belle's last homework entry onto the wall. Belle's turken chicks were growing very well eating the new mixture of food she and Lucas had created.

An hour later Bell put away her datapad. "I can't do any more until Lucas does his part," she said. "We're meeting tomorrow after school anyway. We'll do it together then."

Belle couldn't stop thinking about the raiders. She couldn't help worrying, no matter what her dad said. "I think we should make more Petripuffs."

Belle's Petripuffs were her pride and joy. She'd spent a lot of time working on perfecting them. She'd won first prize with them at her last science fair on Earth. Her parents had been too busy with work to see her receive her award, which made her sad. But she was still very proud of herself.

Now her Petripuffs were more than just a science fair project. They could be very useful in the Wild West of Mars. The small palm-sized balls released a powder that could paralyze anyone who breathed it in. The effect only lasted about thirty seconds. But in a dangerous situation, that time could mean the difference between getting hurt and escaping unharmed.

Melody moved to the cabinet where Belle kept the special ingredients for her puffs. It was kept locked because a special ingredient, the most important one, was unstable, and required careful handling.

"You have already put several puffs in the barn, in case the wolves return," Melody said, as she activated the locking mechanism. There was a quiet click as it unlocked.

"True, but we'll need more," Belle said. "Especially now that we also have to deal with raiders."

Melody had no response to that. They began forming gel balls in silence, adding each ingredient with care. Belle had made so many Petripuffs that she was almost as fast at making them as Melody.

"We're running low on PF-51," Belle said as she completed her fifth puff. "And the gel stuff that binds it all together."

Melody turned to face Belle. Her mouth glowed yellow, which was her sarcastic smile. "Gel stuff? How scientific of you."

Melody was good at sarcasm.

"You know what I mean."

"I will add the 'stuff' to my list," Melody said, still glowing. "It is late now. Time for bed."

As Belle lay in bed, she watched the stars twinkle outside her window. "The universe is so big," she said with a sigh.

"That is a given," Melody said, as she plugged herself into her charging port. "Your point being?"

"Nothing," Belle said. "I was just thinking how there must be millions of aliens out there. There must be all different kinds. Some more different than others."

"Another given." Melody's charger hummed quietly.

"Do you think they all hate each other?" Belle asked.

"That would seem unlikely," Melody replied. "I would need more specific information."

Belle didn't say anything.

"If you are referring to the Sulux and the Nabians," Melody said, lowering her volume, "their fight goes back many generations. Prejudice is seen in their every encounter."

"But their problems shouldn't affect us kids or be brought into our classroom," Belle argued. "Ta'al is a good person, and a great friend. She deserves a chance to fit in. We should all learn to exist together — not let old issues separate us."

"It will take more than the opinion of one little girl to bring them together in friendship," Melody responded.

"I'm not a *little girl*. Besides, I believe a single person can change the world . . . if she cares enough." She yawned and shut her eyes.

"Well quoted, my young friend." Melody's eyes glowed bright pink for a second, just before she powered down for the night.

Sol 112/Autumn, Mars Cycle 105, early morning

I was woken by the weirdest dream last night. I was a Nabian and Lucas was chasing after me. His whole family was trying to catch me. I didn't know why, but I was afraid. I couldn't shake the fear, so I decided to just get up early.

Melody's still charging. No one is awake. But outside, I hear the howl of wolves. I hope they don't come back. Just the sound of their howls is enough to give me goosebumps.

I need to find a way to get Lucas to see how good a person Ta'al is. We should all be friends.

CHAPTER 14

STANDING UP
FOR A FRIEND

After Belle and Lucas had been paired up for the science fair project, the walk to school became a time to discuss their progress. But once they reached school, Lucas usually ignored both Belle and Ta'al.

Belle was determined to change that. Somehow.

"It looks like the fifty percent micro-algae combination works the best so far," Lucas said. As they walked and talked, he kept his eyes on his datapad, which showed their project results. "We should be ready for our presentation today."

"If you don't look up occasionally, you will trip over something," Melody said. The android had decided to walk with them to school today. Belle suspected it was because of the recent incident with the raiders.

Lucas looked at Melody. "I don't think I'll ever get used to talking to an android like it was another person."

"She's not an 'it'," Belle reminded him again. "There's no reason to be afraid of her."

Lucas put the report away, sliding his datapad into his backpack. "Everyone's afraid of intelligent androids. I watched all the old news holo-vids of the fight between robots and people on Earth. It was scary."

"That was years ago, before our parents were even born," Belle said. "And Melody would never harm anyone."

Lucas shrugged. "She'd better not."

"I am a Personal Home Helper," Melody said, looking directly at Lucas. "I am not designed to hurt humans."

Lucas didn't reply.

As soon as the school building came into view, Lucas looked to the right and then ran on ahead. From the path to Belle's right, Ta'al approached, seeming to glide along as if she traveled above the ground. Belle stared at Ta'al's tiny feet as they peeked out from under her long cloak. Belle couldn't work out exactly how Ta'al could move with such gracefulness. It was one difference she'd noticed between the Nabians and the Sulux. Lucas wasn't nearly as graceful as Ta'al.

"Sorry I interrupted your talk with Lucas," she said. She wore layers of light-colored fabric that reminded Belle of fairy wings. Each layer looked fragile and shiny in the autumn morning sun.

"It wasn't you," Belle said, looking over at her android. "He still gets a little freaked out by Melody."

Ta'al waved to Melody, who greeted her in Ta'al's own language.

"That's incredible," Ta'al said. "You have perfect pronunciation."

"*Sia-mi* — thank you," Melody said. "I do my best."

Belle beamed. Her android *was* the best.

"I'll leave you now," Melody said as they reached the school gate. "I will meet you here after school."

"See you then," Belle said, grabbing Ta'al's hand. Together they ran to the gray block building that held the town's school, library, community center, and medical facility.

● ● ● ●

Lucas and Belle's project presentation went very well. Lucas had made all kinds of charts, using the data that Belle had gathered. They spoke with confidence as they explained how their new food formula made turken chicks grow fifty percent bigger in half the usual time.

Ms. Polley was impressed.

Belle was so pleased that she barely paid attention to the next report by Trina and Pavish. Every project had to be about agriculture, and agriculture didn't interest Belle very much. She had to admit, though, that she was starting to like the turkens. When she first got them as a gift from Lucas' mom, she hated how they smelled and their sharp claws. Now they were easy to handle and seemed to smell less.

The last students to present their project were Brill and Ta'al. Brill rushed up to the front and opened a holo-file on his datapad. Everyone could see it was full of notes. Ta'al stayed at her desk.

"Are you the only one presenting?" Ms. Polley asked.

Brill pointed at Ta'al. "She wouldn't help at all. So I did the project myself."

Everyone looked at Ta'al, who examined her fingers.

Belle leaned over and whispered. "What's wrong?"

Ta'al only blinked without looking up.

"Ta'al," Ms. Polley said, in a tone everyone knew meant she was in trouble. "Is this true? Are you being uncooperative?"

Ta'al didn't respond.

"Come on," Belle whispered. "You should tell her the truth."

"Can't ever expect a Nabian to do their part," Lucas mumbled. The others snorted.

"That's really rude," Belle snapped. "You don't even know the whole story."

Lucas stood up. "You can't trust Nabians. They're just a bunch of lazy raiders."

Belle smacked her hand on her desk so hard that her datapad screen fizzled. "You take that back, Lucas Walker!"

"I will not!" he yelled. "Everyone knows that the raiders are Nabians. They want to rule Mars. But they can't, so they make it hard for the rest of us to live here. And they're jealous of the Sulux."

The other kids murmured "yeah" and nodded. Belle could feel her blood pressure rise, making her face hot. She couldn't believe what Lucas was saying. In all her research, there was no hint that the Nabians ever tried to rule Mars.

"Nabians are a peaceful race," Belle said, trying hard not to shout. "Just read their history."

"I don't care about their history," he said. "It's what they're doing now that's causing problems for everyone."

"You're wrong, Lucas!" Belle shouted. "That's illogical — and ignorant."

"That's enough, Lucas . . . and Belle," Ms. Polley said. But it was too late. So many nasty things had been said.

In all of the ruckus, no one saw that Ta'al was now standing. Her eyes were wide and full of rage.

"Ms. Polley," she said. Her voice was steady, but Belle could sense the anger behind her words. "I gave Brill many ideas, good ideas, for projects. But he refused to listen — *si ner toh khan*! He chose to conduct the simplest experiment. There was nothing I could do to make him cooperate."

"Her ideas weren't science," Brill protested. "They were more like magical hocus pocus — weird alien stuff."

"I'd think you'd jump at the chance to learn about alien science. Something new that we don't know anything about," Belle said.

Ms. Polley clapped her hands loudly. The whole class stopped and turned to look at her. She sighed and pushed her curly, black hair away from her face. The red rings around her irises — the rings that all Martian-born humans had — glowed like fire. The class watched her in silence for several long minutes.

"Fine," she finally said. "Brill, you can complete your own project. Maybe pair up with your younger brother. Fourth graders are eligible to enter the fair too." She moved around her desk and sat down. "Ta'al, if you want to compete in the Olympian Science Fair, you'll need a partner. As there are no other Nabians in this school, I don't know how to help you. Is there anyone you're willing to work with?"

Ta'al didn't move. Only her eyes flickered over to Belle for a second.

Fed up with all the fighting, Belle piped up. "I'll work with her, Ms. Polley."

"You can't," Lucas said. "You're my partner."

"I can do two projects," Belle said. "Winter will be so boring anyway, and Ta'al and I can work remotely." She looked over at Ta'al, who gave Belle a slight nod. "If that's okay with you, Ms. Polley."

Ms. Polley threw her hands in the air. "If you think you can handle it, Isabelle Song, you're welcome to enter two projects." Then she exhaled loudly, stood up, and continued with the day's subjects.

At the end of the school day, Lucas ran off toward home with Brill, leaving Belle alone to wait for Melody. Ta'al, who had to stay behind to speak to Ms. Polley, caught up to Belle at the school gate.

"Melody's late," Belle said. "That's not like her."

"She'll be here soon," Ta'al said. "Why don't we meet her on the path?"

The girls walked until they reached the fork in the path that Ta'al took to get home. There was no Melody in sight.

"I'll walk with you," Ta'al offered.

"But it's too far from your home."

"I'll ask Fa'erz to come get me later. We can talk about our science project."

Belle listened intently as Ta'al shared her ideas. They were so different and interesting that Belle was excited to be working with her. She didn't even notice the time pass as they walked along.

Abruptly, Ta'al stopped talking.

"What is it?" Belle asked.

Ta'al pointed ahead. As Belle turned to look, she gasped. There in front of the girls was the Song farm. And it was on fire!

CHAPTER 15
ATTACKED!

Belle stood frozen to the ground. Her hands gripped the farm gate so hard that her fingers had gone white. Black smoke rose from behind the above-ground portion of their home. The air was filled with ash, making it hard to breathe. Loud pops and crackles were mixed with the shrieking of animals. The sight of it all scared Belle too much to move.

"I'll call for firebots," Ta'al said. Her calm voice helped Belle to begin breathing again.

"My parents!" Belle shoved open the gate and ran. As she reached the house, she saw Melody leaning over her dad's body. He was lying on the ground and wasn't moving.

"Is he . . . ?" She didn't dare finish the question.

"He is unconscious," Melody said, as if it were nothing more than an interesting factoid. "He will be fine. I am taking him into the house." Belle was grateful for Melody's lack of emotion. If she said Yun wasn't in danger, then he'd be all right.

Belle watched as Melody lifted her dad up in her mechanical arms and carried him toward their underground home. Then she headed to the back area behind the house. With each step, she felt the heat of the blaze. She couldn't believe her eyes. The field behind the house was on fire. Flames rose almost as high as the barn. Zara was in one corner of the field. She and one farmbot were trying to put out the fire with extinguishers. Their efforts barely made a difference.

"Firebots are on their way," Belle called to her mom. "What happened?"

Zara's face was full of soot and ash, as were her hands. She put down the extinguisher, then ran over to Belle and hugged her tight. Belle could feel her mom's ragged breathing and knew she was trying not to cry.

"It'll be all right," Zara said over and over again.

"But how did this happen?" asked Belle.

"Raiders . . ." She didn't have to say more.

Belle began to cry. It wasn't until she heard the hum of drones overhead that she stopped.

"We should get out of the way," Zara said, waving the farm droids away.

Five firefighting drones hovered over the area where the water tank was buried. White pebbles rained down from above. When they hit the ground, they began expanding into white foam. Within minutes the fire was out. Zara stood bent over, with her hands on her knees, panting.

"Melody took Dad inside the house," Belle said, her voice trembling. Seeing her mom like this scared her.

Zara straightened. She looked as if she'd forgotten all about Yun. "He was stunned when he went after them. But there were too many, and they had weapons." She marched back toward the house with Belle running after her. "We should report this. We need to get Protectors out here immediately."

As they reached the house, Myra Walker and Lucas came running up the driveway.

"We saw the smoke," Myra said. "How bad is it?"

Zara told Myra the whole story. They'd been out in the fields harvesting when they heard the rumble of engines. Two vehicles each carrying half a dozen raiders crashed through their back fences, right where the water tank was. Within seconds, they were pumping out water. Yun had gone to get his sonic blaster as Melody and Zara approached the raiders.

"We used some of your puffs, Belle," her mom said.

"You know about my Petripuffs?"

"Melody told us, so we threw a few at the Raiders," she said. "It kept them occupied long enough for your dad to get his blaster. Then he chased them off. But as they left, one of them threw some kind of explosive device at the tank. There was a terrible explosion, and then the fire."

Zara had her hand on her chest. She was breathing fast.

"All is well now," Myra said, draping an arm over Zara. "Let's go inside and report it. Children, you should all come in as well. Get out of the firebots' way as they finish their work."

Lucas followed his mom without a word. Belle turned around to look for Ta'al. She'd forgotten all about her, but it was Ta'al that had saved them. She had called for the firebot drones. Belle saw Ta'al standing by the farm gate. She looked unsure of what to do.

"Come inside with me," Belle cried, waving to her friend.

Ta'al ran over. Her eyes were wet with tears and reflected the black smoke of the fire. Belle gave her a hug.

"Thank you so much," Belle said.

● ● ● ●

Yun was lying unconscious in his bed when Belle went in to see him. His face was covered in soot, just like Zara's. Melody hovered over him, scanning him from head to toe.

"He should wake up soon," she said. "He has not been permanently damaged."

In a moment Yun blinked his eyes open. Belle held his hand in hers. She fought back the tears. She wanted to be brave for her dad. When he saw her, he smiled.

"That was quite an experience," he said. "I've never been stunned like that before." He pushed himself to a sitting position, but held his hand to his head. "And I don't think I ever want to be stunned again." He chuckled weakly.

"Why are you laughing?" Belle asked.

"What else can I do?" He rubbed his head. "If I think about what we've lost, I might cry like a small child. And what good would that do?"

He ruffled the top of Belle's head, making her feel like that small child. She hated how her dad seemed to think that kids were weak. But she didn't correct him. He had earned a pass to express his old-fashioned ideas. Just this once.

In the kitchen, Zara was already talking to the authorities. When she saw Yun, she insisted he sit back down again.

"They're sending a Protector out today," she said, signing off the holo-vid.

"One Protector?" he said. "Is that enough?"

"Have you ever met a Protector?" Myra said. She was busy making tea for everyone. "They do the work of ten humans combined. Or Sulux."

"Are you all right?" Lucas said to Belle, when she joined her friends in the living room.

Belle patted Ta'al on the shoulder. "I am, thanks to Ta'al's cool-headedness."

Ta'al's face went purple. She almost matched Lucas. "I just did what anyone else would have done."

Lucas looked at Ta'al in a way Belle had never seen before. It was almost a smile. "Well, I'm glad you were there to help," he said. "Belle, I should've walked you home. I'm sorry."

Belle couldn't believe her ears. Lucas was being nice to both of them! She leaned in closer to her two friends.

"We need to come up with a plan to stop these raiders," she whispered. Her parents wouldn't approve, but she couldn't sit back and be helpless. "Will you help me?"

Ta'al's eyes widened. Lucas' eyes narrowed.

"Come on, Lucas," Belle said. "You don't really believe Ta'al's family is involved in the raids, do you?"

"Not them, specifically," he said, looking down at his hands. "But, you know, the rumors about Nabians —"

The doorbell rang before she could answer Lucas. She was surprised to see Paddy Walker walking down the stairs, talking respectfully to So'ark, He'ern, and Fa'erz. He gestured for Ta'al's parents to enter first.

After checking to see if Yun and the others were okay, Paddy coughed to get everyone's attention.

"I've called for a meeting of all seven of the neighboring farm families," he said importantly. "Everyone has agreed to be at our house tomorrow night." Paddy nodded to So'ark. His face was redder than Belle had ever seen. "It's about time we stand up to these monsters once and for all."

Belle went over to her friends.

"Rumors about the Nabians need to be proven before I'll believe them," she whispered. "In the meantime, we should work together to stop the raids. Kids too, not just adults. Agreed?"

Both Ta'al and Lucas looked over at their parents, then back at Belle. They nodded. Belle's heart skipped a beat. This was her chance to get back at the raiders for what they had done to her family and her home.

Sol 113/Autumn, Mars Cycle 105, early morning

I have to come up with a plan to help fight the raiders. I've got my Petripuffs, and I can teach my friends how to make them. But they're not enough. We need other defenses too. I'm hoping there will be other kids at the neighbors' meeting tonight, and we'll be able to come up with more inventions.

The Protector arrived just after midnight, but my parents wouldn't let me go out to watch the inspection of the damage. So I'm stuck in my room. They said I would get in the way. How rude! I was a witness too. But my parents wouldn't listen.

Well, I refuse to sit back and let others protect us. This is my home too. I also need to do more research. I can't believe the Nabians would have anything to do with the raiders. Everything I've read tells me they're a peaceful people. Why does everyone believe they're bad?

CHAPTER 16
NEIGHBORS UNITED

The next morning the shiny silver and black Protector stood in the Walkers' living room as neighbor after neighbor fired questions at it. Belle hadn't taken her eyes off the android. It was the biggest one she'd ever seen.

This Protector was humanoid in shape, like Melody. But it was three times bigger than her. It had all kinds of gadgets attached to its body. Belle was sure it probably had several hidden weapons and instruments in its body as well. It had one roaming red eye that seemed to constantly scan its surroundings. This android was definitely intelligent. And no one seemed to mind it being in the house. How were Martians not afraid of these huge androids, yet still afraid of an old robot like Melody?

"When will the authorities start to care about the farmers?" asked Mr. Park, one of the oldest neighbors. "Without us, people in the cities would have no food."

"We need real assistance out here, especially as winter approaches," Paddy added.

The Protector didn't answer. It just kept repeating the same phrase, "Investigations are underway. We are close to finding the criminals."

"Can you share the results of your investigations?" Yun said.

"That information is classified." The red eye blinked over at Belle and the other kids sitting in the corner.

One farmer, who had been silent for most of the meeting, stood up. He pointed to So'ark, He'ern, and Fa'erz, who had also come for the meeting. "Before we go on, how do we know you lot aren't here to spy on us? You might go telling the raiders what actions we're going to take."

Yun put a hand on his shoulder. "Now, Harry, let's not turn on each other. We're all in this together."

"And there's no evidence that the Nabians are even involved in the raids," Zara said. "They're just rumors, spread by ignorant, frightened people." She went to sit with So'ark.

"So how come they've never been raided then?" Harry said. "And I've heard that some Nabians around here have gone missing 'cuz they've joined the raider gangs. Isn't that enough to make anyone suspicious?"

He'ern stood up, his hands clasped tightly in front of his body. He spoke in deliberate, measured tones. "The missing Nabians have been reported to the authorities. Their families are worried for their safety. And we have a security system that is far beyond your technology. I hardly think that is evidence of our involvement with the enemy."

"Yun is right," Paddy said, surprising everyone. "Nothing will get done if we argue among ourselves. We're in this together. Let's get on with this meeting, shall we?"

Harry sat back down, grumbling.

"So, Protector, tell us what exactly the authorities will do to help us," Yun said. "Please be specific."

The Protector repeated the stories of how other farms had formed neighborhood patrols. They used farmbots to keep watch at night. Neighbors also kept an eye on each other's farms when families were traveling. Each suggestion was greeted with complaints that it wasn't enough.

"The raiders are getting more violent," Mr. Park said. "Didn't you see the damage done to the Song farm?"

"Investigations are underway —"

"Yeah, yeah, we get it. 'You are close to finding them.'" Paddy rubbed his face with both hands, as if he was trying to keep himself awake.

The farmers tried to pry suggestions out of the Protector for the next hour. When they got no satisfactory answers, they shook their heads. They had to accept the fact that they'd be on their own to stop the raiders.

"We cannot condone violence," the Protector said.

"But if you won't help us, we'll have no choice." Yun walked right up to the giant android. "You've given us no guarantee that anything will be done."

The Protector repeated his usual line again.

Yun threw his hands up. "I guess we're on our own."

"Can't you do something, Melody?" Belle whispered to her android.

Melody moved over to the Protector while the neighbors were busy talking amongst themselves. As they made plans to patrol the farms, Belle kept her eyes on Melody as she communicated with the Protector.

Just as the schedule was set for the farmbots to patrol the farm borders, the Protector spoke up. Its deep voice vibrated through the underground home, and right through Belle's body.

"I will authorize five drones to fly regular routes over the farms in the Sun City area," the Protector said. "They will patrol all day and night, until the first day of winter. Is that acceptable?"

No one said a word in response. They were all too shocked and surprised to speak.

"Well, it's a start," Paddy said eventually. He walked up and shook the Protector's hand. "If you'd said that in the beginning, you'd have saved us all a lot of trouble."

Belle patted Melody on the back. "Well done," she said with a grin. She felt very proud of her oldest friend.

"I simply reminded him of his duty to serve and protect," Melody said. "And I highlighted some Protector actions taken in Utopia, when they had similar troubles. I find that previous practices make for a strong case."

"Well, now it's our turn," Belle said.

Belle nodded to Lucas, who gestured for all of the the kids to follow him to his room. Her classmates had come with their parents that night. They'd all agreed to join Belle in her scheme.

Belle stood in front of the group with a holo-document displayed on the wall and a digital pen in her hand. "First, we need to figure out what weapons we can use against the raiders. We need something that won't get us in trouble with our parents," she said. Everyone looked at her nervously. "Don't worry. We'll be defending our homes, not going on the attack. Now let's think."

There was a collective sigh of relief. Then Ta'al spoke up.

"I've built a sonic disrupter device. It creates a very loud, high-pitched sound," she said. "It will disable someone instantly, without permanent damage."

"But won't that hurt the user's ears too?" Lucas asked, looking skeptical.

Ta'al pulled two round objects out of her pocket. "These are auditory shields."

Belle squinted at the rubbery things. "Ear plugs?"

"I suppose you could call them that." Ta'al demonstrated by shoving them into her ears and yelling, "If you wear them, you are protected from my disruptor!" That was the loudest Belle had ever heard her speak. She laughed. Ta'al laughed too, and soon everyone was chuckling.

Lucas shared his idea for a slingshot that used pellets of a gel-like substance. "As soon as it hits the target, the gel expands to cover a large area in sticky goo. It's awesome!"

"I like that you use ingredients that can be found at home," Belle said. "We have to be careful not to spend money. It'll make our parents suspicious." Even as she said it, she knew she'd have to pay for the PF-51 that Melody had ordered. It was the one ingredient for her puffs that couldn't be found at home.

Trina and Pavish thought of booby-trapping their water tanks with tripwires that set off a blaring alarm. Brill suggested filling his paintball pellets with itching powder. The two youngest kids wanted to fill bags with alpaca manure and set them around the water tanks. If the raiders stepped in them, the smelly manure would make them stink and hopefully chase them away.

Belle applauded everyone's ideas. "Great! We'll spend tomorrow making as many of our weapons as possible. Then we'll meet in my barn to share them. Deal?"

"Deal!" Everyone clapped.

● ● ● ●

As the Song family walked home that night Melody lit the way with her brightly shining eyes. Belle skipped along the path ahead of her parents.

"You seem happy tonight," Yun remarked.

Zara stopped in her tracks. "Wait. What have you got up your sleeve, Belle? I know you."

"What are you thinking, Belle?" Yun said.

"Nothing," Belle said, trying her best to look innocent.

Yun put his hands on Belle's shoulders. Somewhere in the distance two scavenger birds cawed at each other.

"Listen to me," Yun said sternly. "Raiders are no joke. They're vicious. Trust me, I know from personal experience. I don't want you getting involved and putting yourself or your friends in danger. Do you hear me?"

Belle nodded, avoiding her dad's eyes.

"Promise me you won't do anything stupid, Isabelle," he said.

"I promise." Belle bit her lip in frustration. She thought her plan was anything but stupid. In fact, it was brilliant.

Sol 113/Autumn, Mars Cycle 105, evening

Tonight the other kids and I put together a list of weapons we can use to defend our farms. If we all share what we have, we can be prepared for another raid. I believe we kids can help fight back against the raiders. After all, these are our homes too!

On another note, I think I'm making progress on getting Lucas to be friends with Ta'al. He actually spoke to her at his house. It's a first step.

CHAPTER 17
AN UNEXPECTED GUEST

The next morning Belle jumped out of bed, devoured her breakfast, and ran outside before her mom could ask what was up. She walked past the charred backyard that looked like a giant black and grey pancake. Belle was thankful that at least the barn had been spared from the fire.

"I can prep the puffs ahead of time," she said to Melody, who met her by the barn. "Then when the PF-51 arrives, all we have to do is the final assembly."

"But first, you must complete your homework assignment," Melody reminded her.

For the first half of the morning, Belle measured and weighed her turkens, and then recorded all the information in her datapad. The birds eating the special diet were growing fast. Their big, brown feathers were silky and strong. Their red wattles were beginning to grow, and they were loud and enthusiastic when it came to feeding time.

"Compared to the other birds eating regular feed," Belle said, shutting off her datapad, "these are like super-chicks."

"Your project appears to be doing well. You have a good chance to represent your school in Tharsis City next summer." Melody leaned over the pens, taking holo-images of each turken for Belle's charts. The android's eyes glowed a deep pink. Melody was proud of Belle's work.

"I hope so," Belle said. "But there's also my other project with Ta'al. I wonder what we'll be doing?"

"Nabians are more advanced than Sulux and humans," Melody said. "I am curious why they bother with a planet like Mars. We are quite far behind them, technologically."

"Well, I can't wait to find out what ideas Ta'al has," Belle said. "Now, on to making more Petripuffs."

Melody assisted as Belle worked on making the delicate weapons. Belle began by making a gel-like substance, mixing it together with her hands. Then Melody used a special pump attached to her arm to gently blow the gel into small, thin-skinned bubbles. Three gel bubbles would fit in each Petripuff. Belle injected ground pebble dust into one set of bubbles.

Melody filled another set of bubbles with a pressurized gas. The third set of bubbles would be filled with PF-51. The chemical would create a paralyzing gas when mixed with the other two ingredients. Since the PF-51 hadn't arrived yet, Melody placed the empty bubbles in trays. They glistened in the bright sunlight that shone through the open barn doors.

They worked quietly, concentrating on the process. As Melody reached out to place a delicate bubble onto a tray, she paused. Her neck joint extended upward and her head spun slowly all the way around. Belle was so absorbed in her work that she didn't notice Melody's movements until she tried to hand the android another dust filled bubble.

"What are you doing?" Belle asked.

"Silence," Melody said. Her eyes turned dark red. She was scanning the area.

Belle's heart skipped a beat. Melody rarely gave orders like that. She stood very still and tried to listen for what had alerted the android. She heard the turkens squawking as they shoved each other away from the feeding bowls. Outside, an alpaca shrieked. There was a shuffling sound just beyond the rear barn door, but that wasn't anything unusual. Then she heard it.

Something was whining outside the barn.

Belle froze. During the summer she'd had an encounter with some fierce predators. They were huge and scary, with long, sharp teeth and glowing eyes. At the time she'd thought they were wolves. But after that first encounter, she did some research about the animals' origins. A long time ago, humans had created hybrids — animals that were part dog and part wolf. They wanted pet dogs that could better survive on Mars. But some of the animals got loose, and their descendants had lived in the wild ever since. And like almost every animal on Mars, these creatures grew enormous. That's why they looked more like wolves than dogs. They were terrifying when hungry or scared.

"Wolves?" Belle asked. She still thought of them that way.

Melody's red eyes turned yellow, which meant that she was still analyzing the sound. "Just one."

"I don't want it to kill any of the chicks."

The creature whined again. This time it sounded long and very sad. Belle's curiosity got the better of her. She had to know what was going on outside. Why was the animal whining like that? She moved to the back door.

"Wait!" Melody called.

Belle cracked open the door and peeked through the gap. There was a wolf, a wild dog, sitting out there. It was gray and scruffy, and one ear looked like it had been chewed up. Belle's heart jumped to her throat. Quickly, she considered how fast she could get to one of her hidden Petripuffs if the dog showed its teeth.

Belle took a step back. The dog whined again. It was such a sad sound. She peeked at it again. The dog's tongue hung out of its mouth. It was panting heavily. She pushed the door open wider. When the dog saw her, it lowered its head. Then it lay down. It seemed that the dog wasn't here to attack Belle or her birds.

"I think it's thirsty," Belle said quietly and slowly, so she wouldn't scare it. "It doesn't look dangerous."

"Famous last words," Melody said.

"Get me some water, please. In a bowl or something."

"Why do you insist on taking such risky actions?" The android brought over a bowl filled with water.

Very carefully, Belle moved to the dog and set the bowl down an arm's length from its head. The dog moved closer and sniffed at the water. For several seconds, the only sound was that of the dog's tongue lapping up water. When the bowl was empty, it looked up at Belle and shook itself. Belle stepped back but was splattered anyway.

"Eew!" she laughed. "Dog drool!"

"You forget that this is a wild animal," Melody said, moving to stand between Belle and the dog.

Belle walked around her android. "It seems friendly. Look, it's wagging its tail."

"That alone is not a sign of tameness."

The dog took a step forward, lowering its head. Belle moved closer, holding her open hands out toward it. The dog sniffed her hands and then licked one palm. Belle giggled. She scratched the dog on its chin. It rubbed its face on her hand and then rolled over on its side.

"It is a male dog," Melody said.

"He's tame!" Belle rubbed his tummy. "I wonder who he belongs to?"

Melody's eyes went red again as she scanned the dog. "There are no implanted microchips or any other sign that he belongs to a person."

"Wait right here," Belle said to the dog. It stayed in position, as if it understood her.

Belle hurried into the barn and scooped up some mealworms. From her last encounter, she remembered that the wild dogs liked to eat worms. They also liked turkens, but she wasn't going to sacrifice any of hers. Not this time.

Belle tried not to squirm as the dog chomped down hungrily on the worms. When he was done, she petted him again.

"Do you think we could keep him?" she asked.

"It is highly unlikely that your parents would approve," Melody said.

"I've always wanted a dog." Belle picked up a stick and threw it across the yard.

The dog jumped to its feet and ran to get it. He trotted back to her with the stick in his mouth. Belle threw it again and again, and each time the dog brought it back.

"His behavior indicates he must belong to someone," Melody said. "I shall search all media for requests to find a lost dog."

"Okay, but if no one claims him, I'm keeping him."

Belle threw the stick again.

"I hear something," Melody said.

The dog reached the place where the stick fell and stopped. It pricked up its ears.

"What is it?" Belle asked.

"A whistle, outside the range of human hearing," Melody replied. "There it is again."

The dog cocked its head to one side. He whined, looked back at Belle for a second, and then took off.

"Wait!" Belle ran after it.

"Belle!" Melody followed after Belle. "He is being called home. You cannot hear it, but I can."

Belle turned back to Melody. "We have to make sure he gets home safely. I want to know who owns him."

Belle took off after the dog. Melody activated her hover function, rose into the air, and followed them both.

"This is not wise," she said. "Your parents will be angry."

Belle pretended not to hear her android. She was determined to find out where this dog lived. She pushed her legs to go faster. In the distance, she caught sight of the dog's tail. He looked back at her and barked once, as if he was asking her to chase him.

So she did.

CHAPTER 18
A MAJOR DISCOVERY

If it had been dark, Belle would've stopped the chase much sooner. But because the sun was shining, she didn't think twice about entering the forest across from their farmland. She followed the dog through the thick trees, hopping over bulging roots and skipping around wide ferns and prickly branches. Somewhere behind her she heard Melody hovering. That sound gave her the courage to keep going. Her android wouldn't let anything bad happen to her.

Emerging from the trees, Belle blinked in the bright sunlight. All she could see were more farms. She heard the dog panting somewhere up ahead. She picked up her pace as Melody floated along behind, quietly complaining.

Belle caught a glimpse of a wagging tail disappearing behind some hedges to the left. She followed. The narrow path in front of her was lined on both sides by tall hedges. It seemed to stretch all the way to the horizon. Belled jogged along the path. At times the hedges gave way to small lanes to her right. These led into wide, grassy fields. There was no sign of the dog. Only a few paw prints in the dusty ground told Belle that she was on the right track.

She paused to let Melody catch up to her. That's when she heard the sound of trickling water. Alongside the path was a small stream. It seemed to emerge from somewhere underground.

"Belle, this is far enough," Melody said.

"I think he's almost home." Belle didn't take her eyes off the path ahead.

She kept going, past several empty fields.

"You are the most stubborn human I know," Melody said.

Belle stopped. She had completely lost sight of the dog. Even the paw prints had disappeared. Her heart sank.

"I can't lose him now," she panted as she caught her breath.

Melody made a creaking noise. She extended her head upward about a meter to scan the area. "I hear the whistle again. It is coming from the northeast, roughly two kilometers from here."

Belle looked up at her android. "I thought you wanted me to go home."

"Well, since we're here . . ." Melody said, throwing her hands up to imitate human behavior.

Belle held up her hand. "First, I need a drink." She bent down by the stream and cupped her hands.

"I don't think —" Melody began.

But Belle wasn't listening. She scooped a handful of water into her mouth, and then spat it back out.

"Yuck!" She spat several more times. "It's so salty!"

Melody walked over, opened one of her storage compartments, and offered Belle a bottle of water. "I believe your mother has mentioned before that the water on Mars is salty. It is why we have desalination plants in every town."

Belle gulped the fresh, clean water. "Thanks for waiting to remind me," she said sarcastically.

Someone in the distance shouted. Belle choked on her water. Melody put a finger to her mouth, which was a flat line that glowed red. She was in stealth mode.

"The barn ahead is registered as abandoned," she said in a low volume. "Yet, I detect many people present. And dogs."

Melody hovered ahead of Belle to see the open space beyond the hedgerow. Belle caught up and peeked around her friend.

"What is it?" she asked.

"Those vehicles are from the raid on our farm," Melody said.

"Raiders?" Belle whipped back behind the hedge. "Raiders are here? Have they seen us?"

"I do not believe so," Melody said. "But I believe the dog belongs to them."

Melody scanned the area, and then turned to face Belle. "We should leave immediately. I will contact the authorities to alert them of the raiders' location."

Belle nodded. She'd found the raiders' hideout. Her parents would be so pleased. But as she turned to follow Melody home, a warm, wet nose nudged her leg.

"Dog!" She gave the dog a hug as he licked her face. "I'm glad you've found your home, but your master is not a good person."

Someone whistled. Belle heard it this time. Then she heard the crunch of pebbles beneath boots. The footsteps were coming this way! Melody stepped in front of Belle to protect her. The dog licked Melody.

"Come on, boy!" a voice shouted.

The footsteps grew closer. Belle and Melody edged quietly back along the hedgerow. The dog followed them.

"Come here, you stupid dog!" The voice was gruff.

Belle froze. This was it. She'd be discovered by raiders. And who knew what they'd do to her? Her parents would be so mad.

Melody opened her side storage compartment and produced the livestock prod that she carried there. She held it ready.

The dog looked at Belle and cocked its head to the side. Then he turned and ran to his master. Belle let out the breath that she had been holding.

"Come on now, boy. Let's go," Belle heard the voice say. Then she heard footsteps walking away.

"Wait a minute," Belle whispered, more to herself than to Melody. "The raiders have dogs. But Nabians don't keep pets. They consider them unsanitary."

Belle couldn't resist — she had to see for herself. She crept to the end of the hedgerow and peeked around the corner.

Belle saw the raider walking next to the dog. More importantly, she could see his face. He was human! Not Nabian, as everyone suspected.

Wait until her parents found out!

CHAPTER 19

GROUNDED

Melody led the way home. By the time they arrived, it was early evening. Before she even saw her farm, Belle heard her parents calling for her. They sounded frantic, as if they'd been calling for hours. Belle swallowed hard. She knew she was in big trouble.

But she was certain that once her parents learned that she'd discovered the raiders' hideout, they'd be so proud of her.

"Here I am!" She ran to her mom.

Yun and Zara hugged her and then started to yell at her.

"Do you know how dangerous it is out here?" Yun asked.

"How can you run off without telling us?" Zara said. The anger and fear were obvious in her voice.

"The barn door was open and you were missing," Yun scolded.

"You gave us a terrible scare," Zara said.

"But you know I have Melody," Belle said. "Nothing will go wrong if she's with me."

Yun wiped his sweaty face. "I wish that were true."

Belle tried hard to calm her racing heart. "I have something important to tell you," she said.

Zara shook her head. "No more talk. You're grounded."

"That's right, young lady," Yun said. "You've given us enough worry for one day."

"But, I found it . . ." Belle began. Her mom raised her hand to stop Belle. Her dad turned away to lock up the barn.

"That's enough," Zara said. "Your dad and I are going to visit the Park family. They're really worried about the raids, so we're going to help them secure their water tanks."

Yun walked back and bent down to meet Belle's eyes. "You head straight to your room and don't come out until we get home. Do you understand me?"

"But —"

"No 'buts,'" Zara interrupted. Her parents wouldn't hear another word.

The words she needed to tell her parents were stuck in her throat. She wanted to explode with the news. But every time she tried, she was shut down. When they got back to the house she ran to her room and slammed her door shut. She heard her parents order Melody to keep Belle inside and not let her out of her sight.

"We'll be back late," Zara said. "And we need to trust that Belle is in good hands."

Melody didn't reply. She had to obey. That's what androids did.

Sol 114/ Autumn, Mars Cycle 105

I am fuming mad! Mom and Dad wouldn't even let me talk!

They just can't believe a child would have the answers to their problems. Just because I'm 12. When will they start to take me seriously?

I can't believe they grounded me. Melody won't let me out of my room. She tried telling me bad jokes to cheer me up, but I didn't hear a word she said.

Sol 115/ Autumn, Mars Cycle 105

I'm still grounded. Mom and Dad won't even let me go above ground. And they won't let me tell them what I know. This is awful! At least the PF-51 arrived and I've finished making more Petripuffs. But what good will they be if I can't get out?

Sol 116/Autumn, Mars Cycle 105

I'm so, so, so, bored! I've been stuck in the house for two whole days. I don't think I remember what sunlight looks like!

Melody said she reported the location of the raiders' hideout but nothing has been done so far. So that means they didn't believe her.

I have to get out of here and get proof. But how?

DING – DONG!

Belle looked up at the sound. Someone was ringing the doorbell. Finally! After two days of being grounded, she was desperate for a visitor. Her parents were acting so unreasonable. They refused to hear a word about her discovery. Every time she started to say something, they talked on and on about how dangerous Mars was.

"Melody, who is it?" Belle called from her bed. Her parents were out again.

"It appears to be Lucas Walker," Melody said.

Belle jumped out of bed and ran to the front door.

"Mom said I can't go out, but she didn't say anything about others coming in," she said.

"Belle! Are you here?" a boy's voice called.

Belle unlocked the door. Ta'al stood there beside Lucas.

"Ta'al!" Belle was so happy to see them both.

"Our parents are all at the Parks' house again," Ta'al said. "Their farm was raided last night."

Belle's jaw dropped. Her parents hadn't said a word about that. Why were they keeping secrets from her?

"We got bored at their meeting," Lucas said.

"It's not the same without you there," Ta'al said.

Belle told them about being grounded. "But you have to hear what I found out!"

Lucas and Ta'al were captivated as Belle told them about her adventure chasing the dog. Then she surprised them with the information about the raiders' hideout.

"No way!" Lucas said.

"But if Melody told the Protectors, why haven't they done anything?" Ta'al said.

Melody brought them a tray full of snacks. "According to the authorities' site, they investigate tips from the public in the order they are received," she said. "Apparently, there have been a lot of recent raider attacks."

The three friends munched on their snacks in silence, each in deep thought.

"By the time the Protector gets to the raiders' hideout, they could be long gone," Lucas said. "They might already be gone. It's been two days."

"But it's in the hands of the authorities now," Ta'al said. "There's nothing we can do."

Belle looked at her two friends. "Nothing? Are you sure?" An idea was growing in her head.

Belle stood up quickly and grabbed her bag hanging on the wall. Then she went to her closet and began stuffing the bag full of her Petripuffs. "Do you have any of your gel pellets here?" she asked Lucas.

"Yeah, some," he replied, pulling some pellets from his pocket. "I usually carry some with me, just in case."

"Ta'al, do you have your sonic disrupter with you?" Belle asked her friend.

"Yes, it's in my bag, along with some spare hearing protection," Ta'al said. "With all of the raider activity, I thought it best to bring it along on our way here."

"Good," Belle said. "Because we're going to get some proof to show where the raiders are hiding. Then our parents will have to listen to us."

"I cannot allow that," Melody said. "Your parents gave strict orders that you are to stay here."

"But that was *days* ago Melody," Belle argued. "I've been stuck in this room for two days already. I think I've served my sentence. Besides, they only said you can't let me out of your sight, not that I can't leave the house. If you come with us, you won't be breaking their rule."

"You make a logical argument," Melody said. "But I do not think you should investigate the raiders without any adult supervision."

"That's why you're coming with us. Besides, we need you to record what we see as proof," Belle argued. "Our parents might not listen to us. But they'll believe you, especially when you show them a recording of the raiders' hideout."

"I see that no matter what I say, you will do exactly as you please," Melody said. She proceeded to load up her central storage compartment with water bottles and a first aid kit.

Belle hugged her android. "As long as you're with us, I know we'll be safe."

CHAPTER 20
A DANGEROUS PLAN

Trudging through the forest in the evening was scarier than it was a few mornings ago. The trees felt much closer together, and the air was damp. Belle's feet kept sinking into the forest floor, coating her shoes with ice-cold mud. Even Ta'al, who was usually so graceful, stumbled a couple of times. Lucas, however, was too excited about their mission. He ran through the forest faster than all of them.

"Be careful not to drop any puffs!" Belle warned him.

By the time they emerged from the forest, the sky was dark. The moon Phobos only provided a dim glow. It was barely enough to light their way through the paths. Melody was careful to keep her eye lamps dim, just in case there were raiders around.

Just past the salty stream, Belle crouched down and signaled for the others to do the same. Melody dimmed her light beams even lower. Then they crept up as close to the hedge row as possible, listening for the raiders' voices.

At first, everything was silent.

"Maybe they've moved on," Ta'al whispered.

"I knew it. We're too late!" Lucas said.

They stood up to stretch their cramped legs. But then the sudden boom of a loud engine made them jump. It was followed by whoops and laughter. Something began to rumble, sounding like a giant with a bellyache.

"That's a water pump," Lucas said. "They must be filling a water tank."

"Do you think it's the Parks' water?" Belle asked.

"We should contact the authorities," Ta'al said. "I don't think we can handle this ourselves."

Melody's large eyes turned a light blue color. She was sending a communication to the Protector. "It is done," she said. "Now we should head home."

"Wait," Belle said. "There's something you two really need to see first."

Belle stepped to the end of the hedgerow and poked her head around. She waved for her friends to do the same.

In front of the abandoned barn stood at least a dozen raiders. They cheered as their truck unloaded a tankful of water into the ground. The raiders were draped in layers of coats and cloaks. Every part of their bodies was covered, including their faces.

Drats! Belle needed them to remove their scarves to prove to Lucas that the Nabians weren't the enemy.

"Okay, we saw them," Lucas said. "Now let's go."

"Oh!" Ta'al suddenly gasped.

Belle whipped around to see her friend standing with her hand over her mouth. Ta'al's eyes were wide and almost completely black.

"Look over in the corner, there," Ta'al said, pointing to a small group of people on the far end of the pump.

Belle and Lucas squinted. Nabians! Four of them, standing and watching. Belle's heart dropped to her feet. Had Lucas been right all along?

As the water continued to be pumped, it seemed as if the raiders became bored. The group began to break up, and one raider unwound the scarves around his head. He was human. He walked over to a pile of sticks and got a fire going. Others were attracted to the fire's warmth and gathered around it. They too removed their scarves. More humans. The only ones who didn't move to the fire were the Nabians.

Maybe they weren't cold? Then Belle looked at Ta'al. She had her arms wrapped around herself. Ta'al looked cold. So why did it seem that the others weren't interested in the warm fire?

"*Hantu* — wait!" Ta'al said. "Those Nabians are not a part of the raiders."

Belle stretched over Lucas to get a better look. Ta'al was right. The reason the Nabians hadn't moved was right behind them. Two large raiders, still wrapped in cloaks and scarves, were holding blasters pointed at the Nabians.

"They're prisoners!" Belle said in a hoarse whisper.

"I know them," Ta'al said. "They're the ones who've been missing." She hadn't taken her eyes off the Nabians. "We have to save them."

"We can't do anything for them," Lucas said. "Those guards have blasters."

"They're moving," Belle said.

The raiders with the blasters prodded the Nabians in the back. The prisoners shuffled ahead, slowly and clumsily.

"Their feet are chained," Ta'al said. Her voice rose with each word. Belle put a finger to her lips to remind her friend that they had to stay quiet.

The prisoners were herded toward a tent to the far left of the tanker truck. The raider guards checked the restraints on the Nabians before shoving them into the tent. They secured the entrance, then walked over to the fire.

Belle shivered. She wasn't sure if it was because of the cold or what she'd just seen. She'd proven her point. Perhaps it was now time to let the adults take over. She moved away from the hedge and gestured for her friends to follow. They'd only taken a few steps when they heard someone wail.

The cry echoed through the chilly night air. Belle felt like it stabbed her right in her chest.

"What was that?" she said.

They all froze in place.

"From the sounds I am hearing," Melody said, turning to scan the scene beyond the hedges, "there are dogs in the tent with the prisoners."

"No!" Ta'al said. She had her hands over her ears and was shivering. Was it fear, or anger, or both?

Standing in the cold and listening to the wailing of the prisoners, Belle knew they had to do something. They couldn't wait for the Protector.

"We'll sneak around the camp, behind the tent," Belle said. "Melody can cut an opening in the material. Right?" She looked at her android.

"I can use my laser to burn a hole in it," Melody said.

Belle nodded. "We can save the prisoners, at least."

Ta'al nodded so hard it looked like her head might fall off.

"No, we should wait," Lucas said. "We could make things even worse."

"I agree with Lucas," Melody said. "I am not prepared to sacrifice your safety, Belle."

Belle wasn't listening to either of them. She shoved plugs into her ears, and then pulled out two Petripuffs. Ta'al held her disruptor at the ready.

"Lucas, you stay here and be our lookout," Belle said. "If the raiders decide to head our way, try to distract them. Make some noise, and then get out of here. We'll meet up back at the entrance to the forest."

She turned to Melody. "You'll come with us, okay?"

Melody's eyes and mouth went red. Belle smiled. Her android was in stealth mode.

CHAPTER 21
A DARING RESCUE

Belle and Ta'al waited for Melody to signal that all of the raiders were looking away from the hedges. Crouching low, the girls dashed across the path to the hedges on the other side and stopped to listen. They were closer to the captives' tent now — so close they could hear dogs snarling . . . and more wailing.

Belle didn't want to think about what was going on inside. She just knew that they had to do whatever they could to help the prisoners. She didn't want to think about the danger or how angry her parents would be if they knew what she was doing. Or worse, how awful it would be to get caught by the raiders. But she pressed on in spite of her fears.

The last dash to the tent was going to be out in the open. They had to stay low and run one at a time. Melody went first. Hovering with all her lights turned off, she was almost invisible in the dark. Belle wished she had that power. She was glad that she was at least wearing dark colors. Ta'al, though, was wearing a lot of bright yellow and pink clothing.

"You go next," Belle said to her friend. "When Melody signals, run fast."

Ta'al tucked in all the loose fabric around her middle. Then she began rubbing her clothes with both hands. The fabric began to change color. Within seconds, she was cloaked in darkness.

"That's clever," Belle said. Ta'al grinned. Nabian technology was truly incredible.

Ta'al dashed over to Melody like a ghost. Belle could barely see her. Then it was her turn. She took a deep breath and swallowed her fear. With her eyes fixed on the tiny red light on Melody's head, she ran.

Belle took several large leaps. But because of Mars' lower gravity, her legs sent her flying as high as the corral posts. In the distance, someone shouted. She couldn't hear the exact words. Then more people were shouting. She hit the ground and crouched down behind a post that was too narrow to hide her. Her heart pounded so hard in her chest that she couldn't hear anything else. She pulled out an earplug and opened her eyes.

The raiders had abandoned their fire and were running. Belle stretched up a little to get a better look. *Were they coming for her?*

"Belle! Run to me!" She heard Melody call.

It took all her strength to force her legs to keep moving. But she did until she collapsed into Melody's hard arms.

"Should we run?" she said, in half breaths.

"Lucas must have made a distraction, like you suggested," Ta'al said.

"They are headed the other way," Melody confirmed.

Belle let out her breath. Lucas was doing a great job. She leaned up against the side of the tent to catch her breath. Meanwhile, Ta'al had her ear up against the tent wall. She waved Belle and Melody over to her side.

"This might be a safe place to cut through the fabric," Ta'al whispered. "I don't hear anything on the other side."

Melody agreed and pulled out a small laser. Belle held on to her Petripuffs, ready to throw them at the dogs inside the tent.

"There's one guard left on the other side," Ta'al said. "Give me some of your puffs. As soon as you're through, I'll paralyze him." Ta'al moved around the side of the tent and took a stance, ready to take action.

Melody's laser burned through the fabric, scorching it like fire. Immediately they heard sniffing sounds and low snarling. Belle heard Ta'al huff as she hurled a Petripuff at the guard. He cried out briefly, and then there was silence.

As soon as a flap was cut through the tent wall, Belle caught a peek inside. Two angry wolf-dogs stood ready to attack them. Belle lobbed a puff at each dog. The first dog fell immediately, yelping pitifully. But the other puff missed its mark. The second dog jumped through the hole. Baring its teeth, it pounced at Belle.

Belle crouched on the ground and covered her head with her arms. She squeezed her eyes shut and braced herself for the pain. Why had she chosen to do such a stupid thing? How would this night end?

Nothing happened. She waited a few seconds, in case she'd misjudged the dog's attack.

She opened her eyes to see the dog lying on the ground, just inches from where she crouched. Ta'al stood on the other side of the dog, looking terrified. In one hand, she held her disruptor. She held her other hand in front of her, frozen in position after throwing a puff at the attacking dog.

Belle stood up with wobbly legs. She gave her friend a thumbs-up. Ta'al didn't respond. She kept staring at the dog.

"I've never harmed a living thing in my life," Ta'al said shakily. "And already tonight, I've hurt two."

"Don't worry. They'll be fine in a minute," Belle said, trying to sound confident, and failing. "I designed the puffs so they wouldn't do any permanent damage to anyone."

Melody had already stepped inside the tent. She was using her laser to cut the shackles off the prisoners. They were speechless at what was happening.

Belle began helping the Nabians out of the tent, one by one. As the first one emerged, Ta'al spoke to them in their language.

"This was too dangerous for you," one of the Nabians said in the common language, so that Belle understood too.

"You should have just told the authorities," another said.

"We couldn't let you suffer while we waited," Belle said. "We don't know how long it would have taken the Protector to arrive."

"*Sia-mi* — thank you." The Nabians patted Belle on the back. She could see the cuts and scrapes on their skin, even in the darkness.

"We should move," Melody reminded them all.

"We'll head this way," the first Nabian said, pointing away from where Lucas was waiting for them. "Our homes are in this direction."

"All right," Belle said. "But please tell the authorities what happened as soon as you can."

The Nabians nodded, giving Belle and then Ta'al an odd look. Ta'al nodded back with an expression that said she understood their meaning. Belle was confused. But there wasn't time to ask questions. They had to get back and meet up with Lucas.

They ran back the way they'd come. The raiders were nowhere to be seen. Where did they all go? Had they simply run off at Lucas' distraction?

The pump engine was still humming when they reached the place where they'd left Lucas. He wasn't there. He must have moved on to the forest.

But when they reached the forest meeting point, Lucas wasn't there either. They called out cautiously, but there was no reply.

"We lost his tracks a while ago," Melody said. "Perhaps he took a different way into the forest."

"Or maybe he went to your house?" Ta'al said.

Belle didn't like this one bit. Something wasn't right. Lucas wouldn't change the plan like that, would he? But Ta'al had a point. They hadn't planned for this possibility. Surely Lucas would head to her house.

They ran on as fast as they could. As they crossed through Belle's farm gate, she fully expected to see a smiling Lucas sitting on her porch step, wondering what had taken them so long.

But the porch was empty.

Belle's stomach twisted. *What if something bad had happened to Lucas?*

"Melody, call Lucas' home," she said. "See if he's there."

"No one is answering," Melody said. "They're all at the Parks' house tonight."

Belle took off in the direction of the Parks' farm. It was on her way to school, and she knew all the short cuts.

They ran around the small barn where Loki slept, and then on through the back fields.

When they reached the Parks' house, the meeting had finished and all the parents were on their way out.

"What are you doing here, Belle?" Yun said, startled.

It took Belle a full minute to catch her breath. She was almost in a full panic. Most of her words were garbled. Once again, it was Ta'al's calmness that saved the moment.

Ta'al explained what they'd done. With each sentence, more neighbors gathered. Gasps of horror filled the air around them.

"And now we can't find Lucas," Ta'al finished telling them. "We need your help."

Myra broke down crying and fell into Paddy's arms. He looked pale.

"The raiders have our son!" he said. "Show us the hideout. We have to get him back."

Every neighbor stood ready to help. There was a lot of shouting and cursing.

"Wait!" Yun said, waving his arms. "We need to calm down and think for a moment."

People quieted, but Myra was weeping loudly. Zara went to her side.

"The Protector left our meeting in a hurry, didn't he?" Yun said. "Perhaps that's when he received Melody's call. So that's good news. The authorities are on their way."

"Yes, but those raiders would've been alerted when they found our boy," Paddy said, getting redder in the face with every word. "We have to go now!"

Yun nodded. "I agree, but let's be smart about this."

"We'll need a wagon," Zara said. "It'll be faster."

Mr. Park hitched his wagon to two giant horsels and everyone piled in. Yun and Zara insisted that Ta'al and Belle sit inside the wagon while Melody directed Mr. Park to the raiders' hideout.

The ride was bumpy as the horsels ran as fast as they could. The wagon was packed with neighbors. They all looked at Ta'al and Belle as if they were the naughtiest girls on the planet.

Belle felt like she could cry at any moment. But she was determined not to show any tears in front of the others. This had been her mistake. She had been so stupid to think that she could solve the raider problem herself. What did she think would happen? That she and her friends would catch the raiders, free the Nabians, and be hailed as heroes?

However this night turned out, she was sure the adults would always see her as a foolish, disobedient child.

CHAPTER 22
SAVING A FRIEND

The wagon stopped just outside the abandoned farm that served as the raiders' hideout. Quietly, everyone stepped out and formed into groups of three or four. Some of the farmers were armed with blasters. Others just held sticks and shovels.

"You two stay inside the wagon," Yun warned Belle. "And I mean it."

Belle couldn't look her dad in the eye. She blamed herself for this mess. Ta'al was silent. Her parents were among the neighbors getting ready to save Lucas too. They hadn't said a word to her this whole time. Belle wondered if that was worse than being scolded.

"Do you understand me, Belle?" her dad asked.

Belle nodded, looking at her feet. She hated the idea of not being able to do something — anything — to fix her mistake and save her friend.

She and Ta'al peeked through the wagon's small window at the raiders' barn. Everything was silent now, eerie under the cloak of night. Even the sound of the water pump was gone. Had the raiders moved on so quickly?

"There!" Belle heard someone say. Her gaze turned to where everyone else was looking.

The Protector, with its bright-red scanning eye emerged from the barn ahead. Belle was surprised at how quietly the large android moved. She and Ta'al pressed their ears against the window so they could hear the conversation with the big android.

"There is no one in the area," the Protector said. "But there is evidence of recent human activity here."

Several murmurs of "Human?" arose from the crowd.

"Where could they have gone?" Paddy shouted at the Protector. "They have our son!"

The Protector pointed to the sky. "The drones are scanning the area. We should have results soon."

"That's not good enough," Paddy said, looking around at the others. "I'm forming a search party. Who's with me?"

Everyone voiced their support. Paddy proceeded to organize people into groups. Each group moved off in a different direction. Melody was instructed to stay, with strict orders not to let Belle or Ta'al leave the wagon.

Belle collapsed into a seat. She dropped her head into her hands. Ta'al sat next to her and stroked her back soothingly.

"He'll be fine," Ta'al said. "They can't have gone far." Belle could hear the uncertainty in her friend's voice. But she appreciated her for trying to help.

The horsels whinnied. Belle looked up. The big creatures stomped their hooves. Then something yelped. Belle jumped up and stuck her head out the front of the wagon. There, next to the horsels stood a dog with one chewed up ear — her dog! The one she'd found and followed. She'd know him anywhere.

"Melody, look!"

Melody was already coming around the wagon. The dog trotted up to her and gave her a lick.

"You are right," she said. "It is our friend, the dog."

The dog turned its head and whined. Belle knew exactly what that meant.

"Do you hear the whistle?" she asked Melody.

"I do," she said. "It is coming from the south."

"Melody, you know what this means, don't you?" Belle said. "We have to follow the dog. It can lead us to Lucas!"

Belle climbed down from the wagon, followed by Ta'al. Belle stroked the dog's head, then held on to the thick fur around his neck. He whined again. His owner was calling him.

The dog struggled against Belle's grip. Not wanting to hurt him, she let go. He took off.

"You stay here, while I follow him," Melody said. "I will inform your father."

Belle watched as Melody and the dog faded into the darkness. She wasn't sure what to do. She didn't want to disobey her parents again. After all, her impulsive actions had gotten Lucas into trouble in the first place.

Belle turned to Ta'al. She didn't have to say anything. The determined expression on Ta'al's face told her what she had to do.

"I still have my disruptor. And I have one puff left," Ta'al said, patting her pocket.

Belle nodded and set her jaw. She'd gotten Lucas into this, and she was going to get him out. "Right. Let's go."

At first, the girls followed the sound of Melody's mechanical feet trudging over the rough ground. Then they heard the approaching footsteps of a search party. Everyone had received Melody's message and were gathering for a showdown with the raiders. Belle and Ta'al hid as well as they could, staying far enough behind not to be seen.

They climbed a nearby tree and lay still to watch. In the distance was a circle of vehicles and several shadowy figures. Dogs barked and howled as raiders spoke in harsh tones. They didn't see the farmers circling around them. The huge Protector was nowhere to be seen.

Suddenly the farmers let out a loud cry and charged. The raiders were stunned, but only for a moment. A blaster went off. Belle cringed.

"We have to help," she said.

Ta'al was already climbing down. They hit the ground and ran into the fray. The scene was chaotic, with raiders and farmers tangled in a messy fight. Dogs growled and barked, but most of them ran away as soon as blaster fire was heard.

Belle signaled to Ta'al to circle around the chaos and head for a small nearby barn. Light poured through the bottom of the door.

"I bet Lucas is being held in there," Belle said.

They were almost to the barn door when a large raider stepped in front of them.

"Where do you two think you're going?" he roared.

Belle and Ta'al froze. The raider was a mountain of a man, with dark curly hair that stuck out everywhere. He reached out his hand and grabbed Ta'al by her cloak. He wore gloves with the fingers cut out and he smelled like old fuel. With his other hand, he pulled Belle off the ground by her jacket. She kicked him with all her might but he just laughed. Both girls screamed.

Belle's arms flailed helplessly until one hand smacked against her pocket. Inside was her last Petripuff!

"Hold your breath!" she shouted to Ta'al as she pulled out the puff and lobbed it at the man's chest.

The puff hit its mark, releasing its white powder into the big raider's face. He let go of Ta'al and dropped Belle, who fell to the ground on her knees. Although her skin burned, she dared not take a breath. Belle crawled as far away from the man as she could. He choked and gagged, then fell to his knees. He collapsed onto his side, eyes wide open in disbelief. He couldn't move a muscle.

Belle scrambled to her feet and ran for the barn door before she dared to breathe again.

Ta'al met Belle at the barn door. She hefted her disrupter and gave Belle a knowing look. Belle nodded to show she understood. The girls shoved their earplugs into their ears, and then Belle quickly swung the barn door open.

Lucas sat crouched on the floor of the old barn. His hands and feet were bound with rope. But he was alone. The raiders were all outside fighting the farmers.

"I'm so sorry," Belle said as she looked for something to cut the ropes. She found a rusty old saw blade and began cutting him loose. "Are you all right? Did they hurt you?"

Lucas shook his head. His face was streaked with dried tears and dirt. He looked too frightened to even speak. Ta'al helped lift him to his feet as soon as he was free. Together, the three ran back to the barn door.

But suddenly the same mountainous raider appeared at the door in front of them. He'd recovered from the Petripuff and looked furious.

"Nice try, little ones," he growled. "But it takes more than some kiddie powder to stop me."

He lunged at them, hands stretched out, trying to grab anyone within his reach. Belle jumped out of his way, as did Ta'al. But Lucas was too slow. The man grabbed him and yanked him off the floor so his feet were dangling.

"Please put me down!" Lucas cried.

Belle looked at Ta'al. Her friend looked back and nodded. The girls instinctively knew what to do. Belle stepped up to the man.

"Don't you hurt him!" she screamed.

She looked right at Lucas. She placed her hands over her ears. Lucas seemed to understand. He imitated her. Then Ta'al pointed her sonic disruptor at the man and pushed the button. Belle only heard a shrill tone, thanks to her ear protection. Lucas squirmed, but the effect on the raider was worse. He yelped and dropped Lucas. He slapped his hands over his ears. At that moment, Ta'al lobbed her last puff at him. The huge man didn't see the puff in time. It burst in his face, and he once again dropped to the ground — paralyzed.

Belle ran out of the barn with Lucas and Ta'al. Her heart was pounding. They were out of ammunition, and there were many more raiders to deal with. What would they do now?

They were greeted by bright lights shining from the sky above. Floodlights — and the sound of drones.

The Protector stood in the center of the floodlights. Every opening in its armor held some kind of weapon. The weapons all pointed at the raiders kneeling on the ground with their hands behind their heads. Farmers stood behind each one, pointing whatever weapons they had at the raiders.

"Lucas!" Myra cried as she came running. She hugged Lucas so hard, he started to laugh and cry at the same time.

Paddy soon joined his family in a group hug. Meanwhile, the drones dropped nets over each of the raiders. The drones lifted them into the air and carried them away.

After the drones left and the whole place fell into silence and darkness, Yun and Zara walked up to Belle. She expected to be yelled at by her parents for disobeying them again. But they too huddled into a group hug, and no one said a word.

"We're all safe," Yun finally said, as if he knew what Belle was thinking. "That's all that matters now."

Sol 117/Autumn, Mars Cycle 105, night

What a night! I'm still shaking from all that's happened. I just thank the universe that Lucas is safe. I feel so bad — this was all my fault. But no one has said anything to me about it. Right now, all the parents are just happy that we're safe and the raiders have been arrested. I want to go to sleep. I'm so tired. But my brain is racing. I keep replaying everything that's happened in my head. It's over. I just need to let that sink in.

Sol 118/Autumn, Mars Cycle 105, morning

I haven't slept this much in ages. When I woke up, it was almost lunchtime!

Dad says that now the raiders have been dealt with, we have to focus on fixing our tank and restocking it with new water. Ta'al's parents have generously offered to share their security technology with us, as well as any neighbor who wants it. They really are the nicest people. I feel so awful that I put Ta'al in danger too.

One good thing has happened though. I think Lucas may actually think of Ta'al as a friend now.

CHAPTER 23
RAIDER COMES HOME

"The raiders who were arrested will stand trial in Tharsis City," the Protector said. The huge android was meeting with the Songs, the Walkers, and Ta'al's family, who were gathered in Belle's house. "You may be asked to give testimony through holo-vid. But they will not bother you anymore."

"Thanks to our kids for discovering their hideout," Paddy said. His arm had been around Lucas the whole evening. Even though several days had passed, Paddy and Myra still hovered over Lucas like he might disappear at any moment.

"But I hope you've learned your lesson," Yun added, turning to Belle. "Some adventures aren't safe for children."

"I'm not a child," Belle said. "I'm almost thirteen."

"Maybe so, but some adventures aren't safe for teens, either," Zara said.

Belle smiled at Ta'al and Lucas. They made a good team.

"I'm just grateful that no one was hurt," So'ark said. Ta'al's other parents nodded vigorously in agreement. "But I do admire your resourcefulness. We would be interested to study your Petripuffs. Perhaps we can make some improvements on the technology."

Belle beamed with pride.

"Maybe we can do that for our science fair project," Ta'al said. "Your puffs with some Nabian improvements."

"That's a great idea," Belle said. "It would be amazing if the Petripuffs won on Mars, like they did back on Earth."

She looked over at Lucas, who was watching them.

"Maybe both our projects could win," Belle said quickly. She didn't want to offend Lucas.

"You never know," he said with a laugh. "Ever since you showed up, so many things have changed."

"In a good way, I hope," she said.

He shrugged. "More like scary and exciting. You need me and Ta'al to keep you out of trouble."

"Wonderful," Melody said. "More mischief to contain."

Everyone laughed. Belle liked the sound of that. Lucas had begun to treat Ta'al as if they were all one group of close friends. Things were changing — for the better.

All three families walked outside with the Protector as he took his leave. After the big android was gone, Zara invited everyone back into the house for a light lunch. As they turned to head inside, Belle heard a whine.

There by the fence was her friend with the chewed-up ear. She ran toward him.

"Wait, Belle!" she heard her dad say. "It's a wild animal!"

"It's my dog!" Belle bent down and rubbed her face in its soft fur. The dog licked her face. "He must be missing his owner, now that he's in jail."

Belle led the dog to her family. He sat very still, panting, while everyone stared at him.

"He's friendly," Belle said. "Pet him and see."

One by one everyone petted the dog. Ta'al did too, but her parents just stood back and watched.

"He seems friendly enough," Yun said.

"Can we keep him?" Belle looked at her parents. "Please?"

Zara shook her head. "We don't have room in our home."

"What if we kept him in the above-ground front porch area?" Belle asked. "He could be a guard dog for us."

Zara and Yun looked at each other. The other parents were already smiling. They knew what the answer would be.

Belle squealed with delight when her parents agreed.

"What will you call him?" Lucas asked.

Belle thought for a while. She looked at the dog, who panted eagerly at his new owner. Then a huge smile spread across her face.

"I know exactly what his name is," she said. Her friends waited, excited to hear. Even the parents stopped chatting.

"His name is Raider."

Sol 125/Autumn, Mars Cycle 105

I have the pet I've always wanted. And all my friends and family are safe. Still, when I think of what we did, I shiver. Things could've gone so wrong. I think Mom and Dad know how bad I feel though. Thankfully, they've chosen not to punish me.

Tonight, Raider is sleeping above ground. He seemed happy when I left him with a large blanket, along with some food and water. I think over time, Mom and Dad will get used to him. Hopefully, he'll be sleeping in my room very soon.

PART THREE:
JOURNEY TO THARSIS

Martian winters are especially cold and harsh. Most people wait out the long winter months in their protected, underground homes. The Songs have survived their first winter on Mars. Now the weather is growing warmer and spring is in the air. Belle's mom is about to get exciting news that will lead the family to Tharsis City – the wonder of Mars. Belle is excited about their trip, but unknown dangers lurk on the city's streets . . .

CHAPTER 24
A SURPRISE

Belle watched with Lucas and Ta'al as their parents installed a new computer panel over the Songs' brand-new water tank. After their underground tank was destroyed by Water Raiders the previous autumn, they couldn't afford to replace it right away. And over the winter, the land had frozen over, so no work could be done on repairing it. Thankfully, the neighboring farmers were kind and generous. They helped provide for the Songs' water needs during the long winter.

But as soon as spring arrived and the ground thawed out, Yun was able to install a new tank. And thankfully, Ta'al's family had again come to help. Belle wasn't strong enough to do much of the work. And Belle's mom hadn't been feeling well for several weeks. However, Melody was very useful. She was especially helpful when it came to communicating with the computer that controlled the tank and its pump.

Belle crossed her fingers and held her breath as her dad prepared to flip the pump switch. Yun had already made several attempts. But the pump had failed. Twice in the last week the alarm that told them the pump had gone offline had triggered for no reason. Once, it even went off in the middle of the night, waking the Songs from their sleep and scaring them half to death.

"Here we go," Yun announced. He flipped the switch.

There was a moment of complete silence. Then the pump came to life, humming smoothly. It was a good sound. Everyone cheered.

"Third time's the charm, or so the saying goes," Lucas said.

"That's an odd saying," Ta'al said. "I don't believe there's any mathematical proof of its truth." Ta'al was very clever, but sometimes she took things too seriously.

"Well, so far, so good," Yun said, turning to Ta'al's parents. "And your gift of the extra security system will certainly help us sleep better at night. We can't thank you enough."

The Songs couldn't have asked for a better gift. A secure water tank was a necessity for an Olympian farmer. Without water, none of them would survive.

So'ark crouched by the tank's control panel. She made a few adjustments to the security program.

"You are most welcome," she said. "We can share this technology with all of our neighbors, if they desire it."

Paddy Walker slapped his thigh. "Well, that'll certainly help us keep those pesky raiders away. Thank you!"

He'ern was watching nearby. He nodded his agreement and nudged Fa'erz. Fa'erz pulled out a palm-sized disc. "I will make a note to download our technology for the Walkers' farm."

The Nabians' tall, lean bodies swayed like trees in a light breeze as they watched So'ark tweak the tank's control panel. Belle knew this meant they were a little nervous. They'd been worried that their technology would not work with human technology. So'ark had spent all winter trying to fix that problem. And now they would test it together on the security system.

"It's ready," So'ark said, rising to her full height and towering over Belle's dad. "Try it now."

"Here we go again," Yun said. He entered the passcode that So'ark had given him.

An energy field, which reminded Belle of a bubble, rose around the perimeter of the underground tank. The energy field's reflective surface glistened in the bright spring sun as it grew to meet in the middle. When all the sides touched in the center, the shield sizzled. It sounded just like a turken leg being thrown onto a barbeque grill.

"Go ahead," So'ark said to Yun. "Try touching the force field."

Belle gaped at So'ark. She didn't like that idea. Why would So'ark encourage her dad to touch something that was meant to keep the bad people away? Wouldn't he get hurt? He'd already been knocked out once before when raiders had attacked their farm. She remembered how frightened she'd been seeing her dad unconscious and lying on the ground. She really didn't want to see him hurt again — or ever.

Yun gave her a mischievous grin and stuck his hand into the shield. "Aaggh!" he yelped loudly, and began shaking like a rag doll in a dog's mouth.

"Dad!" Belle screamed. "Help him!"

Yun pulled his hand out of the shield and burst into laughter. "I'm fine, Belle! I was just teasing. But it's amazing. I can't reach in far enough to touch the tank."

Belle glared at her dad. "That's not funny!" She couldn't believe he'd tricked her.

He wiped a tear from his cheek and cupped her face in his hands. "I'm sorry. But I couldn't resist. The look on your face was totally worth it."

Belle squirmed out of his hold. "Stop it. I'm not a baby." She hated that her dad always treated her like she was a child. She was thirteen after all.

Her face was hot and everyone was watching her. She disliked being in the spotlight and wanted to hide. Ta'al came to her rescue.

"It looks like the shield works," Ta'al said. They watched as the energy bubble settled flat over the surface of the tank. It made a sucking sound, as if it had vacuum-sealed itself to the water tank. Turning to face Belle, Ta'al said, "Why don't we go and finish up our science fair project?"

Belle took a deep breath and swallowed the irritation she was feeling toward her dad. She nodded, but couldn't speak just yet. She was still fuming from her dad's silly prank. But she also remembered that Nabians treasured good manners, so she pushed her feelings aside to thank Ta'al's parents.

"Without your help, our farm would not be a safe place," Belle said in Nabian. She had learned the correct words and gestures from Melody, her android. This morning Melody had gone into Sun City with Zara. But Belle remembered what Melody had taught her.

"Your generosity is more than we deserve. *Sia-mi* — thank you." Belle rolled her hands around in a dance-like movement, a Nabian expression of thanks.

Ta'al's parents clapped when Belle was done.

"How thoughtful of you to learn our ways," He'ern said, returning the hand gesture. "You honor us."

Belle looked over at Ta'al, who was beaming. Even Yun looked impressed by his daughter. It made Belle feel better, just a little.

The sound of hooves told Belle that her mom had returned. Since Zara hadn't been feeling well, Yun had insisted that she go to the doctor in Sun City for a checkup. Their horsel, Loki, was pulling the Songs' hover wagon up to the house. The huge half-horse, half-camel creature neighed when he came to a stop. Melody stepped out of the wagon, carrying some supplies for the week. Zara climbed down slowly. She looked pale, but Belle thought she detected a smile on her mom's face.

Zara handed the reins to Belle, who unhitched Loki from the wagon. Together with Ta'al, she led him off to his stable to feed him. When Belle opened the stable doors, Raider came bounding toward her. His one chewed-up ear, the result of a previous fight with another dog, flopped to one side.

"There you are!" Belle cried. "Were you sleeping in Loki's stable all this time?"

"You know, a year ago I wouldn't have believed that I'd be taking care of animals this size," Belle said to Ta'al. "It's hard to believe I used to be afraid of them."

"I still am," Ta'al said nervously, keeping her distance. Most Nabians weren't fond of animals, and they didn't keep pets. But Ta'al tried to be accepting of Raider.

When Belle was done settling Loki, the girls headed back to the Songs' underground home.

"So, what did the doctor say?" Belle heard her dad ask her mom as the girls entered the small kitchen. Zara was putting away the supplies. Melody was helping her.

"Would you like me to project the physician's report?" Melody asked, turning to Belle, Yun, and their guests.

"No," Zara said abruptly. Her face was flushed. Belle was puzzled. It was a little crowded but it wasn't that warm inside their house. Was her mother seriously ill?

"Perhaps we should leave," So'ark suggested. "Ailments are a private matter to humans."

Zara laughed nervously. "It's not that. I can scarcely believe it myself." She moved to the living room and sat down. A strange look of disbelief crossed her face. Yun looked worried, which made Belle even more worried.

"What is it, Mom?" Belle asked, sitting next to her.

Zara took Belle's hand. She looked at her and then at Yun. "It's a nice surprise, really," she said. "Our family is about to get bigger."

Belle looked from her mom to her dad. It took a few seconds for the news to sink in.

"You're going to be a big sister, Belle!" Yun exclaimed. He hugged Zara as their friends gathered around to congratulate her.

"How do you feel?" Ta'al asked Belle a few minutes later. "Nabians rarely have more than one child. I've often wondered what it would be like to have a sibling."

Belle wasn't sure how she felt. "I don't know," she said. "I suppose it's good news. And I'm old enough to help take care of a baby. It could be fun."

"You're going to be busy helping your mom," Lucas added. "That's what I hear from other kids anyway."

"Should we not tell them about the physician's advice?" Melody asked after all the congratulations were done.

Zara shook her head. "It's nothing," she said. "The doctor suggested that I see a specialist in Tharsis City. Since this is my first pregnancy on Mars, she thinks that a more complete checkup is necessary."

"The differences in atmosphere and gravity sometimes cause complications for humans in this condition." Melody spoke with such authority, it alarmed Belle a bit.

Zara laughed at how seriously the android put it. "It's not that bad. Besides, Tharsis is so far away, and we can't leave the farm for that long. I'm sure I'll be fine."

Yun took his wife's hand. "Nonsense. We've been cooped up all winter. We deserve to take a break. A visit to the capital is just what we need. I say we should make it into a short vacation. What do you say, Belle?"

"That would be great!" Belle said excitedly. School wouldn't start for a couple more weeks. And they really had been cooped up all winter. A trip to the city would be a welcome change from the boring chores and routine of the last several months. "Can Ta'al and Lucas come too?" she asked.

Ta'al looked up at her parents, who spoke with each other in their language.

"We're expecting Paddy's family to visit in a few sols," Myra said. "It's their annual vacation with us."

Lucas looked disappointed.

"Maybe next time," Zara said, smiling at Myra.

"We have never seen the capital," Fa'erz said. "If you have no objections, we would like to join your expedition."

Belle jumped for joy.

"I'm not sure I'd call it an *expedition*, but we'd welcome the company," Yun said, laughing. "It'll be fun. We'll camp in our wagons, and in two days, we'll be in Tharsis City, capital of Olympia. I've heard it's a wondrous city."

Zara insisted that everyone stay for dinner to celebrate the good news. Melody cooked up a delicious meal combining Nabian spices with roast turken and lots of vegetables. Zara didn't eat much. She still looked pale, but she seemed happy. And that made Belle happy too.

Sol 12/Spring, Mars Cycle 106

I'm going to have a baby brother or sister. I've never thought about our family as being more than the three of us — and Melody, of course. I guess it could be fun. I just hope Mom will feel better soon. Having a baby seems like a lot of trouble to me.

I'd rather think of our road trip! I can't wait. Tomorrow, we're heading out to Tharsis City. I'm so happy that Ta'al is coming too. It's too bad Lucas couldn't come along. His dad offered to take care of our animals while we're gone. We're really lucky to have such good neighbors.

I looked Tharsis City up on the map. It's a long journey by wagon, but we can't afford to take a shuttle. We'll travel closer to the three volcanoes and Mount Olympus than I've ever been. Also, we'll be crossing the Marine Valley River and Dad says we might stop and visit a desalination plant.

I wonder what Tharsis will be like? In the holo-vids it seems like an amazing city of the future. When we landed on Mars I saw a bit of Utopia, the capital of Eastern Mars. It was big, but it didn't seem as grand as Tharsis.

I really need to get some sleep, but I'm too excited!

CHAPTER 25
ROAD TRIP

The next morning, Melody had the wagon packed and ready to go before anyone got out of bed.

"What would we do without you?" Zara asked Melody as she wrapped a warm blanket around the half-asleep Belle.

"A day without an android is like a day without food." Melody was trying out one of her bad jokes. "You'd survive, but it would be most uncomfortable."

"Ugh, that's awful," mumbled Belle. "It's not even a joke, really." But Zara laughed anyway.

"I am still learning about humor," the android said. "Your mother was amused."

Leaving before dawn meant that they'd be able to camp right by the Marine Valley River that night. But being up so early was hard for Belle. She grumbled all the way to the wagon, climbed inside, and fell straight back to sleep in her cot. Raider lay on the floor by her side, and she could hear his soft panting as she drifted off. Even Loki's whinny and odd gait didn't wake her.

Belle didn't wake up again until the sun rose and shone down on her through the wagon window. Melody was still charging in her portable station when Belle blinked her eyes open. She felt something weighing down her feet. When she sat up, she saw Raider asleep at the end of her cot, snoring quietly. He stirred when she moved. She scratched his ears and wiggled her feet out from under him. Slipping out of her cot, she tiptoed to the front of the wagon where her parents sat to guide Loki on the journey.

"Where will we meet up with Ta'al's family?" Belle said, stifling a yawn.

"They said they'd meet us at the campsite tonight," Yun said. He checked the navigation system. "That should be sometime this evening. We're gaining a lot of time with Loki's speed."

"You should probably wash up and get dressed," Zara said. She looked pale but seemed cheerful.

Dressing in a moving hover-wagon was harder than Belle expected. And with Raider constantly nudging his head under her hand for attention, it took Belle longer than usual to get ready. When she sat down to breakfast, the dog laid his head on her lap and stared at her with his large brown eyes. He whined a few times.

"What is it, boy?" she asked.

"Perhaps he needs to go outside," Melody said, as she unplugged herself. "He has been indoors longer than usual."

When Belle asked her dad to stop, he reluctantly pulled over to the side of the road. Belle opened the back door to the wagon, and Raider jumped out before she could blink.

"I guess he really needs to go," she said, following him outside.

Melody climbed down too, ready to go with Belle.

"Melody, wait!" Yun called. "I think something has come loose under the hover-wagon. I could use your help to fix it."

"I'll be fine, Melody," Belle said. "We won't go far."

Raider stopped at the first bush he found and relieved himself. Belle breathed in the cool morning air, glad for the chance to get out and stretch her legs too. She picked up a stick and threw it for Raider several times. Each time, he brought the stick back and wagged his tail for more. He even barked a few times when she was distracted by the small stones at her feet.

"I could use some of these for my Petripuffs," Belle said to herself, picking up a handful of colorful pebbles.

Raider's ears pricked up. Even his floppy, chewed-up ear stood straight up. He sniffed the air, cocked his head, and whined. He turned into the wind, and whined again.

"What's wrong?" Belle asked.

The fur around Raider's neck stood on end. A low growl rumbled from his chest. The sound sent a chill up Belle's spine. She'd heard that sound before, when she'd first encountered wild wolf-dogs. Looking around, she saw nothing but a slightly raised hill, dotted by low bushes and a few scattered trees in the distance.

"Come on, boy," Belle said, patting his head. "We should get back inside."

Raider took a few steps away from Belle. Her heart skipped several beats. She was sure he sensed danger.

"Raider, come on," she called again.

He trotted off in the other direction.

"Raider, come!" She called out more firmly. "It's time to go."

Raider stopped in his tracks. He took a stance — his back legs spread out, and ears flattened back against his head. He shifted his weight forward, lowering his body. Something in the distance, something Belle couldn't yet see, was approaching. Another low, warning growl vibrated through Raider's chest.

Belle held her breath.

One by one, a pack of five wild wolf-dogs appeared over the low hill. They had enormous heads and big muscular bodies. They stood only a few yards from Belle. They bared their teeth in a snarl and moved toward her.

But Raider had taken a stand, right between Belle and the wild animals.

Raider was crouched low and giving a warning snarl to the wild dogs. His fur twitched across his body as his muscles rippled, preparing for a fight. Belle had never seen him like this, and she couldn't tell which was more frightening — the pack, or her Raider trying to protect her.

For the longest time, the wolf-dogs stared at Raider, and he stared right back. Two of the wild dogs took a step closer to Belle. Raider adjusted his position, blocking their advance. Raider bared his teeth and barked several warnings at the pack.

Their wild, orange eyes shifted from Belle to Raider and back again. Belle could almost see them thinking about whether she was worth eating, especially if they had to fight Raider for her.

Raider took a step toward the pack. He threw back his head and howled one long note. What was he telling the pack?

Whatever it was, it seemed to work. Most of the wolf-dogs changed their stance. They seemed to relax and began to wag their tails. Two of the dogs whimpered quietly. A third even laid down. Raider seemed to relax too.

But the largest of the wolf-dogs decided that Belle was too easy of a meal to pass up. As the rest of the pack took their eyes off Belle and Raider, the big one leaped at her.

Raider must have expected the move, however. As the big wolf-dog pounced, Raider jumped sideways and threw himself at the attacker. Raider's head connected with the wild dog's middle, sending him crashing sideways to the ground. The big dog let out a loud yelp of pain and shock.

The whole thing happened in the blink of an eye. Yet to Belle it felt like forever. She managed to squeal, alerting Melody. A moment later, Melody appeared by her side. A livestock prod stuck straight out of Melody's central compartment. Its electric blue tip sparked dangerously as it pointed at the pack of wolf-dogs.

The others in the pack whined pitifully when they heard the crackle of the livestock prod. They turned tail and ran, disappearing from view. The big one was still on the ground. His breath had been knocked out of him, and he struggled to get back to his feet.

Raider advanced toward him, barking madly. His eyes were bulging out of his head, and his fangs flashed in the sunlight.

This time, outnumbered and outmatched, the big wolf-dog decided Belle wasn't worth the fight. He lowered his head and backed away, never taking his gaze from Raider. At the top of the ridge, the big dog turned and ran off after the rest of the pack.

Raider straightened up. He shook his body as if he'd just come out of a dip in a river. Then he trotted back to Belle, panting like nothing remarkable had happened.

Belle crouched down and gave him a big hug. "You saved my life!" she cried, burying her face in his fur. Her heart hadn't stopped racing yet, and his warmth was comforting.

"He is a good dog," Melody observed. "I am glad he was here to protect you. You were in great danger."

Belle stood up. "You won't tell Dad, will you?"

She looked over Melody's shoulder. The wagon was quite a distance away. It was a miracle that Melody had covered that distance in such a short time.

"How did you . . . ?" Belle pointed to the wagon.

"I was on my way to get you," Melody said, anticipating her question. "Your father is almost done with the repairs."

Belle could see her dad as he emerged from under the wagon.

"I don't want Mom and Dad to worry," Belle said, looking at Melody. "We've only just started on our road trip. And Mom isn't feeling well. There's no sense in making things worse for her."

"I agree," Melody said. "But from now on, I go everywhere you two do."

Belle smiled. She was lucky to have two protectors. There was little chance of her getting into trouble on this trip. But she also couldn't wait to tell Ta'al all about how Raider had chosen to protect her against his own kind.

As they climbed back into the wagon, Melody paused. Her eyes turned blue.

"I am simply checking on the weather reports," she said. "It looks like we shall have a smooth journey to the campsite."

That suited Belle just fine. She climbed into the wagon after Melody. Raider jumped in behind them, and the family continued their journey toward the river. As soon as Belle fed Raider his breakfast, he curled up at the foot of her bed and fell asleep. His encounter with the wild wolf-dog had tired him out. Belle stroked his soft fur with one hand while she read some information about Tharsis City. They stayed this way for the next few hours.

"Do you know any wolf jokes?" Belle asked Melody, when she was tired of reading. She scratched Raider's ears as he slept. The wagon hovered smoothly under Loki's steady pace.

"What did the wolf say when someone stepped on his foot?" Melody was happy to indulge in her favorite activity.

Belle knew this one. "Aaoooooowwwww!" She laughed quietly, careful not to wake her dog.

"What did one wolf say to the other wolf at a party?" Melody asked.

Before Belle could answer, Raider stirred. He sat up, as if something had changed. It took Belle a moment to realize that Loki's pace had slowed. Belle looked up toward the front of the wagon to see what her parents were doing.

"Look!" Yun said, pointing. A small cabin with a large holo-sign by it signaled the entrance to the official riverside camp area. The sky was beginning to turn pinkish orange. "We've arrived at the camp."

Yun slowed Loki down to a walk. They went through the registration booth, and then to the campsite that was assigned to them. Ta'al and her family had already arrived. They were just starting to cook dinner when the Songs pulled up beside them.

After a delicious meal, the two families enjoyed some time talking by the campfire and watching the stars. While the girls and Raider explored their campsite, the adults shared stories about life on their home worlds.

When it was time for bed, Belle and Ta'al begged their parents to have a sleepover. They agreed and Ta'al slept in Belle's wagon that night. It was the first sleepover for both girls, and they stayed up and talked late into the night.

Sol 13/Spring, Mars Cycle 106

Ta'al and I are snuggled up on the floor of our wagon. She loved my story of how Raider had saved me. Funny, I didn't expect that Nabians would be so like humans in how they sleep. Ta'al and I talked for ages, and then she went silent. Instantly! She's completely asleep and looks so comfortable. I wish I could fall asleep that fast.

It's too dark to see the river, but I can hear it. It's loud, so it must be big. The sound of the water flowing is soothing. Dad says we'll try to visit the nearby desalination plant tomorrow before we take the ferry across. But they don't allow animals inside, so Raider will have to stay in the wagon. I'm a little bit mad at that. Raider saved my life. He should be allowed to come with us. I hope he won't be too bored in the wagon, all by himself. Right now he's sleeping with Dad because Ta'al is afraid of animals. I can just hear his soft panting from inside my parents' makeshift room. I miss his soft furriness at my feet. Oh well, I guess it's just for one night.

CHAPTER 26

DISAPPOINTMENTS

The next morning Belle woke to Raider licking her face. She snuck him out of the wagon without disturbing anyone else. It was a bright morning, and the air was crisp. Raider chased Belle around and in between the wagons. They were both glad for the exercise.

The air here smelled different from the farm. Belle knew it was because of the salty water in the river. Mars' water was naturally salty, which was why the desalination plants were so important. The whole desalination process fascinated Belle. The way they worked to change the salty water to sweet, clean water, was science and technology at its best. She had watched every documentary that Melody could find about the plants. She couldn't wait to visit one later that morning.

By the time the sun had warmed everything up, Ta'al and all of their parents were finally ready.

"Come on!" Belle cried, growing impatient. "I read the plant's brochure, and they only take a certain number of visitors per day."

An hour later they reached the desalination plant. It was enormous! It was a towering round building with no windows. Miles of pipes snaked around the building, leading to huge tanks of water that surrounded the plant.

The building sat on a flat area overlooking the Marine Valley River. The river was so wide and misty that Belle could barely see the other side. The wind near the river was cold and strong. It almost knocked Belle and Ta'al over a few times as they tried to stay warm in their thin coats.

There were many visitors to the plant that morning, and the line to buy tickets was long. While He'ern and Yun stood in line, the others found a bench under a large tree to wait. Belle noticed that a few visitors were Terrans. Many were red-eyed, Martian-born humans.

Other tourists were Sulux. Belle knew that some Sulux people didn't like Nabians very much. So she wasn't surprised, only disappointed, when she saw the stares as the Sulux tourists passed their bench. Some smiled at Belle, but when they saw Ta'al and her family, their smiles turned to frowns. Once or twice, she even heard a Sulux say a word she didn't understand.

Ta'al and her family didn't hear any of it. Or at least they pretended not to. When Belle had had enough, she couldn't contain her questions anymore.

"Don't you get angry with people who are rude to you?" she asked Ta'al's mom. "They don't even know you and yet they treat you like an enemy."

Belle could tell that Ta'al was mad. Her friend was completely still and staring at the ground as if she was trying to burn a hole in it with her eyes. So'ark put a hand on her daughter's shoulder and looked at Belle.

"It is not our place to tell people what to think," she said in a low voice. "If they choose to be narrow-minded and ignorant, nothing we do or say will change that."

"We can only hope that they will eventually learn more about us and see that we all have a place on this planet," Fa'erz added. "The universe is far bigger and more diverse than any human can imagine. We must be patient."

"I couldn't do that," Belle said. "I'd rather yell at them to stop being so stupid."

So'ark smiled, but her eyes reflected the ground and not the sky, which Belle knew meant that she was sad. "Nabians are far more ancient than either Sulux or Humans. We must bear this burden of knowledge and wait."

"We will endure," Ta'al said, under her breath. So'ark patted her hand and nodded.

Yun and He'ern returned from the ticket booth. They were both frowning.

"It looks like we won't be able to tour the plant today," Yun said with a grunt.

"The ferry terminal just announced that the next sailing will be their only one for today," He'ern said. "They are worried about the weather forecast for later in the day."

"We had to decide," Yun said. "We could stay another night in the camp and tour the plant tomorrow. But we thought it best to leave for Tharsis now and get there sooner. Besides, I think your mother would prefer to sleep in a real bed tonight, don't you?"

Belle couldn't believe it. They were so close to the plant, and she wouldn't be able to go inside? She felt the anger grow in her chest, and her face grew hot.

Yun put his hand on her shoulder. "Maybe we can stop on the way back," he said. "There'll be plenty of opportunities to take a tour. Some other time."

Belle wanted to yell at someone. But Ta'al caught her eye. Her friend was disappointed too, but she was taking the disappointment with calm acceptance. Belle wanted to be more like her Nabian friend. So she took a deep breath, pressed her lips together, and just nodded. She was thirteen years old. She shouldn't behave like a spoiled child.

"Okay. But if we can't tour the plant," Belle said, trying to stay calm, "could Ta'al ride with us on the ferry, at least?"

"I don't see why not," Yun said, looking to So'ark for permission. Ta'al's parents talked amongst themselves for a long time. When Ta'al came back, Belle could tell the answer was going to be no. Everything was going wrong. This trip was turning out to be a huge disappointment.

"I have to stay with my family when we get on the ferry," Ta'al said. "It seems Nabians have to go through a separate entrance. And we all have to stay together."

Belle didn't like the news at all. "That's not fair! How can they do that?"

"Those are the rules. I don't like it either, but there's no point in fighting it," Ta'al replied.

Belle wanted to fight it. That fire in her chest burned hotter. She hated that she couldn't do anything about the situation. She stomped into her family's wagon behind Raider and Melody. After taking her seat, Belle poked her head out the window so that she could wave to Ta'al.

"See you on the Tharsis side of the river," she called to her friend. She tried her best to sound cheerful.

Ta'al waved back, but she didn't look very happy either.

●●● •

A little while later, a question kept lingering in Belle's mind. She turned to Melody. "I don't understand it. Why do the Nabians seem to get treated so badly by others?"

"A long time ago, Nabians refused to help terraform Mars, although they had the technology," Melody said. Her eyes were green. She was accessing her internal archives. "They believed that humans should learn and create their own advanced technology. But the Sulux had no problems with simply giving their technology away. This caused a rift between the different races. It seems that many Martians have not forgiven the Nabians for their decision."

"That does sound kind of selfish," Belle said. She filled Raider's bowl with food and watched him attack it hungrily.

"I would disagree. Think about what you are doing now," Melody said. "You learned to take care of your turken chicks because Zara refused to let me help you. You hated them in the beginning, but you learned to be responsible. All that work taught you to care for bigger creatures with greater needs, such as Raider and Loki."

"Mom did say that if I could handle the smaller responsibilities, I could be trusted to move on to more important tasks." Belle was beginning to understand. "So, the Nabians thought humans needed to be more mature?"

"Precisely. But we will never know if the Nabians were right, because the Sulux helped humans make Mars livable anyway," Melody said. "Since much of that technology came from the Nabians, it caused problems between the two races. Still, without both the Sulux and the Nabians, humans would not be living on Mars today."

Belle tried to see all sides of the argument. But she couldn't decide who was right. Thinking about it made her head hurt. She left Raider to his meal, and went to sit up front with her parents so she could see the ferry terminal as they arrived. Yun paid a small fee, and they waited while androids scanned their wagon.

"Their job is to make sure nothing dangerous is brought onto the ferry," Yun explained when he saw Belle's worried look.

"It's quite a long ride on the ferry," Zara said. "Even though this is the narrowest part of the river. If you look carefully, in the distance you can see the outline of the city on the other side."

Belle stood up on her tiptoes and squinted. Sure enough, she could just make out tall structures along the horizon. She couldn't wait to see the capital city.

Once they passed inspection, they moved on to another series of lines to wait for the ferry. A loud horn blasted through the air.

"This will be the only ferry of the day." The holo-image of a Martian man appeared in front of the waiting wagons, reminding them of what they already knew. "If you miss this ferry, please be back in line tomorrow morning for the next ferry to Tharsis City."

"I'm glad we decided to skip the tour," Zara said, looking a bit ill. "I hope we make it onto this ferry."

Belle frowned. "I hope Ta'al's family makes it too."

She and her parents watched in awe as the giant ferry approached the dock. It was bigger than any shuttle she'd ever seen. It had fan-like propellers whirring on its surface, like a monster insect with many wings. It also had two huge hulls that, according to Melody, could cut through the water very smoothly.

"The propellers allow it to skim over the water in case of bad weather conditions," Melody explained. She had poked her head out of the wagon to watch the arrival of the ferry. "The main hover engine is below."

"We're lucky that the river is calm today," Yun said. "We should make it to Tharsis in plenty of time, if we can get on this ferry." He counted the number of wagons in line in front of them.

"And because the water is calm, the ferry will be sailing as a regular sea-going vessel," Melody said. "It should be quite an interesting experience."

The Songs were one of the last wagons allowed onto the ferry. Belle tried to find Ta'al's wagon, but there were too many other wagons to locate her friend. She crossed her fingers and hoped they had made it on board the ferry.

Once they were safely secured, packed tightly among hundreds of other wagons, another loud horn blasted through the air. This told the lucky passengers that they were pushing off and beginning to cross the river. Zara took the opportunity to nap. Belle, Yun, and Melody took Raider for a walk around the ferry. Loki looked like he was asleep at the end of the harness like most of the other horsels around them.

The breeze from the river was strong but refreshing. Belle leaned against the railing while her dad held onto her from behind. Raider trotted up to their side and stuck his head between the railings. He stuck out his tongue as if he was tasting the salty air. Melody stood with her arms and legs spread wide, as if she was daring the wind to knock her over. Belle thought it was the funniest sight she'd seen in a long time.

They watched the dark waves float up and down. As the ferry cut smoothly through the water, white mustaches of foam formed on the tips of the waves. Water stretched as far as the eye could see.

Only when they moved to the front of the ferry could Belle make out the skyline of Tharsis City. In the distance, beyond the city, the sky was dark, like a giant shadow. But right over the city, the sun was shining. It lit the city up, showing off its many red and gray buildings. Some of the tallest buildings glimmered in the sunlight. Belle's heart raced.

"Tharsis City looks like a fairyland from here," she exclaimed.

Yun laughed. "From what I've read, it is quite a city. It's the most impressive city on Mars."

Sol 14/Spring, Mars Cycle 106

    Standing on the front deck of the ferry was fun, but my face froze after a few minutes. I loved looking out at the city as it grew bigger with each passing minute. It looks like an amazing place! We finally gave in when we couldn't feel our faces anymore and headed back to the wagon. Dad decided to take a quick nap with Mom. Raider is tired out from all the excitement. The hum of the ferry engines is quite hypnotic. But I can't sleep. I'm going to play 3D chess with Melody.

    I can't wait to get to Tharsis City. I just hope Ta'al and her family made it onto the ferry too. The city won't be any fun without my best friend.

CHAPTER 27
THARSIS CITY

Belle rode up front with her parents as they drove off the ferry and followed the lines of wagons into the main city. Signs of city life greeted them long before the city gates came into view. Along the roadside, as each wagon passed sensors, holo-banners popped up from the ground. They advertised all sorts of wonders to be found in Tharsis.

Best Hotel in Town
Stay at the Desert Inn!

Topamei Medical Center.
Most advanced medical facility on the planet!

Give your android a SPA day!
Restoration facilities available in many areas.

Have you tasted lab-grown steaks?
Give it a try at Borealis Planitia Steakhouse!

Belle gaped in awe as each banner popped up in front of them. She wanted to try everything they suggested.

"Just ignore the ads," Yun said. "We've already decided where we're staying and which hospital we're going to."

More and more banners popped up as they got closer to Tharsis. Belle eventually grew tired of them.

"There it is," Zara said as they rounded a small hill.

Belle gasped as Tharsis City came into view. Buildings taller than she'd ever seen, even on Earth, rose into the sky. The buildings were of all shapes and varying heights. Some looked like cylinders jutting up into the sky. Others were shaped like prisms and slender pyramids. Several buildings had disc-like tops with many windows that looked like viewing galleries. Belle wondered what the view was like from such a high place.

The roar of a shuttle engine flying overhead caught her off guard, and she grabbed onto her dad's arm.

"Lots of air traffic here," he said with a laugh.

Belle looked up. The sky was dotted with aircraft of all shapes and sizes. Many were coming in low to land. A few smaller craft landed on top of buildings.

As they neared the city boundary, the level of noise surprised Belle. She had grown used to the stillness of the farm. Here the air was filled with a continual humming sound. Then there were the constant roars of engines, the clanking of wheels, horsels grunting and whinnying, and the chatter of hundreds of voices. These all gave Belle a chill of excitement.

As they came to the city gate, they were stopped for a short interview about why they had come to Tharsis City. Large silver and black Protectors asked Yun several questions. After Yun had answered their questions, the Protectors waved them through into the city. Large signs floated out of the sky, declaring:

Welcome to Tharsis City
The Wonder of Mars!

The Songs had booked a room at the Starry Skies Motel. It was one of the few motels that allowed pets to stay with their families.

Their guidance system led them through Astronaut Avenue. It was a long street that was broken up by several cross junctions. At each intersection, they had to stop to allow other traffic to cross.

At each stop, Belle checked out the decorative storefronts along both sides of the four-lane road. She'd never seen so many stores in one place. She swept her head back and forth, trying to take in the sights in every store window. They passed a large toy store that had all kinds of flying gadgets on display. Another store sold the latest in home wares. Belle pointed out what looked like a self-cooking device to her parents. Fully prepared meals appeared within it every few seconds.

"I'd love to have that at home," Zara said, nudging Yun. "Melody and I would never have to cook again."

He laughed and shook his head. "Maybe so. But only if we won the lottery first."

At the seventh cross-junction, they turned onto a smaller street — Starry Way. Loki slowed to a snail's pace as they searched for their motel. Belle spotted a blue and silver sign floating above their heads:

Starry Skies Motel
Sleep Among the Constellations

After checking in at the motel's front desk, they rode a glass elevator to their floor. Their room made Belle feel as if she were in the middle of a colorful cloud in space. The walls were swirled with pinks and purples, and artificial stars twinkled every few seconds.

"It's quite soothing," said Zara.

"And hypnotic," added Belle.

Raider wasn't sure about it, however. He barked at the fake stars whenever they twinkled. *Poor Raider*, Belle thought. She hoped he'd get used to the city and its strange sights and sounds. Otherwise this would be a miserable vacation for him.

Once they got unpacked and settled in their room, Yun suggested that they go out and explore the city.

"But Ta'al and her parents aren't here yet," Belle said. She didn't want to go out exploring without her friend.

"I'm sure Ta'al's family will show up at some point," Yun said. "Come on, let's get some dinner. I'm starving." Even Zara was feeling hungry.

Tharsis City at night was just as busy as it was in the daytime. But it was colder. Belle was glad she'd brought along her coat. She even wrapped an extra scarf around Melody's neck.

As the Song family stepped out of their motel, they were met by crowds of people hurrying from one place to another. The larger transports that were present earlier were now replaced by smaller craft. Several of these were open top carriages — some pulled by horsels, others by unseen engines. The noise level, though, hadn't changed at all. The city was still loud and unstoppable.

As they wandered about the city, Belle noticed that they were the only family walking with a wolf-dog and an android. She also noticed many Sulux and Nabians. They often acknowledged each other with a nod or a hand gesture of greeting. Belle was surprised. The two races seemed to be a lot friendlier to each other in Tharsis than back home.

Belle was also surprised at how many other alien races were here too. The first person they met was the driver of a horsel-drawn carriage. He, or she (Belle couldn't really tell), offered to show them the city for a rather steep price.

"He is Parsiv," Melody told the Song family as they were approached. "They come from a star system very far from here. There are not many Parsiva on Mars."

The Parsiv made a sound, as if he were singing.

"That is the Parsiv way of welcoming visitors," explained Melody. "I downloaded the more common languages spoken in Tharsis into my memory banks. I thought it would be helpful."

"It is," Belle said. She smiled and waved at the friendly Parsiv carriage driver.

"Welll-coome!" He said the word in a sing-song voice, as if it was a part of his greeting song.

The Parsiv had a long, narrow face with three eyes. His four arms ended in hands that looked like fins with very fine skin. "See the night lights by rrr-omantic ca-rrr-iage. I have many blankets to help keep you warrrm."

The Parsiv driver emphasized the 'r' in his speech. He sounded a little like a purring kitten. Belle liked him instantly and was sorry that they couldn't afford a ride.

Suddenly the air was filled with the blaring of an alarm. The carriage driver's horsel whinnied, and Raider barked. Belle had heard alarms like this before, back in Sun City. It meant that everyone had to run for cover, preferably underground. Belle couldn't believe it. A dangerous dust storm was coming — here in Tharsis City!

CHAPTER 28
UNEXPECTED SURPRISES

Belle looked to her parents. They looked almost as nervous as she felt. The carriage driver, on the other hand, just shrugged. He stroked his horsel with his two finlike hands to calm it.

"Where do we go?" Yun asked him.

The alien nodded. "Ah yes. You arrre new to Tharrrsis." He pointed to the sky. "Watch."

Looking up, Belle watched as an energy bubble grew across the sky above them.

"It's just like the new security system over our water tank!" Belle exclaimed.

Sure enough, the bubble grew until it formed a dome that covered the entire city. Other people in the streets stopped and watched the shield form as well. For a moment, the city went quiet. Once the shield was complete, everyone went about their business.

"Tharrrsis is prrro-tected," the alien carriage driver said. "No worrries. Enjoy yourrr stay."

"That is incredible," Yun said, as they headed back out to Astronaut Avenue. "It must be Nabian technology."

"It must use a lot of energy," Zara said.

Melody confirmed Zara's guess, but the numbers went right over Belle's head. Within minutes, the dust storm hit the shield. It sounded like distant thunder that never stopped. Belle and her parents found a bench and sat down to watch the storm as it swept over the city. Raider crawled under the bench and whined quietly. He didn't understand what was happening.

"This is such a rare opportunity," Yun said. "To see a storm up close and not be harmed by it."

"Indeed," Melody said. "There is only one other shield like this on Mars. It is in Utopia. Tharsis City must be very important to have expensive technology such as this."

Belle was mesmerized by the storm, until she realized that her friends might be out there in it.

"Ta'al and her family!" she cried. "What if they're stuck outside the city?"

Zara gasped. "That's right! I hope they're okay."

"Don't forget," Yun said. "They're Nabian. They're probably better prepared for storms than most of us."

Belle hoped her dad was right. She didn't like the idea of her friend being out in this storm.

After about ten minutes, Belle became bored with watching the storm. And her stomach was growling. The Songs continued their walk to find something to eat.

"Look who we've bumped into!" Yun cried, as they crossed Astronaut Avenue.

Parked in front of a large store called Sol's was Ta'al's family's wagon. So'ark and He'ern jumped down as soon as they saw the Songs. Ta'al ran up to Belle.

"We've had quite an adventure," Ta'al said with a big grin.

"Indeed," So'ark said, coming up behind her. "We misunderstood the ferry line system. We thought the Nabians were being sent to the end of the lines."

"Instead, we were allowed on the ferry ahead of others," He'ern said. He flapped his long sleeves, straightening out his robes.

"Apparently, in Tharsis City, as in Utopia, Nabians are given extra privileges," Fa'erz said. "We arrived late because we were given a tour of the city's power grid."

Ta'al pointed at the shield above them. "It uses Nabian technology. Tharsis authorities are so grateful for it that all Nabians are treated to a free tour of how they use it." She spoke quickly and excitedly. She took a deep breath. "That's why we're late."

Belle was pleased for her friend. Tharsis seemed like a good place for people from all planets to live. She wanted to hear all about her friend's adventure, but right now she was too hungry.

"Well, you couldn't have arrived at a better time," Yun said, clapping He'ern on the back. "We were just out looking for some dinner. We're all starving."

A few blocks away they found a traditional Nabian restaurant. Ta'al seemed excited by this so they all went in. The Nabian hosts greeted them all in the usual way. But the main host kept glaring at Melody and flicking his chin in her direction. He said something to Ta'al's family in their own language.

"I think I should wait outside," Melody said.

"Why?" Belle asked.

"They do not allow androids inside."

So'ark looked embarrassed. "We could go elsewhere."

"It's all right," said Yun. "Rules are rules." He told Melody to head back to the motel and wait in the room.

"You might as well take Raider with you," Zara said. "I'm not sure they'd like a big hairy wolf-dog in their restaurant either."

Belle tried not to show her displeasure. Melody and Raider were a part of their family and she didn't like to exclude anyone.

Dinner soon made her forget her bad mood. She was famished, just like everyone else. And the food was delicious. Melody's Nabian food wasn't nearly as good as this.

After dinner, the two families walked down the street, looking for dessert. They found a small store that sold frozen sweets. The server was another type of alien Belle hadn't met yet. She watched as he folded several flavors together with his four arms, creating a colorful and edible flower. Belle didn't want to ruin it by eating it, but she couldn't resist. As she took a bite, all the flavors burst in her mouth with the most amazing sensation.

"I'd eat this every day if I could!" she declared. She and Ta'al slurped their special desserts as they walked back to their motel.

At the motel, the Songs waited for Ta'al's family to check in, and then returned to their own room. When Yun opened the door, Belle expected Raider to bound out to greet her. But the room was completely silent.

"Raider? Melody?" Belle called.

There was no response.

She walked through the room. As the automatic lights came on, she realized that the room had been untouched since they'd left for dinner.

Yun called down to the lobby to ask if anyone had seen Melody and Raider return. But nobody had seen either of them.

Belle felt sick. All that food she'd eaten threatened to come back up again. Her heart raced, and she felt cold and hot at the same time. What had happened to Melody and Raider? Where could they be?

Sol 14/Spring, Mars Cycle 106, evening

I can't sleep. Dad went out again to look for Melody and Raider. He wouldn't let me come. But I hate waiting. I keep thinking about the kind of trouble they could be in. They'd be expecting me to come to their rescue.

Mom said she's worried too but she's fast asleep now. So it's just me in this room, all alone.

If anything happens to them, I don't know what I'd do.

Sol 15/Spring, Mars Cycle 106, past midnight

Dad came home empty-handed. He said Tharsis City has a midnight curfew during dust storms. He promised we'd try again in the morning.

CHAPTER 29

MISSING!

Belle was the first to wake the next morning. She could barely wait for her dad to get ready so they could look for her missing friends.

"We have to take Mom to the hospital for her checkup first," he said. "Then we'll set out to look for Melody and Raider. I already reported them missing to the authorities last night."

Belle stomped her foot and was about to yell at her dad, but then saw how pale her mom looked. She was torn. She desperately wanted to find Raider and Melody, but she was also worried about her mom.

"Melody is resourceful," Yun said to comfort her. "And Raider has a great sense of direction. I'm sure he'll find his way back to us."

Belle was afraid her android and dog could be in trouble, and that someone might have harmed them. To say it aloud would've made it impossible for Belle to get through the day. So she pushed the thoughts to the back of her mind and went quietly with her parents to the clinic.

The hospital was only a few blocks away. Zara was feeling weak, so they walked slowly across Astronaut Avenue, and turned down Main Street. Then they looked for Healthcare Avenue. Belle took the opportunity to ask everyone they passed if they'd seen Melody or Raider. She walked into one store that sold antiques. All kinds of ancient things were stacked almost to the ceiling. She showed the shopkeeper a holo-image of Raider and Melody. But the Martian lady shook her head sympathetically.

Most people Belle met didn't believe that Raider was tame and worried that a wild animal might be loose in the city. Belle had to convince them that he was safe.

"If you see him, please contact me at this motel," she said to an alien working in a store that sold holo-vid programs. "If you feed him some mealworms, he'll stay with you. He won't hurt anyone, I promise."

Belle had expected people to be uneasy about looking for a wolf-dog. What she didn't expect was the negative attitude people had about Melody. Most people didn't seem to care that she was missing. It didn't seem to matter when Belle told them how much Melody was loved by her family.

"We don't need androids that try to be human," one storekeeper said. "Not after what happened on Earth."

Belle couldn't believe people were still afraid of something that had happened so long ago. How could she convince them that Melody was her best friend?

At the hospital, Belle sat in the waiting room while her parents went in to see the doctor. After half an hour of waiting alone, Belle became restless. She began exploring the hospital. Soon, she found herself standing outside of the main entrance. As people arrived at the hospital, she showed them holo-images of Melody and Raider.

"Have you seen my friends?" she asked.

Most people were kind enough to look, but all shook their heads. No one had seen either a wandering android or a big hairy wolf-dog.

Then one elderly Martian stopped and stared at the holo-images for a lot longer than the others.

"Hmmm, that chewed-up ear . . ." the man said, thoughtfully rubbing his chin.

"Yes?" Belle said. This was the first person to even think about Raider's appearance. Her heart raced. "He's always had this one strange looking ear. My Dad thinks he may have been injured in a fight with another wolf-dog before he lived with us."

The man nodded. "I heard someone say something just like that last night."

Belle bounced up and down. She was finally getting somewhere in her search. "Please, can you tell me where you heard that?"

"I believe it was last night, at dinner," he said, staring at the image of Raider. "There's an old diner just down this block."

He squinted in the direction he'd just come from. "I went there for a bite to eat last night. I have to stay near the hospital, in case my wife needs me. She's not well, you see. Anyway, there were three men at the table behind me. They were loud, and I couldn't help but overhear them. It isn't polite to listen in on other people's conversations, you know?"

Belle grew impatient. She wanted to tell the old man to just get to the important part — where was Raider? But at the same time, she was afraid to interrupt him. This man had her only clue to Raider's whereabouts.

"Do you remember what they were saying?" she asked, as politely as she could manage.

The man looked up at the hospital as he thought about the previous evening. "One of the men, the loudest one, was bragging that he'd found a new dog. He was talking about the dog having a chewed-up ear and how he must have gotten into a fight in the past. It seems similar to what you said about your dog. Maybe it's the same one."

The man looked back down at Belle and rubbed his chin again. "I could be wrong, I don't know," he finished.

"No, I think you're right!" Belle said, a little too excitedly. "I think that's my dog he was talking about. His chewed ear is very distinctive. Can you describe what the man looked like for me?"

The old man nodded. "He was still bragging about how strong this dog was when I got up to leave. I remember that a Protector walked into the diner, just as I left. It was strange because the men at the table went completely silent. Their sudden silence made me turn to look at them."

Belle could barely contain herself. "What did this man look like?" she repeated.

"He was big," the man said. "He had a fuzzy beard and wore several layers of clothing. Seemed a little dangerous to me."

It wasn't much of a description, but it was the most she'd received all day. Belle asked for directions to the diner, then thanked the old man and took off running. She knew she should have waited for her dad, but she didn't want to lose the only clue she had.

I'll find out more at the diner, and then come back and tell Dad what I learned, she told herself.

The diner was called The Dirty Pig. A hologram of a giant pig rolling around in the mud glowed on the outside of the door. Without another thought, Belle pushed open the door.

The foul smell of old cooking oil and sweat hit her right in the face as she walked in. She tried not to gag. It was a bright morning outside, but only a few streaks of sunlight made it through the grimy windows. The whole place looked dim, old, and dirty. There were only a few people inside — most of them were sitting at tables. One man leaned heavily against a counter inhaling the steam from whatever was in his large cup.

An odd-looking android rolled back and forth behind the counter. It was cleaning the countertop with a rag, stopping once to refill the customer's hot drink. This android looked nothing like Melody. It had no head . . . only arms and a narrow cylinder for a torso. It reminded Belle of a metal broom with arms.

They obviously don't want to interact with intelligent androids, thought Belle.

She showed the broomstick droid the image of Raider. She wasn't sure the android could see, but she had to try. "Did you overhear a large Martian with a beard talk about this dog last night? He might have mentioned a chewed-up ear."

The android stopped in front of Belle. The customer next to her looked over too.

"You are underage, with no adult supervision," the android said in a flat, robotic tone. "Children are not allowed to purchase goods on their own. Please return with an adult."

"I don't want to buy anything," Belle said, annoyed. She was old enough to enter a diner on her own. She hated that people treated her like a young child. Mom said it was because she was petite. She pressed on. "I was told a tall man with a beard was here last night. He was talking loudly about this dog. Did you see him? Do you know where he went?"

The android stopped in front of Belle. It scanned Raider's image with a green light that fanned out from the top of its body.

"The man you mention was here," it said. "His group became silent when the Protector entered. They left soon after."

"Yes, that's the one!" Belle was thankful for the old man's long story now. "Do you know where he went after leaving here?"

The man at the counter looked up from his cup. "Those men were laborers," he mumbled.

Belle turned to him. He took a long gulp of his drink, and then wiped his mouth with his sleeve. He blinked at her with tired, bleary eyes.

"They're the ones who built most of what you see in this city," he said. "They live at the old miners' camp on Sulphate Way."

"Where's that?" she asked.

The man rubbed his face and shook his head, just like Raider did after his encounter with the wild wolf-dogs. Her heart ached for her pet.

"The camp's at the edge of the city," the man said. He slurred his words, so Belle had to move in closer to hear him. His breath stank, so she tried hard not to inhale.

"It's unprotected from the weather," the man continued. "When a storm's coming, most of the people there seek shelter inside the dome. That's probably why they were here last night."

"Sulphate Way," Belle said to herself. She didn't want to forget that name.

Belle turned to leave the diner. But then a thought occurred to her. She turned back and showed the man another image, this time of Melody. The broomstick droid was back behind the counter, and it scanned the image as well.

"Have you seen this android?"

"We do not serve androids," the simple droid said. "All unaccompanied androids are sent to the SPA facility."

"What's that?" Belle asked. She was sure it was not as relaxing as the name sounded.

The man at the counter blurted, "Humanoid robots get picked up by the authorities, especially if they're out in the streets mucking around on their own."

"All unaccompanied androids must be taken to the SPA facility," the service droid repeated.

Belle walked out of the diner into the fresh air and bright sunlight. She squinted. She had two places to find, and had no idea where either one was. She needed help and knew just who to call.

Sol 15/Spring, Mars Cycle 106

I have to find the SPA facility and the miners' camp. But I don't know how to find these places. I usually rely on Melody to find that type of information.

I met my parents back at the hospital. Ta'al was there too with her parents. When I told them about the clues I'd found, Dad was awfully mad that I'd wandered off on my own. But he was glad to get the information about Melody. He agreed to go to the SPA facility to get her.

Dad told me to stay with Mom while she rested back at the motel. The doctor gave her some medicine to get over her sickness. But it's knocked her out. I can't just sit here in the motel and watch her sleep, can I? Not when Raider's in trouble.

So I've talked Ta'al into sneaking out with me. I promised her we wouldn't do anything dangerous. I told her that if we found Raider, I'd call my dad right away.

I just hope we're not too late.

CHAPTER 30

THE SEARCH FOR RAIDER

Ta'al downloaded an interactive guide map of the city onto her comm device. Together, she and Belle found where the mining camp was on Sulphate Way. This is where the man who had Raider probably lived. It didn't seem to be too far from the hospital. Ta'al started the guide program and a green arrow was projected onto the ground by their feet. It showed the direction they needed to go.

"Did you bring the Petripuffs?" Belle asked, as they crossed the street in front of the hospital. The arrow pointed to the right.

Ta'al patted her pockets. "We have plenty. And our new improvements should come in handy if we run into any trouble."

Belle shivered at the thought of meeting the large Martian and his friends. Her Petripuffs were really just a security blanket. They made her feel safe, but she hoped she'd never have to use them.

The streets were busy and crowded. Transports zoomed down the wide streets, kicking dust into the air. Impatient drivers rose above the ground to pass over other vehicles ahead of them. Drivers on the ground blasted their horns and swore loudly at those above them. It was chaotic. Crossing the streets on foot required a lot of courage. No drivers obeyed the pedestrian crossing signs. So the girls held hands and waited for an opening in the traffic.

"Ready . . . go!" cried Ta'al. The two girls dashed across the street as fast as they could. Ta'al was much faster than Belle. She barely kept up with her Nabian friend and was breathing heavily when they reached the other side.

The girls crossed two more main roads in the same way. Then the green arrow at their feet led them down sidewalks for several blocks. Because there were so many tall buildings, the sun was hidden and they walked in cold shadow most of the time. Belle had to pull her thin coat snugly around herself and tuck her hands into her pockets to keep warm.

"This is Museum Walk," Ta'al said, reading the guide information on her comm device. "It says there are several historical buildings and artifacts here. Once Raider and Melody are safe, we should come back. It would be fascinating to learn more about the history of the city." Belle knew that Ta'al was trying to distract her from her anxiety over losing Raider. It wasn't working, but she appreciated her friend's efforts.

The girls kept following the green arrow on the ground. The traffic stop at the next junction was unlike the others they had seen.

Along with the usual warning lights were barriers that rose out of the ground. The girls had no choice but to wait.

The ground began to rumble beneath their feet. Suddenly a large panel in the road slid open — and a train flew out of the underground! It was very long and fast, and it created a strong wind that blew the girls back a few steps.

"What is that?" Belle cried.

Ta'al tapped on her comm device. "It's the public transportation train!" she said, shouting because the rumble got louder with each train car that emerged. "It functions mostly underground up to this point. From here it continues on its route by hovering about three stories above the ground." She looked up. "Amazing!"

After the train had completely emerged and the barriers were removed, the girls continued on.

As they passed one large window, Belle simply couldn't resist stopping to look. A salesperson was waving a wandlike device over some dull jewelry with boring gray stones. But as soon as the wand touched them, they came to life. The stones lit up in a wide range of colors and tiny holo-images popped up from each one. They looked like dancing fairies. Belle had never seen anything like it. She imagined her mom wearing such a necklace and how beautiful she'd look. The salesperson behind the window gave her an inviting smile, but Belle knew her family could never afford anything like this incredible jewelry.

"Come on, Belle," Ta'al called. "The arrow is blinking. Sulphate Way is just around the next corner."

The girls followed the arrow to the end of the street. At the corner, the arrow turned into a red circle. The sign above them showed that they had arrived at Sulphate Way.

"Which way now?" Ta'al said. "We don't have a full address, only the street name, so the guide program can't take us any further."

Belle tried to remember what the man at the diner had said. "We have to find a miners' camp. Maybe we should ask someone."

The girls stood on the street corner, trying to get someone's attention. But people were walking by too quickly. No one made eye contact. Everyone just went about their business without acknowledging the two girls.

Belle decided to duck into the first building they came across to ask someone for information. It was a banking facility. The outside of the building looked like most of the other buildings in Tharsis — massive and reddish brown. Inside, however, everything was bright and shiny white.

"This is ancient marble!" Ta'al exclaimed, running her hand along the floor. "This kind of stone isn't found on Mars. They must have imported it from Earth. Amazing."

Belle had no idea what marble was, but it certainly was shiny. Their boots squeaked against the floor as they crossed the large lobby to a high counter. Two droids that looked like Protectors stood at attention by the counter. A large, purple Sulux man stood on the other side. He looked down at the girls as if they were tiny bugs.

"May I help you?" he said. Then seeing Ta'al, he added it in her language. "*Kra-ni-toh-ku?*"

Ta'al giggled. "His accent is terrible," she whispered.

"We're looking for the miners' camp on Sulphate Way," Belle said, sounding more nervous than she felt. The wide space and brightness of this place made her appear small and scared. "Could you tell us where it is?"

The Sulux man stared at Belle for a long time. "Why would a child such as you have business in a place like that?"

"My dog ran away," she explained. "And he was last seen there."

The man exhaled loudly and slowly. "If I were you, I'd report it to the Protectors and let them do their jobs. The mining camp is no place for a child."

That just got Belle's blood boiling. She glared at the man and stood as tall as she could. "I'm not a child."

The Sulux man shrugged. "Have it your way," he said, and then programmed the directions into their guide. The camp was at the very end of Sulphate Way.

"Thank you for your help," Belle said drily. Together the two girls dashed out of the building.

CHAPTER 31
THE END
OF THE ROAD

The closer they got to the camp, the more excited Belle became to see her dog again. They picked up their pace.

Sulphate Way was a very long road. With each passing block, the buildings grew shorter and farther apart. Fewer and fewer tourists walked along the street. It felt more industrial here, as if this area was where all the real work of the city was done.

Suddenly the paved sidewalk came to an end, as did the roads. It was as if the city builders had run out of material at this very spot. Over the girls' heads, the hover-train swooshed by and disappeared into the encampment that lay before them.

Across the dusty unpaved road, the girls saw a rough stone wall with an ominous looking gate in the center. The wall surrounded a camp of large tents. There were rows and rows of them inside.

"I suppose 'camp' was a literal term," Ta'al said, sounding a lot like her mother.

Belle sighed. "How are we going to find Raider in there?"

She wished more than anything that Melody were with them. Her android would've been able to hear Raider from this distance. Belle thought of all the times she was rude to Melody and regretted every one of them. She missed her friend. If she ever got Melody back, she promised herself, she would treat her like a precious jewel.

"I wonder if I can program this to emit a frequency like a dog-whistle?" Ta'al said and began tapping on her comm device.

The girls approached the gate slowly. Ta'al slowly waved her device back and forth as they moved forward. At the gate, they stood and listened. There must have been hundreds, even thousands, of people living inside. Voices filled the air, as well as the sound of animals — birds screeching, shoats bleating, and dogs barking.

Belle's heart sank. The camp was like a huge maze. Without help, they'd never find Raider.

Ta'al groaned and tapped at her comm device again.

"I don't know what I was thinking," she said, frowning. "I can't reprogram my comm to do anything." She gave Belle an apologetic look. "And my parents are demanding we return to them."

"But, Raider . . ." Belle wouldn't budge. She gripped the sticky gate bars tightly. She didn't want to think about why it was sticky.

"Belle, you promised we wouldn't do anything dangerous." Ta'al's voice rose. "If we don't head back now, our parents will never trust us again. We should go."

"When our parents find out what we did today, they're not likely to trust us anyway," Belle said sharply. She was frustrated. She was going to be in trouble for sneaking out. And worse, her sneaking hadn't produced anything useful.

Belle shook the gate to see if it would open. Two rough-looking women walked by and glowered at her.

"A bit young to be coming for the fights, aren't you?" One of the women sneered at Belle.

Belle's heart jumped into her throat. "Wha- what fights?" she squeaked.

"If you don't know, then I'm not telling!" the woman laughed.

Then the other woman charged at Belle, yelling something at the top of her lungs. Belle was so shocked, she couldn't move. The grubby woman grabbed onto Belle's hands, pinning them to the gate. Belle winced at the pain.

"Pretty little girls like you should stay away from places like this," the woman hissed. Belle leaned away because the woman smelled bad, like old fish and something sour.

"I . . . I'm . . . looking . . . for my dog," Belle whimpered. She couldn't pry her hands away from the woman's grip.

The other woman watching from behind the gate laughed wickedly. "Your dog is likely gone, missy," she cackled. "Most of them don't survive a day in the ring."

And then as quickly as she had charged, the woman at the gate let go of Belle's hands. She hobbled away into the camp. The only thing Belle could hear was their mocking laughter and the pounding of her own heart.

"See? We can't do this on our own," Ta'al said urgently. "We need to get help."

Belle shivered. This wasn't a nice — or safe — place. But she was sure her dog was inside. And he was in danger.

Belle shook the bars of the gate again with all her strength. But the gate wouldn't budge.

"Belle! Let's go!" Ta'al sounded desperate.

More people inside the camp passed by the gate. They were headed in the same direction as the two women.

"What fights are you going to?" Belle called out to them.

Most people ignored them and just kept walking.

"I'm leaving, Belle," Ta'al warned. "I'm telling your parents what you're trying to do." She tapped something into her comm device.

"Wait, please," Belle pleaded. "Let me just find out where they're going."

She called out to the people in the camp once more. "What fights? Where are you going?"

A younger man looked their way. He flicked his chin up at Belle and winked. He put a finger up to his lips. "Shh!" he said. "Don't tell now. We're heading to the dog fights!" Then he disappeared into the crowd.

Belle froze. She couldn't move a muscle. Her heart dropped, and she felt like she was going to be sick.

Dog fights?

The man who'd taken Raider was going to force him to fight other wolf-dogs? Or other creatures? Or even a person? Belle had no idea what a dog fight was, but she was sure it was the worst thing in the universe.

How was she going to save Raider? The gate was locked. She couldn't find a way in, and Ta'al was sending a message to tell her parents where they were. A fat tear rolled down the side of her nose and into her mouth. The saltiness gave her small comfort. She felt Ta'al tug her sleeve.

"We need help," Ta'al said. "And if we tell our parents the whole truth, I'm sure they'll come back with us."

Belle wasn't sure there would be time. She allowed her friend to take her hand and pull her away from the camp. It was as if all the strength in her body had flowed away. She couldn't stop thinking of Raider being bitten and scratched by another animal. She pictured him lying on the ground, injured, bloody, and confused. She wondered if Raider felt let down by her. Did he think she had abandoned him to this horrid life?

Her mind was so full of thoughts about Raider that she didn't even realize that they'd arrived back at the hospital. She finally began to focus when she heard her dad's voice.

"And just where have you been young lady?" he demanded — very loudly.

Ta'al's voice came next, and Belle knew she was explaining the whole story to him, but no words registered in her mind.

Her dad was yelling again. Belle didn't understand what he was saying, but he was clearly very angry. Still, she didn't care. Raider was in serious trouble, and she felt responsible. Without thinking, she wrapped her arms around her dad and began to sob, her tears soaking his light jacket.

Sol 15 / Spring, Mars Cycle 106, evening

I think my dad carried me back to the motel. I don't really remember much. I felt like such a failure today. We went all the way to the mining camp and couldn't do a thing. I can't stop thinking about what might be happening to Raider.

I'm glad Ta'al was with me, though. She stays so calm and positive. She's sure that we'll be able to find Raider tomorrow.

Ta'al's mom gave me something sweet to drink. She said it would help me to rest. She said I'd need my strength tomorrow if we're all going to save Raider and Melody together.

CHAPTER 32

AN ANDROID IN PIECES

The sky was dark outside by the time the Nabian medicine wore off. Belle heard low voices coming from the sitting area on the far side of the room. Yun and Zara were on the sofa, talking quietly.

"Have we found Melody?" Belle asked.

Yun nodded, without looking at Belle. "She's at a SPA facility a few blocks away from here."

"Then let's go get her." This was the first good news Belle had heard all day.

"She's scheduled to be dismantled," Zara said, twisting her fingers together. "I'm so sorry."

"What?!" Belle cried. "We can't let them do that."

"They're not responding at all to my request to speak to them," Yun said.

"Then let's go to the facility." Belle couldn't understand why her parents didn't think of that.

"It's really late now," Yun said. "I'll send them a message to say we'll be there first thing in the morning." He began dictating a message into his datapad.

"NO!" Belle screamed. She hadn't meant to. The word had just come out that way.

She rushed to the door. "Dad, we have to go *now*. If they kill Melody, I'll never forgive you!"

"Melody can't be killed," Yun said, looking a little hurt. "The worst they can do is wipe her memory."

"Can't you see that's the same thing as killing her?" Belle cried. "Without her memories, she wouldn't be Melody!"

Zara nodded. "She's right, Yun. Melody belonged to my mother, and she has all the memories of my mother's life, my childhood, and Belle's too. We can't let them reset her to nothing."

Belle stomped her feet. "You were the one who told Melody to head to the motel on her own. This is your fault, Dad."

"Now Belle, that's not fair," Zara said, shooting Belle a serious warning look.

"But she has a point." Zara turned to Yun. "It wasn't your fault, but there's no harm in going to the facility to find out what's happening. We're all awake anyway."

Belle was so relieved that her mom was on her side. She looked over at her dad with tears in her eyes. Yun rose out of his seat and picked up the coat that was slung over the back of the sofa.

"Come on, then," he said with a sigh. "Let's go find our android."

After persuading Zara to stay and rest in the motel, Yun and Belle rushed to the SPA facility. It was too far away to walk, so they hopped into a tiny hover-cab. The driver was another broomstick droid, like the one in The Dirty Pig diner.

"Dad, do you think they're going to turn Melody into one of these simple droids?" Belle couldn't bear to think of her friend without a head, legs, or body with lots of secret compartments.

"Don't worry, Belle," Yun said. "We'll get there in time to stop anything bad from happening. Trust me."

Belle wished she could trust her dad. But she was so mad with him for not acting right away. This was turning out to be the worst vacation ever.

The SPA facility was another giant bulky structure. But this building had tall glass doors that opened into a bright lobby area. Large letters lit up the wall before them as they walked in. It read:

Department of Planetary Protection: Security Protocol for Androids.

"So that's what SPA stands for," Belle murmured.

People in blue uniforms walked about while staring at their datapads. Several broomstick droids rolled around on their wheels helping customers. One such droid rolled up to Yun and Belle.

"May I be of assistance?" it asked in the same flat, robotic voice as the diner droid.

Yun showed the droid Melody's order number, and it led them to a room at the back of the lobby. There was a bench against the wall by a closed door with the number one on it.

"Please wait here," the droid said. "You will be served momentarily." Then it rolled away.

Belle fidgeted in her seat for several minutes. "No one is coming to help us," she grumbled.

Yun got up and went to ask another droid for help. It told him the same thing as the first droid. At the same time, a Nabian girl in uniform approached the door beside Belle. She tapped a pattern in the control panel and the door slid open. Belle got up to follow her.

The girl held up her hand to stop Belle. "Authorized personnel only. Please wait here," she said. The door closed.

"I have to do something," Belle said to her dad, as he sat back down. She looked around to make sure no one else was coming, then tapped the control panel and entered the same pattern the Nabian girl used. The door slid open.

"Belle!" Yun followed her as she walked through the door. "You can't just barge in there. There are proper ways to do things."

Belle wanted to tell her dad that she rarely did things the *proper* way. Nothing would get solved if she did.

"You can't do this!" he whispered.

She looked up at her dad. "I just did."

The room behind the door was a laboratory. The lighting was bluish-white and there were transparent pods in rows down the sides. Computers and robot parts sat neatly on counters and benches. A couple of workers were focused on android parts on the counters in front of them. More cylinder droids stood in the pods, likely waiting to be activated or repaired.

Belle tiptoed through the lab, searching for Melody, but there was no sign of her. Her stomach twisted painfully. She began to look for robotic parts that might have been a part of her friend.

Then she found Melody's arms.

She squealed in fright, and the nearby workers turned around.

"Hey! What are you doing in here?" a man asked. He rushed up to Belle.

Yun stopped the man before he reached Belle. "We're here to get our android back. Where is she?" He showed the man the holo-document with Melody's information.

"You should be waiting outside," the man protested, pointing to the door.

"We're not going anywhere until you show us where Melody is!" Belle yelled so fiercely that the man took a step back.

He frowned and looked over the holo-document again.

"Fine," he said. "She's been cleansed anyway."

Cleansed? What does that mean? Belle thought, terrified.

The man led them to a bench along the back wall. Androids of all kinds were stacked in piles, completely dismantled! At the far end was a pile of parts where Melody's head sat on top. Belle wailed so loudly that everyone in the lab stopped to stare. She wrapped her arms around her android's head and glared at her dad.

"You did this!" she yelled. "This is all your fault!"

Yun's face went a deep red and his nostrils flared. He demanded an explanation from the man in the uniform. The man took Yun into a different part of the lab to see his supervisor, while Belle began to put Melody back together. The Nabian girl from earlier came by to help her.

"I'm sorry this happened to your droid," she said. "I had a Home Helper when I was younger, and I really liked it too."

"Melody is more than a Helper," Belle said quietly. "She's my oldest friend."

The girl sighed. For the next few minutes they worked in silence, putting Melody back together. By the time Yun returned, Belle had Melody fully assembled.

"I need her memory chips," Belle said, afraid to look her dad in the eye. She knew in her heart that it wasn't his fault that this happened. But she'd been so angry. Her mom was sick. Then she lost Raider. And now her oldest friend was in pieces. It was all too much to bear. She hoped her dad knew she still loved him.

Yun opened his hand. He had Melody's chips in his palm. Belle inserted them into Melody's central processor, behind a panel in her head. Then she pressed the power switch on Melody's back. It took several tries before her eyes lit up a bright green. Melody turned her head left to right and back again. She stopped when her eyes met Belle's.

"Where am I?" she said. "What happened to me? The last thing I remember is . . ." she trailed off.

It wasn't a good sign. Melody should have recorded everything that happened up to the moment they powered her down.

"Do you know me?" Belle was worried that the SPA people had wiped her entire memory. Everything that they'd done over the years, all their adventures together, it would all be gone. Without her memories, Melody would be just another droid, like the ones rolling around this lab. Belle held her breath.

Melody's eyes scanned Belle. Then moved toward Yun and scanned him too. For the longest seconds in the universe, the android was silent.

"What did one wolf say to the other at a party?" she said at last.

Belle stared at her. Slowly, Belle's lips curled upward into a smile. Then she laughed.

"We are having a howling good time," Melody finished.

"Have you completed your science fair homework, Belle?" Melody continued, standing up. She was a little wobbly. Belle tightened a few of her joints. She hugged Melody, squeezing her middle with all her might. Her android was back!

"I missed you so much," Belle said.

"And I have several hours missing in my memory, it would seem," she said.

The man who had caught them in the lab earlier returned with a holo-document. "It seems this droid was dismantled by mistake," the man said. "It's a 3X model, quite harmless. We apologize, but it's only a droid, after all."

Belle glared at the man and wanted to yell at him. Melody was more than just another droid. But Yun took her hand and led her away.

"Dad?" Belle said, as they walked back out into the evening air. "I'm sorry for screaming at you."

He put his arm around her shoulders. He was looking up at the stars that were beginning to appear in the clear, dark sky.

"I know how scared you were to lose Melody," he said. "I was too."

After finding a cab and climbing inside, Melody asked, "Where is Raider? The last time I saw him, he was growling at a large Martian man." Belle told her android what had happened to Raider.

"We should go and find him then," Melody said.

"Oh, no," Yun said sternly, after giving their destination to the driver droid. "No more adventures for you two. We'll leave that to the authorities."

Belle looked at Melody. Melody's eyes turned blue. She was searching for information on Raider. Belle leaned over toward her android. "First thing tomorrow," she whispered.

"We will go in search of Raider," Melody whispered back.

Sol 15/Spring, Cycle 106, night

It's so good to have Melody home. She seems fine, but only time will tell if she's completely back to her old self. Ta'al's family was in our room with Mom, waiting for news. They were so happy to see Melody too. The more I get to know them, the more I love them.

Mom looked a lot better tonight. She laughed and chatted like her old self when she saw Melody. The only thing that I need now is Raider. Tomorrow, Ta'al, Melody, and I are going to go find him.

Note to self . . . don't tell Dad!

CHAPTER 33

A RISKY REUNION

As soon as Yun and Zara left for the hospital the next morning, Belle and Melody snuck out. Ta'al met them behind the motel.

"I hate lying to my parents," Ta'al said. "But I know this is important."

Belle gave her friend a quick hug, and the threesome went off to rescue Raider.

"Wolf-dog fighting has been a problem in several cities on Mars," Melody said. "But Protectors have a hard time catching them in the act." She was still a little wobbly from being reassembled and walked more slowly than usual. Her eyes turned blue for a moment as she accessed the Tharsis City public database.

"Dangerous criminals run these fights," Melody continued. "The man you described may be one of the ring leaders. His name is Hans Punkin. There is an arrest warrant out for him. There is also a reward for his capture."

"A reward?" Ta'al said. "Is it a large one?"

Belle didn't care about any reward. The news about Hans Punkin meant that Raider could be in real trouble.

Finally they arrived at the end of Sulphate Way, and stopped outside the wall of the camp to survey the area.

Belle turned to Melody. "I was hoping that you could scan for signs of Raider."

"That would be hard," Melody said, extending her head and neck upwards so she could scan the camp. "There are several wolf-dogs here. Raider does not have a distinctive voice. Nor does he have a tracker chip."

Belle's heart sank. She was sure that Melody would be able to find him.

"Wait. Look!" Ta'al exclaimed.

Ta'al pointed to where the wall turned the corner. Belle couldn't believe her eyes. A wolf-dog with a chewed-up ear was trotting out of another gate. It was Raider! He was being led on a short, thick rope held by a giant Martian man with curly hair and a messy beard. Melody scanned them both and confirmed that this was indeed Hans Punkin.

Ta'al gasped. "We have to do something. Call the Protectors!"

"It's too late for that," Belle said. Without thinking, she ran toward Punkin and her beloved dog.

Ta'al called out her name. "Belle, wait!"

"If we wait, Raider and Punkin will be gone!" Belle replied, charging forward.

Raider must have sensed her coming. He stopped in his tracks and barked happily. The man glanced up at Belle and scowled.

He pulled Raider behind him. The dog yelped. " What in the . . . ? Are you the nosy kid who's been pestering everyone about me?" he roared, baring his ugly teeth.

Belle froze. Even from this distance, she could smell him. He smelled of old food and sweat. She gagged.

"I just want my dog back," Belle said, surprised that she wasn't at all afraid of the huge man. From behind him, Raider tilted his head to look at her.

Ta'al ran up beside Belle and secretly handed her two Petripuffs. Melody ambled up and stood at her other side.

"I've reported our situation," Ta'al whispered.

"*Your* dog?" the man growled. "I found him wandering the streets. He's a born fighter. I'm going to train him to be a champion. Go play with your dolls and leave us alone."

Belle stepped forward. There was no way she'd let him turn her dog into a killer.

"The Protectors are on their way," Ta'al said. "You'll have no use for a dog when you're in jail."

"They haven't found me yet." Punkin spat at the girls. "And they never will." He began to march off in the other direction. He pulled so hard on the rope around Raider's neck that the dog's front feet rose off the ground.

"Stop that!" Belle shouted. She couldn't bear to hear the yelp that came from her dog. The big man was hurting Raider.

She charged forward. Holding her breath, she lobbed one of her Petripuffs at Hans Punkin. But he ducked, and the puff exploded behind him. He stomped toward Belle angrily, nostrils flared. He was so big, his body blocked out the sunlight. Belle was caught in his shadow.

"I'm gonna teach you a lesson, kid," he snarled.

He reached out and tried to grab Belle by the hair. She screamed and twisted out of his reach.

Then Belle heard a growl, low and sinister. Raider stepped between her and the giant man. The hairs on his neck rose and he growled again. Belle was afraid that Raider had turned against her. Punkin grinned.

"Told'ya so. He's a born killer," Punkin said.

Slowly, Raider turned to face the giant Martian. He gave a deep, warning bark, and locked eyes with Punkin.

"Shut up, you mutt!" Punkin ordered.

Raider dug his feet into the ground and held his stance. He lowered his body, just like when he had faced the wild wolf-dogs. His ragged ears perked up and he bared his teeth. He was ready for a fight.

The man looked at Belle and then at Raider. He seemed unsure if Raider would actually attack him.

In that moment of doubt, Melody stepped to Belle's side. She had produced the electric livestock prod stored in her chest compartment and pointed it at Punkin. He glared at Melody as the prod crackled in the air.

Before the android could do anything, Ta'al ran up and lobbed two Petripuffs over Raider. They hit Punkin's chest and exploded, spewing white powder into the air around him. He went stiff as a plank and keeled over to land face first in the dirt. Melody walked over and held her electric prod over the man's paralyzed body.

Belle collapsed to the ground and gasped for air. She didn't realize that she'd been holding her breath. Raider trotted over and began licking her face. She buried her face in his soft fur.

"I've never been so frightened in my life!" she cried.

"Neither have I," Ta'al said, sitting down next to Belle. "At least . . . not this season."

Belle looked at her friend and they both started to giggle. They didn't stop laughing until the sound of drones above told them that the Protectors had arrived.

"I sent a quick message to my parents too," Ta'al said. "To tell them where we are."

"As always, you have saved us all," Belle said. Ta'al was the responsible one. Belle didn't want to think about where she'd be today without her sensible friend.

● ● ● ●

The next day the Mayor of Tharsis City handed Belle's and Ta'al's parents the reward money for helping to capture Hans Punkin. She shook hands with Belle and Ta'al, and patted Raider on the head. She even smiled at Melody when Belle explained the android's part in capturing the infamous dog-fighting ringleader. She congratulated everyone on their heroism and thanked them for their help in stopping Punkin's criminal activities.

As the two families left the authorities' building, they were greeted by a bright and sunny day.

"Today's our last day in Tharsis. Let's do something just for fun," Yun said. "We have much to celebrate."

"And I've had enough adventure to last a lifetime," Belle laughed.

"As have I," added Ta'al.

They spent the rest of the morning at the Nabian natural history museum. Belle and Ta'al enjoyed learning about all sorts of creatures from the Nabian home world.

During lunch, Zara and Yun received a final message from the doctor at the medical facility.

"All is well with me and the baby," Zara announced. "I just needed to adapt to the different gravity on Mars."

Belle heaved a huge sigh of relief. Her mom would be back to her old self soon.

The two families celebrated the rest of the day by doing some shopping. Yun and Zara bought a lovely crib for the new baby. And they bought Belle a real book, made of old Earth paper and ink. Belle couldn't stop smelling it and running her hands over the smooth pages.

Ta'al's parents got her a delicate ceremonial scarf. It changed color and went from purple to green to orange, depending on how it reflected the sunlight.

As they headed back to the motel, they passed the jewelry store that Belle had seen the other day. She whispered something to Ta'al, and then told her parents that they'd catch up with them in a minute.

"Meet us at the café across the street," Zara said. "And don't be too long."

"We won't," she said. As soon as their parents were out of sight, the girls ducked into the jewelry store.

"May I help you?" the Parsiv storekeeper asked. She stared at them with her three eyes.

"I have a bit of money," Belle said. "I'd like to get one of those stones that change color with the wand."

"Ah, you must mean the moonstones." She went to the counter and placed a tray of jewelry in front of the girls.

"They arrre lovely, but verrry inexpensive," she said. "They arrre common on Parrrsiv. I just rrreceived a large shipment of them. I'm hoping they will become popularrr herrre."

After learning how much Belle could afford, the shopkeeper picked out a simple necklace with several moonstones placed in a heart shape.

"It's perfect! That's the one I'll take," she said, holding the delicate necklace against her skin.

The storekeeper wrapped it in colorful paper and placed it in a box.

"You'll look beautiful with this on," Ta'al said.

"Oh no," Belle replied. "This is a gift for my mom."

Ta'al slipped her arms around Belle and gave her a squeeze. Then, arms locked together, the girls raced across the street to rejoin their families.

"You know," Belle said, "I love being on vacation, but I can't wait to get home."

"Oh, I agree completely," Ta'al said, smiling. "I prefer the quiet of farm life anytime."

Sol 17/Spring, Mars Cycle 106

Our vacation is over, and honestly, I can't say I'm sorry to be leaving. Tharsis City is amazing. But it's too much for me, I think. Funny, isn't it? Only a few months ago, I wanted to go back to Earth and the same kind of city life found in Tharsis.

But I think I've had enough adventures for now. I agree with Ta'al — the quiet farm life is just what I long for. As long as I have Raider snuggled at my feet, and Melody and Ta'al nearby, I'll be happy to get back to our boring turkens and shoats, and even school!

PART FOUR:
NEW DISCOVERIES

The Song family has been on Mars for almost one Martian Cycle. During that time, Belle has learned to appreciate the red planet and has made several close friends along the way. However, Belle is about to make an incredible discovery – one that will create serious tensions between her friends and the various races that call Mars home . . .

CHAPTER 34

NEW ARRIVALS

Early summer on Mars was the best time of year. The weather was perfect and warm. The sky was a constant clear blue, with only the occasional puffy cloud floating by. Even the nasty dust storms, common during the later summer season, were nowhere to be seen. Belle didn't even mind being in school twice a week.

"I'm secretly glad your parents had to go away this week," Belle said to her best friend, Ta'al. "I've been dying for some real conversation. All anyone talks about around here is the baby."

Ta'al carried Thea, Belle's baby sister, in her arms. Belle's mom, Zara, had given birth a few weeks before. Belle had been her mom's primary helper ever since. Meanwhile, Belle's dad, Yun, and her android, Melody, tended to the farm. Belle loved Thea. However, although she didn't want to say it out loud, she'd grown rather sick of her baby sister.

Ta'al rocked back and forth on her feet, cooing at the tiny girl, who gurgled contentedly.

"I'd never be tired of this little darling," Ta'al said. She smiled at Belle, who wrinkled her nose as if the baby smelled bad. "But I'm glad to be here with you too. I would have loved to go to Lunar Colony with my parents, but they didn't want me to miss school."

"Well, the results of the Olympia Schools Science Fair will be out soon," Belle said. "If we win, we'll get to go to Tharsis City for the finals. That'll be exciting."

"Only if we win," Ta'al said. She and Belle had worked all winter and spring on improving Belle's Petripuffs.

"Yeah, our turken feed project might win instead, Belle." Lucas Walker bounced into the living room. "Hi Lucas. How did you get in so quietly?" Belle hadn't even heard him arrive.

"My mother says I have to be extra quiet with the baby around," Lucas said, peeking at Thea in Ta'al's arms. "That's a tall order for me. Ha!" He let out a loud chortle, then immediately slapped his hand over his mouth. "Oops, sorry."

Belle jumped up out of her seat. "I need to get outside," she said, pointing to the wallscreen that projected the above-ground scene. The warm, sunny weather outside was perfect.

"We can't stay below on a beautiful day like this," Belle said.

Ta'al had managed to put Thea to sleep. She gently placed the baby into her rocking crib. A mechanism inside sensed the baby's presence and a blanket gently wrapped itself around her little body like a cocoon. The baby sighed happily and stuck her thumb in her mouth. An invisible barrier, similar to a force field, formed around her crib like a bubble. It shielded the baby from loud noises and purified her breathing air. This device had been a gift from Ta'al's family. It used special Nabian technology.

The others could now speak with normal voices without worrying about waking up the baby. Lucas shook himself, as if he'd been restraining himself the whole time. Belle had to laugh. Her friend reminded her of Raider.

"My mom tells me we have new neighbors," Lucas said.

"Yes," Ta'al confirmed. "The Parks have retired and moved to Utopia. They sold their farm to a new family."

Utopia was on the other side of Mars. Belle had been there once before. She remembered it being very dusty. She couldn't imagine why Mr. and Mrs. Park would want to retire there.

"Then let's go see if the new neighbors have kids," Belle said. She went to tell her mom that they were leaving.

"Stay out of trouble," Zara said as they ran up the stairs to head outside. "And don't forget to feed the dog!"

Raider met them at the top of the stairs. He wagged his huge tail and perked up his ears. He licked Belle's hand and then looked to Ta'al to be petted. Ta'al tapped his head once and moved away. Most Nabians didn't really like pets. Raider nudged Lucas' hand instead, knowing that this friend would give him what he wanted. Lucas loved animals.

The three friends raced across the back of Belle's family farm and ran into her dad. Yun and Melody were making repairs to some posts that had been damaged by a dust storm at the end of spring. Raider jumped up on Melody and licked her face. He had always liked the android. Melody petted him in return. As Ta'al and Lucas ran on, Belle told Yun where they were headed. She hoped her dad wouldn't give her a long lecture about how she seemed to get into trouble whenever she went off on her own.

"Do you promise not to get into mischief?" he asked, narrowing his eyes.

"We're only going to see if we'll have new classmates at school next week," she said. "And to be neighborly." She gave him her best pleading face. Even Raider whined a little.

"I believe the family does have children," Yun said. "They were mentioned at the parents' meeting last night."

"Then it's only polite to go and say hello." Belle remembered how Lucas' family had welcomed them when they first arrived. She hadn't appreciated it at the time. But later she realized she was glad to have met at least one person her own age before school started.

"Don't be back too late," Yun said. "And remember, make sure you stay out of trouble."

Belle ran to catch up with her friends. Raider trotted at her side. The three friends climbed over the back gate and headed north along the dirt path that ran among the different farms. They ran past the Walker farm, and another unoccupied farm. Eventually they found themselves among tall, green hedges that formed a wall around the Parks' old farm. Belle felt as if she were in a giant maze.

"There it is!" Lucas said, pointing to the house in the middle of several corrals. Just like Belle's family house, this one was a little run down. But many Martian families didn't really keep their above-ground houses in good shape. There wasn't much point, really, since they lived most of the year below ground.

"Let's go and introduce ourselves," Belle said.

Ta'al fell behind them as they ran ahead. Raider stopped to wait for her.

"Come on," Belle called.

"What if they don't like Nabians?" Ta'al spoke hesitantly.

When Belle had first moved to Mars, she noticed that some people in the Sun City neighborhood were rude to Nabians. Ta'al and her family had firsthand experience with the prejudices of these people.

"Hey, you got me to like you," Lucas said with a grin. "Don't worry. We won't let anyone be mean to you."

Ta'al laughed. Together, they approached the computer panel at the side of the house door. Belle took a deep breath and pressed the intercom button.

Sol 91/Summer, Mars Cycle 106

Our new neighbors are the Senn family. They have three kids — twin boys and a girl. The twins, Alex and Aiden, are a year older than us. The girl is our age. Her name is Ava. She wasn't home when we went to say hello. Alex and Aiden are great. They're funny, like Lucas. And they're Terran, just like me. They moved here from Earth last week and are still trying to get used to things here, like the gravity, and the hybrid animals, and the weird food we eat.

Actually, it sounds pretty familiar to what I first went through. It's funny. I've been here just over a cycle, but I feel like I'm as Martian as anyone else. I don't have the red rings in my eyes like Thea does. That's because she was born on Mars. But I feel Martian. I don't remember exactly when I started feeling like this place is home, but it is now.

Anyway, I understand how the Senns feel. I invited them to walk with us to school tomorrow. Ava will be with them too. Since she's thirteen, she'll be in our class with Ms. Polley. (I can't believe our 6th grade teacher moved up with us to 7th grade!) I can't wait to have another new friend.

CHAPTER 35

BACK TO SCHOOL

The next day was a scheduled rain day. Summer was the only season warm enough to have rain on Mars. Here in Sun City, it usually rained once per week, and it lasted two days. When the Sulux helped terraform Mars, their technology allowed for the creation of a specific water cycle. Rainfall was essential for human life to flourish. So it was made a regular part of life on the red planet.

Belle loved the rainy days. It made everything seem so fresh and clean. She would have happily run through the rain without a jacket to get to school. But her mom insisted that she wear her rain gear that morning.

"It's only just starting, but I want you to stay dry. Hopefully you'll be in class before it starts to rain hard," Zara said. She adjusted Belle's hood and then pressed the knob at the end of her sleeve. The entire raincoat sealed itself snugly around Belle's body from head to toe. She would be as dry as Mars dust when she arrived at school.

Belle kissed her baby sister goodbye. Thea's skin was so soft, and she smelled kind of sweet. The baby gave Belle a big, toothless grin. Sometimes, Thea really was fun to have around.

Raider trotted alongside Belle until she met up with Lucas on the path behind their farms. Then the wolf-dog ran back home where he'd spend the day in the stable with their horsel, Loki. Farther down the road, Ta'al joined Belle and Lucas. They chatted about their homework until they met the Senn twins. Aiden and Alex were walking under a large umbrella. Ava was with them too, staying dry by squeezing between her brothers. She was shorter than the boys, but she had the same bright eyes. Her long, dark hair was in two braids that almost reached her hips.

Belle introduced herself and Ta'al to Ava. She greeted them with a nod, but said nothing. However, when her eyes landed on Lucas, she smiled and became quite chatty.

"What strange raincoats you have," she said, walking straight up to Lucas and running her hand along his sealed arm. Her brothers followed closely behind to keep them all under the umbrella. Lucas looked as if he was having an allergic reaction.

"You can get them in Sun City," Belle offered, staring at the new girl. "They're much more efficient than umbrellas."

"Uh-huh," Ava mumbled. She didn't even look at Belle. She was looking intently at Lucas, who was turning as red as his raincoat.

Belle had a strange feeling about this girl. She looked over at Ta'al. Her friend's eyes were wide, and she had the oddest smile on her face, like she knew something that Belle didn't.

"We haven't had time to do much shopping," explained one of the twins. Belle still couldn't work out which boy was which.

"We'll probably go tomorrow," said the other.

"It might be best to wait until after the rain days are over." Ta'al pointed to the gathering clouds. "Then the roads won't be so muddy."

The new friends trudged through the increasingly heavy rain until they reached the low gray school building at the edge of Sun City.

"Welcome to Sun City School," Belle said to the Senns as they walked through the front door. Lucas ran off ahead of them. Belle and Ta'al took the Senns to the front office. There they received all the information and computer programs they would need to do their school work from home as needed. As Belle had guessed, the twins were assigned to Mr. LeCoq's eighth-grade classroom, and Ava was put into Ms. Polley's class.

"There are so few kids in our class," Ava said, when she walked into room number one and saw that there were only eight desks. "Back on Earth, I had more than thirty kids in my class."

Ava stared at the wallscreen displays, which were changing to match the age of the students occupying the room. Next, she examined the layout of the furniture. Ms. Polley had paired the desks in a semi-circle facing the active holo-board, which displayed a holographic map of the school.

Ava turned to Belle. "Where do you sit?" she asked.

Belle pointed to the middle pair of desks. "Ta'al and I sit there."

"Where does Lucas sit?" she asked.

"At the far left," Belle said.

Belle was about to explain that Ms. Polley would assign Ava to a seat. But then Ava marched to the desk next to where Lucas would be and put her bag down.

"That's Brill's desk," Ta'al told her, as the rest of their classmates filed in. Pavish, Trina, and Brill walked in with Lucas. They were laughing over some joke Pavish had told.

Brill tried to tell Ava that she was in his seat. But Ava didn't seem to care.

"I like this desk," she said. "And since I'm new here, I'd think you'd want to be more welcoming."

Belle rolled her eyes at Ta'al who stifled a giggle. The other students simply stared at the new girl in stunned silence. Lucas tucked his head down and slipped quietly into his seat. His usual light purple skin had blotches of red everywhere.

When Ms. Polley entered to begin lessons, Ava went up to her and they spoke quietly for a long time. Belle strained her ears, but she couldn't hear what excuse Ava had created to pick whatever seat she wanted.

"Ava will sit with Lucas until she catches up with our work," Ms. Polley explained to the class. "Thank you, Brill, for being so generous and giving up your seat."

Brill's face went all red, and he looked really confused.

"I don't know what to think of this new girl," Belle whispered to Ta'al.

"I think she has a crush on Lucas," Ta'al said with a grin. "And she's probably used to getting whatever she wants."

Belle watched Ava during most of Agriculture lessons. She did look at Lucas an awful lot. Belle couldn't quite figure out why Ava was so interested in Lucas, with his messy hair and crooked teeth. She just didn't get it.

"I will be announcing the winners of the Science Fair on our next class day," Ms. Polley said right before lunch.

Belle and Ta'al sighed. It was hard to wait for the results.

"It's a difficult decision," Ms. Polley continued. "So many of the projects are wonderful. The judges need a bit more time."

At lunch, Ava followed Lucas everywhere. She sat by him while they ate. Then she insisted on playing on his low-gravity disc team in the gym afterward. Lucas never voiced his opinion. He just kept turning darker shades of red and doing as she asked.

When Ava went to the bathroom, Belle finally got a chance to talk to Lucas. "Why don't you just tell her to leave you alone?"

"That would be rude," he said.

"You had no problem with being rude to me when we first met," Belle said. "Or with Ta'al either, for that matter."

"Ava's different," he said, chewing slowly on his snack of fried mealworms. "She's . . . very insistent."

Belle laughed. "She scares you, doesn't she?"

Lucas nodded. He slurped down his last mealworm just as Ava returned to his side.

As the school day wore on, Belle felt more and more annoyed with the new girl. She couldn't really understand why Ava irritated her. Maybe it was the way she stuck to Lucas and made him feel scared of her. Maybe it was because Ava barely spoke to Belle, except to ask about Lucas. Even more irritating was how Ava completely ignored Ta'al. She wouldn't even make eye contact with her. By the end of the school day, Belle had had enough of Ava Senn.

But Ava didn't seem to care one bit. The rain had slowed by the end of the day, so Ava and her brothers were able to walk home without their umbrella. This allowed Ava to walk next to Lucas. Belle couldn't believe how Ava kept asking him stupid questions. Then, when her brothers tried to join in the conversation, she ordered them to run on ahead . . . and they obeyed!

Belle rolled her eyes again and turned to Ta'al.

"I forgot," she said loudly to everyone. "I need to pick up some supplies in Sun City. Will you come with me, Ta'al?" She pulled her friend off on a different path, in the direction of the city center.

"What do you have to buy?" Ta'al asked when they were alone.

"Nothing," Belle said. "I just needed to get away from what was going on there." She pointed back toward Lucas and Ava. They didn't even notice that the girls had left.

Belle and Ta'al walked through Sun City in silence. Belle brooded in her own thoughts and didn't pay attention to where she was heading. Ta'al just walked quietly by her side, giving Belle time with her thoughts. Soon, they were leaving the outskirts on the other side of the city. They headed southwest, taking a path they'd never taken before.

Belle and Ta'al walked for a while more before Ta'al finally broke the silence.

"Why does she annoy you so much?" Ta'al asked.

"Because she makes it so obvious that she likes Lucas and no one else," Belle replied.

"I think it's funny," Ta'al replied. "Lucas is so embarrassed by the attention."

"Exactly!" Belle tried not to shout. "She's bullying him into hanging out with her."

"Oh, I don't think he minds too much." Ta'al laughed. Then she stopped and stared at Belle. "Wait, don't tell me that you're actually jealous!"

"Eew, no way!" Belle protested.

They kept walking. Belle was still deep in thought. *Was she jealous of Ava?* But that would mean she liked Lucas too. No. She liked him as a friend, that's all. She just didn't think anyone should monopolize her friend. Yes, that's why Ava annoyed her.

The rain had stopped for the day, and the clouds parted to reveal the bright sunlight. They continued on their path and Belle tried to talk about things other than Ava and Lucas.

"Where are we?" Belle said, suddenly looking at the strange terrain. "We've never been so far out here."

Laid out before them, all the way to the horizon, was flat, barren land. There were clumps of prickly bushes scattered about, but the ground was mostly rocky and dry, even though it had rained all day. It was very quiet too. Nothing seemed to live out here for as far as their eyes could see.

"Facing this way, you'd never guess there was lush farmland nearby," Belle said. She shielded her eyes with her hand. The heat from the ground was making the air wavy. "Terraforming creates such odd spaces."

"It looks like terraforming missed this area altogether. Let's explore a bit more before heading back," Ta'al said. "I'd like to record some of this for study." She pulled out the palm-sized disc that served as her communication device. It doubled as a recording device too. She let it scan the area as they walked along.

"Ta'al, I've been thinking about what you said." Belle watched as Ta'al gathered data of the area. "I think you're wrong about me and Lucas."

Ta'al laughed. "Are you sure?"

Belle opened her mouth to protest. But suddenly the ground beneath her feet shifted. Before she could say another word, the ground opened up and swallowed her!

CHAPTER 36
TRAPPED!

"Belle! Are you all right?"

Ta'al's shrill scream echoed all the way down the hole to Belle. She sounded so far away. Belle opened her eyes, but couldn't see a thing. It was completely dark. She patted the ground around her. It was rocky, sandy, and dry. She rubbed her arms and torso. Luckily, her rain gear had protected her from being scratched up.

What had just happened? All Belle knew was that one second she was talking to Ta'al, and then she was falling. It felt like the longest drop ever. As she fell, the rough, dry ground clawed at her until she landed with a bump at — wherever she was. It was so dark, she couldn't tell.

Belle pressed the button on her sleeve and her rain gear loosened around her body. She stuck her hand under the stiff fabric and rubbed her skin. She didn't feel any blood oozing. That was good. She sat up. Her back ached and her legs hurt. She felt inside her pant leg, but again she felt no blood.

"I can't see anything!" Belle cried out. Her voice bounced off the walls. *I must have fallen into some kind of well*, she thought. *Did they have wells out here?* "Ta'al, can you see me?" she called.

Ta'al was whimpering. That didn't make Belle feel better.

"Ta'al!" She needed her friend's usual calmness, or she would panic too. "Can you see me?"

"No," Ta'al called back. "This looks like some kind of shaft. It's narrow and deep."

Belle could hear Ta'al shuffling around above ground. "Can you climb up?" she called.

Belle got down on her belly and crawled toward Ta'al's voice. The ground rose sharply beneath her. She made some progress but then slid back down again.

"It's too steep," she called up, rubbing her sore hands together. "And I can't see anything."

"I'm trying to call for help, but my comm device says we're out of range," Ta'al said.

How had they walked so far out without even realizing it? The whole Ava situation must have really distracted them.

"Wait!" Ta'al sounded like she had an idea. "My comm disc! It also works as a flashlight. I could throw it to you."

"But we need it to call for help," Belle said.

"It doesn't work out here. So you might as well use it. Can you see my light?"

Belle looked up. All she saw was darkness.

"I don't think the shaft goes straight down," Belle said. "Are you shining your light now?"

"I'm going to throw my comm disc down to you," Ta'al said.

"Wait!" Belle replied, but it was too late. She heard the clunking of the disc as it rolled through the shaft. She waited. Seconds passed but still there was no sign of light. She closed her eyes and took deep breaths. She felt her heart pound in her chest. This was no time to cry or to panic. She had to find a way out. Fast.

She opened her eyes and saw a sliver of light on the ground.

"I got it!" she cried. "Thank you, Ta'al."

Belle gripped the comm device and shined the light over herself first. She'd been right. She had no big cuts and barely any scratches. Her rain gear had served her well.

Belle swept the light around her. She was definitely in some sort of underground shaft or well. It wasn't very big, just wide enough for her to stretch out her arms and touch the sides. The top of the shaft was not straight up. It curved away so that Belle couldn't see the surface.

It's like a long slide. That explains why I didn't get too hurt, she thought.

She pointed the light farther down the shaft. She saw nothing but more blackness. Belle shivered. She bit down on her lip to stop herself from bursting into tears.

"I'm going for help!" Ta'al called down. "Can you sit tight and wait for me?"

"Where else am I going to go?" Belle replied. Truthfully, she was afraid to be left here alone. But Ta'al had to leave, or she'd never get out of here.

Belle heard the crunching of pebbles beneath Ta'al's feet. And then there was silence. It was the heaviest silence she'd ever experienced. She pulled her knees to her chest and tried to breathe normally. She thought about her farm and her dad working on the posts with Melody. She imagined Raider running around them barking in excitement. She thought about her mom, giving little Thea a bath in the kitchen sink. She pictured the sun sliding behind the rain clouds and the soothing coolness of the rain on her skin. She had to think of these things so that she wouldn't begin to cry or scream out in fear. But the tears came anyway, even though she didn't want them to.

She'd never felt so lonely in her life.

Belle had no idea how much time had passed. As she waited for Ta'al to return, her legs began to cramp up. She shined her light around and decided to stand up and stretch her legs.

● ● ● ●

"Okay, Belle," she said aloud to herself. Her voice echoed off the walls. It felt good to hear a sound. "If I have to wait around, I might as well explore a little."

With Ta'al's device in hand, she lit a path farther inside the shaft. She kept one hand above her on the ceiling in case the shaft grew smaller. She didn't want to bump her head. But to her surprise, after a few steps the ceiling seemed to disappear altogether. Belle aimed her narrow beam of light high above her head.

"This is a cave," she said aloud. "Hellooo!"

She knew no one would answer. She wanted to hear the echo. And she was rewarded with several of them.

Hellooo, hellooo, helloooo . . . went the echo. It made her smile, just a little.

Belle pointed her light to the ground at her feet. She took a step, then another. Everything beneath her feet was black and gray. But suddenly, a glint of something silver caught her eye. She bent down to touch it. It was smooth and cold. It was also partially buried. She knelt down and brushed away as much dirt as she could, all the while shining her light on the silver object. Before long she noticed some kind of marking on it.

"That's an N," she said. There was writing on this object. She began to dig with her fingers. "And that's an A."

Belle looked around, found a flat stone, and used it to finish digging out the object. The more she dug, the bigger the object seemed to get.

What are you? she thought. She reached down and swept dirt off the object.

The letters were printed over a circle of stars. There was a red slash behind the letter *A*. There was also a white slash running between the *N* and *A*.

Belle kept scraping at the symbol. The next letter looked like an *S*, but the rest of it was buried too deep. She sat back, panting from her work. "N - A - S," she said. "I wonder if that's NASA, the old Earth space agency?" She'd read about that at her previous school on Earth. Space science had been her favorite subject there. She wished they could learn more about it here on

Mars. But all they seemed to teach at school was agriculture and hybrid biology.

She got back on her feet and dusted herself off. This was probably a relic of history — left here when the first astronauts landed on Mars. Her heart skipped a beat. This was quite a discovery. She wondered if there was more to find down here.

Forgetting her fear, she moved farther into the darkness. She shuffled her feet through the pebbles and dust, just in case the ground gave way again.

Then she heard something like the sound of trickling water, but it was very faint.

She swept her light around her. A hissing noise stopped her in her tracks. Belle thought for a moment that it might be steam gushing out from under the ground, like the geysers she'd read about on Earth. But she didn't see any evidence of that. It was completely dry in the cave. The hissing grew louder, as if something was coming toward her. It wasn't steam. It sounded like a living thing — or several living things.

Belle screamed.

The sound of many feet scurrying and scuttling over the pebbles made her scream again. She turned back and ran. She hoped she was going the same direction she'd come from. It was so dark, she didn't know which way was which. Her foot caught on something, causing her to trip and fall on the hard ground.

"Who's there?" she gasped.

She moved her light slowly in a wide arc while shuffling herself backward. She focused on slowing her breathing, so she could concentrate on whatever was in here with her.

The beam of light flowed over large rocks, cube-shaped stones, and tiny pebbles. Then, just for a second, she saw something. It looked like a spiky tail!

She shrieked.

The tail vanished into a pile of cube-shaped stones.

CHAPTER 37
SPOOKY ANCIENT RUINS

The scuttling sound had stopped. But Belle kept her light fixed on the spot where the tail had disappeared. She was in no mood to encounter a new creature. It had been hard enough getting used to all of the strange farm animals on Mars. She definitely didn't want to meet another mystery creature. Especially not in this dark, spooky cave.

"Ta'al!" She tried shouting again. She did that once every few minutes, each time hoping that someone would shout back.

But so far . . . nothing. Her voice was becoming hoarse, and all her tears had dried up. She took a deep breath and screamed as loudly as she could. She'd had enough of this cave.

"Belle!" She heard her friend's voice. It was faint, but it was definitely Ta'al.

"I'm here! Help me!" she shouted back.

"Hold on," Ta'al yelled. "Melody is here. She was looking for us in town. She sent a message to your Dad. He's on his way here."

"I am sending a mini-drone down to you," came the familiar voice of Belle's android. Melody's flat voice sent a calmness through Belle. She badly needed her friend's steady confidence. It was as comforting as hot cocoa on a cold winter's evening. Everything was going to be fine.

Within minutes, the welcome hum of a mini-drone greeted her. It flooded her area with more light than Ta'al's device could provide. Belle saw that she was indeed sitting before the mouth of a giant cave. And she could more clearly see the mysterious NASA object jutting out of the ground in front of her. It looked like part of a machine, or perhaps a land vehicle. Could it be an ancient rover?

The drone flew around the area where Belle sat, giving those above ground the information needed to rescue her. Melody's voice came through the drone's speaker. "Are you injured?"

"No, I'm okay. My rain gear protected me," Belle replied.

"Are you able to climb up?" Melody asked.

"It's too steep," she said, moving back to where she had fallen. "And it's not straight up. There must be a bend in the shaft."

"You are correct," Melody said. "You fell quite a distance."

"Can you do something? I don't like being down here alone," Belle pleaded.

"I will attempt to come down to you," Melody said.

Belle held her breath as she waited. If her android were down here with her, things wouldn't be so bad.

A trickle of pebbles soon began rolling down the shaft. A few of them bounced off of Belle's shoes. Then a terrible rumbling sound filled the air. It sounded just like the moment when the ground swallowed her.

"No, stop!" she yelled.

But it was too late. A mass of rocks and dirt came tumbling down the shaft. Belle backed away deeper into the cave, tripped over a rock, and fell flat on her back. The rumbling went on for several seconds and then stopped. Silence filled the air again, along with thick dust that caused Belle to cough hard.

She sat up. The drone was shining its light toward the shaft she'd come through. But the shaft was gone. In its place was a wall of fallen rock and dirt.

She was trapped!

"Melody, where are you? Are you all right?" Belle cried. She wiped her face with the back of her hand and her mouth filled with dust. She spat it out onto the ground.

A few moments later the drone rotated to face her. It lowered its light beam.

"The shaft was unstable," the android replied through the drone's speaker. "I was almost buried, but managed to get out."

"What do we do now?" Belle could feel the walls of the cave start to close in on her. She knew it was only her fear that made her feel this way, but it felt too real.

"Don't panic," Ta'al said through the drone. She knew Belle all too well. "Your Dad is bringing help."

"I suggest, in the meantime, that we look for another entrance." Melody was full of good ideas.

"Yes!" Belle got to her feet. "There's a big cave down here. There should be more than one entrance." *Right?* She wasn't sure, but she had to be positive, or else she might just curl up and cry.

The drone and its wide beam of light brought her some relief. She also had Ta'al and Melody's voices to keep her company. She pointed out the NASA object to them.

"This must have been a landing site for the old Earth explorations," Ta'al said, trying to sound cheerful. "That's quite a valuable find."

Belle moved in farther, back to where she'd heard the hissing sounds earlier.

"There's something else down here," Belle said, recalling the tail. She also remembered that loud noises sent them scattering. She stomped her feet with each step. "Melody, are there any native life forms to Mars? Ones that hiss and have long tails?"

"None that I have seen in the databanks," Melody replied.

Belle stepped noisily through the chamber. There was no hissing, and no tails. Then she stopped. The drone's light lit up a lot of stones in front of her. The enormous cube-shaped stones were wider than she was tall. She ran her hand along the smooth surface of one stone. Some stones had cracks in them, forming hand-sized gaps. Belle avoided those, in case there were creatures hiding inside.

The stones could have been created by volcanic lava flows that cooled quickly. She'd learned about that back on Earth. But they could have also been made by humans or aliens. After finding the NASA objects earlier, it seemed logical that someone had crafted these stones. The drone swept its light beam around the area. There were dozens, if not hundreds of these same stones, all roughly the same size. Some were piled on top of each other to form columns. They certainly looked hand-made.

Belle faced the drone and shared her thoughts about the stones with her friends. "Either of those theories could be valid," Melody replied. "Is the cave filled with them?"

"It looks that way from here," Belle said.

She walked farther into the cave. The drone's light lit up a large area of the cave floor. Belle gasped.

Before her wasn't just a cave, but what looked like the ruins of an entire building, or even a city street. The drone flew high over it, lighting up a wide pathway.

"This place must have been lived in by people a long time ago," Belle said. "Amazing!"

"This is a remarkable find," Melody said.

"From what I can see, this looks like an old courtyard." Ta'al's voice was filled with excitement. "And you said there were creatures in the stones that hissed?"

"Yes, but I don't see them anymore," Belle replied. "I hope they're too scared of me to come out again."

Belle craned her neck to see all around her. She was standing in the middle of a large square. It certainly could have been a courtyard from a long time ago. Cubical stones were stacked up high in several places on both sides of her. A couple of stones were cylindrical and jagged at the top, like broken columns. She signaled at the drone to light the ceiling and walls. There were carvings with odd symbols everywhere.

As the drone hummed along and recorded what Belle saw, she heard Ta'al cry out.

"Belle, don't touch anything!" she exclaimed.

"Why?" Belle asked, freezing in place.

"I think you've stumbled upon a Nabian holy site."

Belle's eyes widened. She stared at the symbols on the walls. They looked a lot like the Nabian writing she'd seen in Ta'al's house.

"Belle, those hissing creatures?" Ta'al's voice quivered with excitement, even through the drone's microphone. "I'm not sure, but I think they're guardians!"

"What are guardians?"

"They're legendary creatures," Ta'al said. "I never really believed them to be real."

"Oh, they're real, all right," Belle replied. "I saw a tail and heard them running around. Not to mention the hissing."

"That's incredible!" Ta'al exclaimed excitedly. "Nabians believe the guardians were tasked with protecting sacred relics. Belle, you could be standing right by some of the most holy items of the Nabian culture!"

The drone's light beam panned slowly around the cave. Belle twirled, following its movement. Everything made sense to her now. This was some kind of ancient site, buried underground. The stones might have formed as volcanic rocks, but they had been stacked to be used as columns or parts of buildings.

"I thought Nabians didn't come to Mars until after humans and Sulux came here," she said, looking up at the high ceiling. She hadn't noticed earlier, but there were symbols carved into every part of it. How could ancient Nabians carve symbols so high up? Could they fly?

"That's what I thought too," Ta'al said. "You don't think this was one of the reasons my people fought the Sulux, do you?"

Hissss! Hisssss!

Belle froze. The sound was coming from behind her. It grew louder with each breath.

"Ta'al?" she whispered to the drone. "The guardians don't . . . *eat people*, do they?"

Belle turned around very slowly. The light from the drone dimmed, but only so that it wasn't too glaring. *Was Ta'al doing that on purpose to avoid scaring the creatures?*

As Belle turned, she saw something gleaming in the dark. A pair of round eyes reflected the light from the drone. They were golden-colored, with dark, vertical slits in the middle. All the breath in Belle's lungs seemed to evaporate. Those gold eyes belonged to the biggest, scariest lizard she'd ever seen!

CHAPTER 38

A HISTORIC SITE

"Don't move!" Ta'al's voice came through the drone's speaker. "They only attack if they think you're going to hurt them."

"Um, okay. But what if I think they're going to hurt *me?*" Belle did her best to imitate a statue. "Did you know they have really sharp claws?"

She stared at the lizard. As with everything else on Mars, this creature was huge, about the size of Raider, but with shorter legs. It had sharp-looking ridges running down its back, and its forked tongue flicked at her every few seconds. Its front feet had five long toes tipped with wicked-looking claws. The lizard stretched out one foot with its claws spread out wide, as if it was getting ready to grab her.

The drone lowered to Belle's waist level and placed itself between her and the lizard. Ta'al's voice came through the drone. It sounded like she was singing something very soothing in her own language. The lizard cocked its head to one side. It seemed to be listening to Ta'al's song. For a second, the creature looked quite harmless to Belle.

Suddenly the lizard took a step toward Belle. She took a step back. Some pebbles came loose beneath her feet and rippled down toward the lizard. The pebbles startled the reptile, and it lunged at Belle.

She screamed. The drone turned to face Belle.

"Belle, are you all right?" Melody's voice came through the drone's speaker.

Belle couldn't answer. She was too busy scurrying away from the oncoming creature. The lizard hissed loudly and scuttled up to her feet. The drone rotated to focus on the lizard. Every spike along its back was lit up by the drone's light. The creature flicked its tail around its body, scattering pebbles in all directions. Its tongue shot out and brushed Belle's leg. She screamed again, this time louder and longer. The lizard spun away from her, whipping its tail against both of Belle's legs. The spikes pierced through her pants and scratched her skin. Belle was so scared, she froze. She couldn't scream anymore, and she had nowhere to run. All she could do was shut her eyes and prepare for the worst.

She breathed in . . . and out. In . . . and out.

Nothing happened.

She opened one eye and peeked down at her feet. The lizard stood several feet away and watched her with its head tilted to the side. After a few seconds, it casually turned and ambled away from her, disappearing into the darkness.

"Follow it!" Ta'al called through the drone. "It must know the way out!"

"What?" Belle couldn't believe her ears. She had barely escaped being eaten alive, and now she was supposed to follow the scary creature?

"Go!" Melody agreed with Ta'al.

Belle shoved all her fear aside and ran after the lizard. Its heavy tail swished side to side, creating a visible path through the dusty ground for Belle to follow. Even with the drone to light her way, the path grew darker ahead. Belle was seriously doubting Ta'al's advice, but then she saw a tiny glimmer of light ahead.

Suddenly more hissing sounds filled the cave. Belle froze.

"Keep going," Ta'al said. "They'll leave you alone now."

Belle heard Ta'al add, "I hope," quietly to Melody. That really didn't help.

But with each step, the light in front of her seemed to glow bigger and brighter.

"I see the entrance," Melody said through the drone. "Follow that light, Belle." The drone flew ahead of her.

Belle took a deep breath and counted to three. She hoped Ta'al was right. She ran hard toward the light. The closer she got, the larger the circle of light grew. She'd reached the mouth of the cave!

When Belle burst out of the cave, she gratefully inhaled the fresh air. The warmth of the Martian sun had never felt so good on her face. She laughed and cried at the same time. Behind her,

Melody came hovering over. Belle hugged her android for a really long time. When Ta'al came running up, she hugged her too.

"For a while I thought I was going to be trapped in there forever!" Belle wiped her sticky face with the back of her hand.

"Look at you!" Ta'al laughed. "Your face is streaked with red clay."

Belle laughed too. And then began to cry again. Melody insisted that Belle sit and rest while she investigated the mouth of the cave. She walked around the hole in the hillside that Belle had just escaped from and took holo-images of everything.

"So, you believe this is a sacred Nabian site?" Belle asked Ta'al when she got bored watching Melody.

"It could be," she said. "It would explain the guardian, and how the old lullaby worked to charm it."

Belle wanted to say that it could've all been a big, lucky coincidence. But she didn't want to risk insulting her best friend.

"I found evidence of human activity down there too," Belle said, explaining about the NASA object. "But that would mean that humans knew about the Nabian site long ago. If that's true, why do the records say that no living species existed on Mars before humans lived here?"

"That's a very good question," Ta'al said. "I think my parents would be interested in the answer."

"But that was more than two hundred years ago. Do you think it still matters?" Belle asked.

Ta'al patted Belle's knee. "History always matters," she said. Then she stood up and went to examine the mouth of the cave. Belle lay back down and closed her eyes. She had never been so happy to soak in the sunshine.

A little while later Yun arrived. He brought Paddy and Myra Walker, Lucas' parents, with him. They had Loki and a ton of rope with them. When they saw Belle resting on the boulder, safe and above ground, they clapped and sighed in relief.

"You are one lucky girl," Paddy Walker exclaimed, as he eyed the small cave mouth that Belle had crawled out of.

"I want to know every detail of your adventure," Yun said, holding his daughter. "Your mother is worried sick. She couldn't leave Thea at home alone, but she very much wanted to come too."

"I'm fine," Belle said. "Thanks to Ta'al and Melody."

Yun insisted that Belle and Ta'al ride Loki all the way home. It was a bumpy ride, but Belle was too tired to care.

When they reached the house, Zara had baked a huge batch of Belle's favorite muffins. Belle and Ta'al munched on the muffins as they told their tale. The adults listened closely to every detail.

"Lucas will be sorry he missed this story," Paddy said. "I'll be sure to send him over tomorrow morning so you can retell it."

Myra Walker had been very quiet the whole time. She'd listened very carefully to everything that Belle and Ta'al had described. Just as the Walkers stood up to leave, she turned to Belle.

"I think you have made a very important discovery." She touched Belle's face, staring at her with her large lilac eyes. "We should inform the authorities. I believe they would be interested in excavating this site."

"But if it is a Nabian holy site, we will need our high council to be involved," Ta'al said.

Myra smiled at her, but it was a strange smile. Belle wasn't sure what was going on. Still, she didn't want to be rude to Myra. She really liked Lucas' mom.

That night, before the girls fell asleep in Belle's room, Belle asked Ta'al if she'd talked to her parents about their find.

"I did," she said. "And I sent all our video footage to them." She lay in her bed staring at the ceiling of Belle's room, unblinking.

"And?" Belle didn't want to push Ta'al to talk, but her curiosity was too much to contain. If this site was part of the reason for the feud between the Sulux and the Nabians, excavating it might cause arguments as well.

Ta'al rolled over onto her side to face Belle. She had a very serious look in her eyes.

"My parents have cut short their tour of Lunar Colony," she said. "And they're on their way home as we speak."

Sol 92/Summer, Mars Cycle 106

It turns out my adventure underground only lasted two and a half hours. It felt more like two and a half sols! Every time I shut my eyes, I see those guardian lizards . . . hundreds of them. And they're all chasing me. I can still feel the flick of its tongue on my leg and its sharp tail ridges.

But now that I think about it, I wonder if it actually helped me to get out? I wonder if Ta'al actually communicated with it and asked for its help? In which case, it's not a bad animal. It saved me.

Who knows?

All I know is that I stumbled upon something important. I can't wait to see what happens next.

CHAPTER 39
WHOSE RELICS?

Myra Walker had been correct. The authorities were very interested in Belle's discovery. Two days later, not only had Ta'al's parents returned, but three huge Protector androids also showed up at the Songs' doorstep. Along with them came a representative of the Olympian regional government and a Sulux council member. Their arrival was so unusual that several neighbors came by to see what was going on as well.

There wasn't enough space in the Song house to seat everyone. And everyone insisted on talking at the same time. It was a good thing Thea had her Nabian crib shield. She slept through the entire meeting.

A tall Martian woman raised her hand. The Protectors came to attention and stomped their robot legs loudly. It scared everyone into silence.

"I am Secretary Sukanya, aide to the governor of Olympia," the woman said. "I appreciate everyone's interest in this historic discovery, but Representative Valere and I would like to interview the child who found the relics."

She paused to look everyone in the eye.

"In private," she added.

Belle did not appreciate being referred to as "the child". She was more than thirteen years old, after all.

The Protectors ushered the neighbors out of the Song house. The Walkers didn't look happy to leave. As they walked out, Belle caught Lucas and whispered that she'd fill him in on everything as soon as she could.

"Meet me by the large apple tree at the end of our farm in an hour," she said.

Lucas winked at her as he left with his parents.

The only other people allowed to remain in the room were Ta'al's parents . . . So'ark, He'ern, and Fa'erz. They were the only people in the room who were almost as tall as the Protectors. They towered over the government officials, and looked intimidating in their long, flowing robes.

Everybody listened intently as Belle told her story once more. Ta'al and Melody added details where necessary.

"Can you show us the site?" Secretary Sukanya asked. The red rings around her irises glowed under the dim house lights.

"Of course," Belle said. Ta'al had mapped out the location of the site as they rode home on Loki's back.

"Then we must go immediately," Representative Valere said. He was Sulux, with the same copper-colored hair as Myra Walker. He had very distinct ridges on his head and arms. It made him look as if he had natural armor.

So'ark stepped forward. "There is the matter of jurisdiction." She sounded very serious. "If this is a Nabian site, then it should be our representative that investigates. Sulux will have no place inside."

Secretary Sukanya exhaled loudly. "This is not the place for this argument. Mars is a human colony, and as the governor's representative, I have jurisdiction here."

"If what the child says is accurate," He'ern added, "the relics are located outside of the terraformed area. That makes it *para-ta-num-peia* — no man's land."

Belle cringed at the word "child" again. But she knew it was better to keep silent.

"And access to a sacred Nabian site is not included in the Martian-Sulux Agreement," Fa'erz said.

"Of course it isn't included," Valere said. "That's because no one knew there might be a Nabian site on Mars."

"We don't even know that it *is* Nabian," Sukanya added.

So'ark rose to her full height. Everyone looked up at her. "This is a very troubling argument. According to my daughter, and the holo-vid evidence, it is most likely a holy Nabian site. So, I must insist, quite firmly, that you wait for the Nabian representative before you enter the cave. I am deeply concerned that without our council's involvement, the site may be desecrated."

All three of Ta'al's parents stood together and said, "We cannot allow it."

There was a long silence following the Nabians' stand. Belle was surprised at their reaction. She had never seen Ta'al's family so determined before.

Finally, it was Yun that broke the silence and tension. "Well, how about something to drink? All this talk is thirsty work," he said with a smile. "Besides, I'm pretty sure nobody wants a diplomatic incident this early in the day."

Belle's dad liked to use humor to ease tense moments. She thought it was amusing, even though she sometimes didn't understand what he said. But she wasn't sure it worked this time.

"Yes, why don't we discuss it over tea?" Zara suggested, as Melody entered with a tray of tea and snacks. This was Belle's mom's way of solving problems. It seemed to work better than her dad's attempt at humor.

The two officials appeared relieved by the distraction. Ta'al's family calmly sat down. The tension in the room relaxed and soon they were chatting politely. Meanwhile, the Protectors stood by the wall with their red eyes constantly scanning the room.

About half an hour into the conversation, Belle was growing bored. When Yun put up a holo-map of the region in front of the guests, Belle knew this was her chance.

"I need to feed Raider and Loki," she said to her parents. "Can Ta'al come and help me?"

Nobody seemed to mind if the girls left for a while, as long as Melody accompanied them.

"I couldn't stand listening to them talk anymore," Belle said as they headed for the stable.

"I thought it was interesting," Ta'al said. "It's important to us as Nabians what happens to these relics."

"I found it very interesting as well," Melody added.

"If they *are* Nabian," Belle said.

"Of course they are." Ta'al sounded surprised at Belle's doubt. "I recognized them." She looked to Melody to confirm it.

Melody's eyes turned green as she scanned her inner databanks. "I am unable to find any claims of Nabians living on Mars prior to human colonization. But the carvings did have a strong resemblance to Nabian script."

Belle pulled open the stable door and Raider jumped out at her. He ran around the yard barking happily.

"There are definitely human relics in the cave too," Belle said. "We should have the right to study them as well."

"The Nabian relics are far more ancient and would have been there long before the human ones," Ta'al responded. "For all we know, the humans invaded our site. They may have removed some items too."

"Well, I think the representatives should be allowed to look at everything before making a decision." Belle was getting tired of this argument.

Ta'al didn't reply. Belle could tell she was annoyed.

"Look at us," Belle said, smiling. She wanted to patch things up with her friend. "Let's not fight. Let's leave the decisions to the grown-ups."

"That is the best idea," Melody agreed.

Ta'al smoothed out her robe, and still said nothing. Belle thought it best to leave her alone and went about feeding the animals. She moved on to the big barn to check on the turken fowl that she was raising for her science project with Lucas.

"Oh!" she exclaimed. "I completely forgot about Lucas!"

The girls ran to the end of the Song farm to a cluster of tall, thick-trunked trees. Melody ambled along slowly. Ta'al lagged behind, and Belle reached the trees first. Lucas was sitting up in the apple tree, munching on a giant fruit.

"It took you long enough to get here," he complained. "I've been waiting for you to show me this cave you found."

Belle looked back toward Ta'al as she ran up to them. She knew Ta'al wouldn't be happy with Lucas' idea.

"Come on, Belle, let's go" Lucas said. He took her hand and playfully tugged her in the direction of the site. As he did so, Belle's heart skipped a beat and her face heated up. She kicked the pebbles at her feet.

"I guess I could show you where I fell," she said, looking toward Ta'al. "That should be okay, right?"

Ta'al shrugged. Melody began to protest, but Belle pleaded with her until she agreed to let them go.

"All right!" Lucas was excited. "You're the best, Belle!"

Belle grinned.

"I will send a message to inform your parents," Melody said. Her eyes turned blue as she began to send the message.

"Please wait, Melody," Belle said. "The representatives won't like it, and I don't want to get my parents in trouble."

Melody seemed to accept that argument. "I will give you a thirty-minute head start. But I must message them before we are out of communications range."

Lucas ran ahead. "The Senns want to come too. I'll just go and get them."

What? Belle felt the heat again, but this time it came from a fire in her stomach. Ta'al pressed her palms to her temples and glared at the ground.

"You'd better not let them inside," she warned Belle.

"I *won't!*" Belle was shocked at hearing the anger in her own voice. She had never yelled at Ta'al before. But then, she'd also never seen Ta'al so angry before either.

CHAPTER 40
DISCOVERING NEW TRUTHS

Lucas, Ava, and the twins met Ta'al, Belle, and Melody just outside the school building. Belle led the way to the site. Ta'al lagged behind everyone else, asking Melody questions along the way.

"How far are we going?" Ava complained every ten minutes. Belle wanted to tell her to go home if she wasn't interested in coming along. But she bit her tongue and tried hard to remember her manners.

The twins shoved each other a lot and told silly jokes all the way to the site. They made everyone laugh, and the journey didn't feel so long. When they finally arrived at the hole that Belle had fallen through, she felt dizzy. Looking down into the darkness, she couldn't believe it had actually happened. It felt as if the entire experience had been a bad dream.

"So, there are these enormous lizards in there," Belle said, trying to distract herself from the dizziness.

"Cool!" the boys exclaimed. They took turns sticking their heads in the gap.

"Eew!" Ava scrunched up her nose. She clung onto Belle's arm. "You were so brave to survive down there, all by yourself."

Belle didn't know what to say. All of a sudden Ava was acting like they were best friends. Belle looked for Ta'al to see what she was thinking. But Ta'al was sitting on a rock in the distance, talking to Melody about something. She didn't even look up at Belle.

"Tell me every detail about what happened to you down there," Ava said. "You are officially my hero. Or heroine, or whatever."

Belle repeated her story once again. Even the twins quieted down and listened with mouths open.

"You have to take us inside the cave," Aiden said when Belle finished her tale.

"Oh yes!" Ava clapped her hands. She grabbed Belle's hand with both of hers. "Please! You must."

Alex joined in with the begging. Belle looked over at Ta'al. Her best friend's eyes, which usually reflected her surroundings, were dark and cloudy. She was angry. Not just upset, but seriously fuming. Belle knew she had to refuse the others.

"Is this it?" Belle heard Lucas' voice calling from a distance. While she had been gathering up the courage to say no to Ava and her brothers, Lucas had run off and found the cave entrance.

He was jumping up and down and pointing at the place where Belle had escaped the cave.

"Wait!" Belle ran up to him. The others followed. "We can't go in. We have to wait for the officials first."

"Oh, come on," Lucas said, with a mischievous grin. "We won't touch anything, and we won't tell."

"Absolutely," Ava said. She put her hands together, as if begging for Belle's permission. "You had such an amazing adventure. You'd want to share that with your good friends, wouldn't you?"

"Yeah!" pleaded the twins. "You have to show us how you braved the cave!"

Belle could feel her face heat up. She wasn't used to getting so much attention. She kind of enjoyed it. She twisted back and forth, looking over at Ta'al and Melody, and then at the others. Ta'al wouldn't look at her. Belle was frustrated. All Ta'al seemed to care about was who owned the relics.

"All right," Belle said. "But only to look. Don't touch anything."

Everyone cheered. Everyone except Ta'al.

Lucas and the twins helped pull away some of the rocks around the cave entrance to make room to crawl through. When Belle had climbed out before, she hadn't realized that the gap was so narrow. She was a little surprised that she had squeezed through it. But at the time she had been desperate to get out.

Now she was eager to get back in. Well, kind of eager. She was still afraid of the lizard creatures, and she felt guilty about making Ta'al angry. But she thought she should at least try to act brave enough to show her new friends her discovery.

"Don't forget," she said, as they climbed inside one at a time, "absolutely no touching *anything*."

Alex and Aiden went first, switching on their wrist lamps. Lucas followed. Ava had brought a headlamp, which she strapped to her forehead. Melody had her own lighting, which had the widest beam. Belle hung on to her android, since she was the only one without her own light.

The last person to enter the cave was Ta'al. Her large eyes allowed her to see well enough in the dim light.

"I only saw it through the drone's camera," she said, without looking at Belle. "I want to see it with my own eyes. The representatives may not let me in later."

Belle smiled secretly to herself. Maybe Ta'al wouldn't be too mad at her anymore.

"Wow!" Lucas exclaimed as he aimed his own headlamp at the large cavern in front of them. "Look at those columns. It looks like a giant's house."

Ta'al climbed over a couple of boulders to look at the wall carvings. She ran her hand over some of the symbols.

"I can almost read these," she said. "They're an ancient form of our language. I'm certain now that this is a Nabian site."

She turned to examine the column that Melody and Belle were looking at.

"See this design?" Ta'al said. "We have this same symbol in our home."

Belle nodded. It did look familiar.

Lucas came over to their side. "Huh, that's weird. We have this design in our home too," he said. "I wonder if this could actually be a Sulux site?"

"No!" Ta'al's voice echoed off the cave walls. It made Belle jump. Lucas took a step back.

"Why are you mad at me?" he said. "I'm just telling you what I know."

Ta'al made a scowling face and walked farther into the cave by herself.

"I've never seen her so upset," Belle whispered to Melody.

"Nabians are very serious about their cultural sites," Melody replied. "They lost a lot in the wars."

"Wars?" Belle was shocked. "I thought Nabians were a peaceful race."

"They are," Melody said. "But even peaceful races get drawn into wars when their home worlds are at stake. The Nabian home world is all but destroyed."

Belle noted to herself that she should find out more when they got home. She wanted to know more about the Nabians' home planet and history.

Ava appeared at Belle's side. She wrapped her arm around Belle's shoulders.

"You have to show me these lizards," she said. "I'm scared of them, but I'll hide behind you." She made a silly giggling sound. It grated on Belle's nerves. But she didn't show it. She was curious about Ava's sudden friendliness.

Belle led the group farther into the cave, to where she last saw the lizard that led her out. She put her finger to her lips.

"Stay very still," she whispered. "They don't like loud noises. It scares them."

They kept as quiet and still as possible for a long minute. Melody dimmed her light too. Nothing happened. Ava started to giggle again. She gripped Belle's arm and spoke directly into her ear.

"I don't see anything," Ava whispered.

"Shh!" Belle put her finger to her lips again.

"For how long?" Ava asked.

"I don't know," Belle said.

"Bet they aren't even real," one of the twins said.

"I think you made them up to make things more interesting," the other one said.

Belle couldn't believe her ears. They were being so rude!

"Nah!" Lucas jumped in. "Belle doesn't make stuff up like that. If she said she saw them, then I believe her."

Belle smiled at Lucas. It seemed silly now that she hadn't liked him much when they first met.

"Look over here!" Ta'al's voice echoed through the cave. She was standing over something.

Belle and the others went to her side. Half buried in the dirt was what looked like a set of wheels. They seemed ancient, and Belle could tell they were definitely from Earth. She had seen hologram images of vehicles with these kinds of wheels.

"And over here," Ta'al said. She sounded excited. It made Belle feel better. At least her friend wasn't angry anymore. "Tracks. They go around the perimeter of the cave. They must have been undisturbed for years. They're perfectly imprinted in the ground."

Belle and Lucas walked alongside the tracks. They made an interesting pattern on the ground — a series of dashes and dots.

"This resembles an old Earth code," Melody said, moving next to them.

"Yes!" Belle recognized it. "It's Morse code!" She'd gone through a phase in the fourth grade when she was crazy about spy stories. She'd studied all kinds of codes and encryptions.

She looked closer at the tread marks. After a minute she could make out a pattern. If she remembered the code correctly, it looked like the pattern spelled out N-A-S-A, just like the object she found near the shaft.

"This was definitely made by a human vehicle," she said.

"Do you realize what this means?" Ta'al's eyes were wide as she stared at the tracks. "It means that humans knew about the Nabian site before they colonized Mars. They knew someone else had been here before them."

"So?" Belle wasn't sure where Ta'al was going with this.

"It means they kept it a secret!" Ta'al was clearly angry again. "They told everyone that there was no life on Mars so they could claim it for themselves. Mars should never have belonged to humans."

"What's that supposed to mean?" Lucas asked.

"Yeah, so . . . what? Do you think humans should just leave Mars and go back to Earth or something?" Alex added.

"I didn't say that," Ta'al responded angrily. "But Nabians were here first. We should have had a chance to build our own colony here."

Belle didn't understand what point her friend was trying to make. Before Mars was terraformed, nothing could live there. Nobody else wanted it, so it became an Earth colony. At the time, the Sulux and Nabians were just visitors to Mars. Why was Ta'al so angry?

Ta'al's words didn't just irritate Belle. The Senns and Lucas were also pretty mad. They started to argue with Ta'al. All kinds of opinions were batted back and forth. Belle couldn't stand it. She grabbed Melody and went off to explore on her own.

She trudged past the large columns and walked into a section of the cave she hadn't seen before. There was a large column that was still intact. It was shaped differently than the others. She walked around it, running her hand over the grooves. On the far side of the stone column was a carving of two large faces. Belle had Melody shine her light on it so she could study it more closely.

The faces were familiar. One had two big eyes and a large, dark mouth. Its nostrils were on its forehead, just like Ta'al and her family. It was definitely Nabian. The other face was clearly Sulux. The two faces were close, almost touching. And they were smiling as if they liked each other.

"Hey, everyone, come over here!" she called. She had to shout at the others two more times before they stopped arguing. "You need to see this!"

When the others made their way over to Belle, Ta'al gaped at the sculpture of the faces.

"Doesn't this show that Nabians and Sulux were friends at one time?" Belle asked.

"Let's look for more of these," Lucas suggested. "It's definitely not what I've been taught."

They spread out and began searching for more carvings of Nabian and Sulux figures. Even Ava became absorbed in their mission. Within minutes, everyone had found something. Carvings in the walls, the ceilings, and the floors showed pictures of Nabians and Sulux working and living together. Ta'al even found a full sculpture of what looked like a family.

"I don't believe this," she gasped. "Two parents are Nabian, but the third is Sulux! I've never heard of such a thing."

They stared in silence at their findings.

"So Nabians and Sulux were once friends," Belle said. "What happened to change that?"

Lucas looked at Ta'al, who looked back at him. They both shrugged. Neither knew how to respond.

"Ta'al and I became friends," Lucas finally said. "Maybe we weren't the first."

Ta'al sighed and let a smile sneak onto her lips.

"I will take holo-vid recordings of everything," Melody said.

"Hello! Is there anyone in there?" Somebody was calling from outside the cave.

The adults had arrived. Belle swallowed. She knew she would be in awful trouble. Even Ta'al and Lucas looked nervous.

"We should go back outside," Belle said, fearing what she might have to face there.

They walked carefully around the carvings and tread marks on the ground. Before they reached the mouth of the cave, one of the twins called out in excitement.

"Hey, Alex. Look what I caught!" he cried.

They shined their lights at Aiden. His hands were cupped together and he was grinning mischievously.

"No way!" Alex said, going to his brother's side. "Where did you find it? I want one!"

Belle stepped a little closer. In Aiden's hands was a baby lizard. It hissed loudly and flicked its tongue nervously at the air.

"Put that baby down, *now*!" Ta'al yelled. "Its mother will come after you!"

Suddenly the cave was filled with loud hissing. The sound echoed off the walls and filled their ears. Ava screamed. Melody flashed her light everywhere, but they couldn't see any lizards.

The hissing just grew louder.

"She's right, Aiden. You should put that baby lizard down," Lucas suggested.

"We should get out of here," Belle said.

But instead of putting the baby down, Aiden took a step toward the cave entrance. As soon as he did, the adult lizards appeared. Hundreds of lizard eyes stared at them from every crack in every stone. Tongues flicked, making a crackling sound that sent chills through Belle.

"Run!" Ta'al cried.

Everyone bolted as fast as they could toward the entrance. The lizards followed. Their tails swished against the floor, adding to the sound of their hissing. Then Belle felt the ground trembling under her feet, as if an earthquake was coming.

She turned to look. All the lizard feet shuffling after the kids were causing the floor to vibrate.

"Put that baby down!" Belle yelled one more time. "Or they'll eat us!"

All the others started to yell at Aiden too. As he reached the cave mouth, he turned around and saw the lizards getting closer. In a few seconds, the kids would be surrounded by every creature in the cave.

Aiden yelped and dropped the baby lizard. It fell to the rocky ground with a slap. Then it scuttled toward the adult lizards and disappeared into a crack in the rock. Instantly, the grown lizards scattered. As suddenly as they had appeared, every one of them vanished into the darkness.

The cave was totally silent, except for the sound of the kids' heavy breathing.

"I can't believe we were almost eaten by giant lizards," Lucas said breathlessly.

One by one, each kid began to giggle as the fear of the lizards began to drain from them. As they emerged into the dim evening light, they were all laughing.

However, Secretary Sukanya, Representative Valere, Ta'al's parents, and Yun were all standing outside with stern faces.

They did not look pleased — not one bit.

Sol 94/Summer, Mars Cycle 106

When the adults stopped yelling at us, we explained what we had found. Melody showed them her holo-vid footage. That shut them all up very quickly. Well, most of them anyway.

Dad was furious that I "put my friends in danger." He insisted that I head straight home with him. I tried to explain that Lucas, Ava, and her brothers had practically forced me to show them the cave. But would he listen? No!

When we parted, Ta'al whispered to me that she was disappointed that I had broken my promise not to disturb the site. I think she was just mad about the lizards. (Even worse, nobody believed us about that. They said the lizards were legendary animals and we'd made them up!)

Dad programmed Melody to keep me grounded in the house for the next two sols. Can you believe that? I can't even go above ground to feed Loki and the turkens! Well, two can play this game. I won't just be grounded in the house. I'm going to stay inside my room until I'm ungrounded. Dad won't see me at all. That'll show him!

Discovering the site and the relics has made everyone behave in such a weird way. I wish I'd never found it.

CHAPTER 41

THE COST
OF FAME

Belle was serious about staying in her room. She absolutely refused to leave her bedroom for two whole sols. She even ate in her room. She made Melody bring in trays and take away the empty ones. She refused to speak to her dad too. But that didn't stop him from coming into her room and lecturing her over and over again. He kept talking about the dangers of wandering off to the barren lands and putting herself and others at risk.

But by the third day, her resolve began to wear down. Boredom crept in, and she couldn't wait until it was a school day. At least then she wouldn't have to stay cooped up in her room like this.

Belle also desperately wanted to find out what was happening with the cave and the relics inside. And she wanted to know how Ta'al was doing, as well as what the shared Sulux and Nabian carvings in the cave meant. Her parents wouldn't tell her a thing. Even worse, Melody wouldn't say anything either.

Finally a school day arrived and Belle was allowed out of the house.

"Melody will walk you to school," Belle's mom told her. "And she'll meet you on the way back too."

"*Mom!*" Belle wailed. "I'm not a child. I need some freedom."

Zara put her arm around Belle's shoulders. "I know you're growing up, Belle, but since moving to Mars, you've managed to get yourself into a lot of scrapes. We really just want you to be safe . . . and to obey the rules." She sighed. "It's not just for your safety. This time you put your friends in danger —"

"But they made me!" Belle cut in. She couldn't bear to hear the same lecture from her mom too.

Her mother quickly raised one finger. "Plus, you made a lot of people, very important people, very angry."

Belle had no reply for that. She'd never seen adults lose their cool the way the two government representatives had that day.

"We don't like keeping you in the house for so long. But how else can we get this message across to you? This is a dangerous planet." Zara shook her head. "I really hope you've learned your lesson this time."

Belle nodded. She felt she had learned her lesson. But she had a feeling this wouldn't be the last time she found herself in trouble. Her natural curiosity was just too strong. And trouble seemed to follow her around like Raider did.

Lucas wasn't there to meet her on the way to school. Neither was Ta'al.

"Perhaps they believed you were still confined to your room," Melody said.

It was a long, lonely walk. When she entered the school building, there were a lot of people outside Principal Yuko's office, including Yun. As soon as Belle's dad saw her, he waved her over. Her stomach made a somersault. Was she in trouble again already?

"Belle, there are some people here who would like to speak to you," Yun said. He introduced her to two human Martians, a Sulux woman, and a third person from an alien race she hadn't seen before. This alien was a small, doll-like person.

Ms. Yuko introduced them, but Belle couldn't follow all their names. "They're journalists," she said, "and they would like to interview you about your discovery."

Ms. Yuko explained that everyone thought it was best to meet at the school, since there was more space there.

"And we don't want to upset your little sister," she added. "You may use a spare classroom." Ms. Yuko spoke with a big grin. She clearly enjoyed the attention that the school was getting.

Yun walked with Belle to room number four. As she passed room number one, she peeked through the open door. Her classmates were standing by the door. They waved as she passed by. Lucas was beaming. Ava looked like she was going to faint from the excitement.

"That's my best friend!" Ava yelled to the journalists.

Belle cringed. She looked for her real best friend. Ta'al stood at the back of the line of classmates. She looked very serious. Belle's heart dropped. Ta'al was still mad at her.

Yun sat by Belle through all the questions. One by one, the journalists came into the room and asked her every detail about her fall into the shaft and what she had seen inside the cave. Belle repeated her story for each journalist. She learned quickly to speak to their holo-cameras and not to look at the faces of the journalists. She sat up so straight that her back was aching by the time she began the third interview.

When there was a break between journalists three and four, she turned to her dad.

"Has anyone been back into the cave since we were there last?" she asked.

Yun nodded. He pulled out his datapad. "Secretary Sukanya agreed to wait for the Nabian representative to arrive before entering the cave. They did find human relics, but what was most interesting was this."

He flicked on his datapad, and showed her footage of the different officials exploring the cave. They stopped at the same carvings that Belle and her friends had seen. The expression on their faces was the same as that on Ta'al's. Disbelief and surprise.

"Your discovery made them realize that before their feuds and wars, the Nabians and Sulux were friends." Yun patted Belle on the head. Normally, she would hate that, but today she didn't mind. "And not just friends. It turns out that they may actually be related! They have a lot to talk about over the coming days and weeks . . . maybe even years."

"That's not surprising," Belle said, thinking about all she'd seen. "It makes sense, actually. Their home worlds are in the same solar system. Like Earth and Mars. They were bound to have some kind of connection."

Yun nodded again. "That's an impressive conclusion," he said. "You really are growing up, aren't you?"

"I've tried to tell you!" Belle rolled her eyes. Then she laughed and gave her dad a hug.

"The only ones who might get into trouble are the humans," Yun said as he waved in the last journalist. "They'll have to explain what they knew before colonization, but it was such a long time ago, we may never know."

The fourth journalist came into the room. Belle prepared to repeat her story for the last time — she hoped.

By the time Belle got back to class, Ms. Polley was finishing up the microbiology lecture. She was about to announce the results of the science fair projects. As Belle walked in, she was met with an unpleasant surprise. Ta'al wasn't sitting in her usual desk next to Belle's. Ava was! Brill was back in his seat next to Lucas, and Ta'al was sitting all alone. What had happened?

Belle tried to catch Ta'al's eye but she wouldn't look at her. Belle sighed. A heaviness filled her chest. She had so much to tell Ta'al, but her friend was still mad at her. She didn't care anymore who won the science fair. She just wanted to talk to her friend.

Ava leaned over. "I asked Ms. Polley to let me sit here," she whispered. "I told her we were best friends, and I insisted on sitting next to you."

Belle couldn't even look at Ava. She had no idea why Ms. Polley would listen to her or why Ava thought they were best friends.

"The journalists will be coming to take pictures of you," Ava said. "Maybe you could ask them to take some photos with me too. Then everyone will know we're best friends."

Belle finally understood what Ava was up to. Ava only cared about being famous. But Belle didn't think fame was all it was made out to be. It was tiring.

Before long the four journalists stepped into the classroom.

"Just act normal," the Sulux journalist said. "Pretend that we're not here."

Belle did her best to follow the journalist's advice. But Ava clearly didn't want to. She giggled and talked really loudly. She raised her hand, even when Ms. Polley hadn't asked a question. Even Lucas and the boys started acting like clowns to get the journalists' attention. Ta'al looked annoyed the entire time.

Sol 96/Summer, Mars Cycle 106

I don't know how, but Ta'al managed to avoid me the entire school day. She disappeared at lunchtime. I searched everywhere for her, but I couldn't find her. It didn't help that Ava was hanging around me the whole time. I almost wish she still had a crush on Lucas. But he told me she stopped liking him when he showed her his bug collection. Apparently, she's more scared of them than I was when I first moved here. He thought it was funny.

To make things worse, no one in our class won the science fair. It went to a high schooler who invented some kind of cloning machine. Ms. Polley said that the turken feed project that Lucas and I worked on received a "special mention" — whatever that means. And there was no mention at all of mine and Ta'al's Petripuff project. I guess they're not interested in defensive weapons.

After school, Ta'al ran ahead of me. I couldn't run and catch up to her, because Melody came to fetch me. She insisted I go straight home. Then I spent the rest of the day helping mom with Thea. I still have to help her, but she can almost sit up on her own!

CHAPTER 42
TRUE FRIENDS

For the next few days, Belle's home felt like a tourist destination. Strange people dropped by to talk about the cave find. Scientists and archaeologists from Tharsis City and Utopia kept stopping at the Songs' farm to share the discoveries they were making at the cave. Some of them even brought small artifacts with them. Yun and Zara were very interested, but Belle was sick of them. She missed her best friend. She would have traded all the artifacts on Mars for a chance to talk to Ta'al again.

One afternoon, Belle finally had enough of strangers visiting her house. Her parents must have pitied her, because they actually allowed her to go back to the ancient site to watch the work being done there. However, Melody was given strict orders not to allow Belle to go inside.

When they arrived at the cave site, Belle was amazed at the number of people there. Large crowds mingled around laser fences that had been put in place by the Protectors. The cave had been sealed off to the public, and only specialists and government officials were allowed in. Scientists went back and forth, some carrying large items. But they mostly carried small items in boxes. The scientists all wore facemasks and gloves. Belle asked Melody why they wore the special equipment.

"They do not want to contaminate any of the artifacts," Melody explained. "Once the pieces arrive at the museum, scientists will study them under controlled lab conditions."

"But wouldn't it be better to just leave them alone?" Belle remembered how upset Ta'al and her family were at the thought of the site being disturbed.

"The Nabian and Sulux authorities have given their permission," Melody said. "Apparently, this is a new phase of cooperation between them, and with humans. You started something wonderful."

"It doesn't feel very wonderful," Belle said.

She stood and watched the activity for a while. When people started to recognize who Belle was, they pointed at her and tried to capture her holo-image. Two women approached her and began asking about how she found the site. That's when she decided it was time to head home.

"I assume you were referring to your friendship with Ta'al earlier," Melody said as she creaked along beside Belle. Her leg joints needed to be lubricated. Belle had fallen behind on her duties in taking care of Melody. "I have been wondering where she is."

"She won't talk to me," Belle said. She kicked at the pebbles on the path. "I tried to call her, but her parents always say she's busy. I don't know what I did wrong."

Melody extended her arm high above their heads as they passed under a tall Martian apple tree. She plucked a fruit and gave it to Belle, who took a big bite. The juice dripped down her chin.

"From what I have learned of human relationships, I think it would work best to go to her house and speak to her in person," Melody said. "To get the story from the 'mouth of the horse!' — I believe that is the expression."

Belle looked sideways at her android and smiled. Both because of Melody's strange saying, and because she knew that the android was right.

"That's a brilliant idea," she said. Then she hesitated. "What if Ta'al says she never wants to see me again?"

"I would think by now you should realize that life is about taking risks," Melody said. "If you do not try, you will not know."

Belle laughed. Her android was so wise. "Let's go!"

By the time they reached Ta'al's house, Belle was very thirsty. The apple had been juicy, but it was also sweet. She longed for a glass of water.

The Nabians' above-ground house was nicer than anyone else's in the area. They had rebuilt it from the ground up. The stone they used to build the house was red, like the rocky hills beyond the terraformed areas of Mars. The roof was flat, and there was an extra section on top that looked something like a space ship. The windows were triangular and made the house look like it had eyes.

Belle walked up to the computer panel by the door and pressed the doorbell button. When the panel lit up, she made sure her face was directly in front of the camera.

"I've come to see Ta'al," she said.

"Ta'al is . . . busy." It was Fa'erz who answered.

"I can wait," Belle said. She was determined to see her friend, even if it meant she had to wait outside all day. "Tell her I'll be sitting on the step, right here, until she can talk to me."

Belle heard Fa'erz say something in their language. Then the panel went dark again.

Belle sat down, and the sun beat down on her. It was a hot summer day on Mars. And Melody had not brought along any water. It was just more bad luck for Belle.

"Perhaps we should come back tomorrow," Melody suggested. "That way, you can get your water, and Ta'al will have more time to consider meeting you."

But Belle refused to budge. "I'll stay here until I die of thirst, if I have to."

"I believe that is an exaggeration," Melody said.

They sat in silence for a long time. Drops of sweat beaded on Belle's forehead. Even Melody started to feel hot to the touch. Then they heard a sound. The door was opening. Belle jumped up and turned to look. Sure enough, Ta'al was at the door.

"What do you want?" she asked. She sounded so sharp that Belle suddenly couldn't remember why she was there.

"I don't understand why you're so angry with me," Belle said after she gathered her thoughts. She walked up the steps to meet her friend. Ta'al stepped onto the porch as the door slid shut behind her.

"From what I can tell, the argument between your people and the Sulux and the Martians is being fixed," Belle said. "So . . . I don't know why you're so upset with me for falling into that shaft."

Ta'al tilted her head and frowned. "Is that what you think? That I'm mad at you for falling into a hole?"

Belle frowned and shrugged. Had she done something even worse to make Ta'al mad at her?

Ta'al crossed her arms over her chest and shook her head. It made Belle feel stupid.

"You'll have to tell me," Belle said. "Because I can't figure it out."

"Why aren't you with Ava today?" Ta'al said.

"Ava? Why would I be with Ava?" Belle asked, staring at Ta'al. She felt even more confused than before.

"Isn't she your new best friend?"

Oh! So that's what this is about, Belle thought to herself. She finally understood.

"You think Ava and I are best friends?" Belle said. "And that's why you're mad at me?"

"Well, the two of you seemed pretty friendly at the cave," Ta'al said. "And then you spent all your time with her at school. You even let her take my desk at class. What happened? Did she leave you for someone new? So now you have no one else to hang out with?"

Belle couldn't believe her ears. "Ta'al, after we were at the cave my parents grounded me. I was in my room alone for days. And since then we've been pestered by non-stop visitors and scientists. I've practically been hiding in my house to keep away from all of them. I haven't seen Ava in days, and . . . I really don't care to."

Ta'al glared at Belle for a long time, as if she was studying her face. "So she's not your best friend?"

"Oh my stars, no!" Belle smacked her forehead. "She's so exhausting to be around. She never stops talking about herself, or how wonderful her life on Earth used to be."

"She does talk a lot about Earth." A hint of a smile played on Ta'al's lips. "She should realize that Mars is her new home now."

"Yeah. Earth is old news."

Ta'al giggled.

"Ta'al, I've missed you," Belle said, blinking fast to hold back the tears. "Can we please be friends again?"

Ta'al nodded and Belle threw herself at her friend. She wrapped her arms around Ta'al and gave her a huge bear hug.

"Gently!" Ta'al gasped. "You'll squeeze me to death."

Belle let go and laughed. Ta'al laughed too. It was the best moment Belle had had in days.

The girls sat on the steps and talked and talked. They caught each other up on what they'd been doing.

"I'm disappointed that we didn't win the science fair," Ta'al said.

"Only a special mention," Belle grumbled. "But I'm still glad we got to do the work. I learned so much about Nabian technology."

"And with Lucas, you learned about turkens too."

"Yes, enough to last a lifetime," Belle chuckled.

"I am glad to see that you two are friends again," Melody said. She'd been so quiet that Belle almost forgot she was there. "I believe what you have experienced is known as a misunderstanding."

Belle and Ta'al agreed.

"It reminds me of a joke," Melody continued. "A Martian asked an official how long it took to fly to Earth. The official went to check the schedule, saying, 'Just a minute . . .' so the Martian said thank you and left."

The girls stared at Melody for several long seconds trying to understand the story.

"Oh, I see!" Ta'al exclaimed. "The Martian thought it only takes a minute to get to Earth. He misunderstood!"

Belle laughed and laughed, until her belly ached. Melody's eyes turned bright pink with pleasure.

"I'm just glad we're friends again," Belle said, drying her tears of laughter.

"Me too," Ta'al said. "It was so boring without you."

Belle got to her feet, and turned to face her friend. She put on a somber face.

"I only have one more serious question to ask you."

"What is it?" Ta'al sounded worried.

Belle took a deep breath. "I have to ask you . . . beg you, really . . . for a glass of water!"

Sol 101/Summer, Mars Cycle 106

Oh the relief! I have my best friend back.
Ta'al and I spent the rest of the day talking
and exploring her family's farm. We dug up bugs,
which I didn't really like. But she enjoys it, so I
tried to like it. I tried some of the Nabian fruit
they grow in their gardens too. It was delicious!

Later, we practiced throwing empty
Petripuffs at posts. My aim is definitely getting
better. I helped Ta'al with her chores, and we
finished our homework too. We were so good that
our parents agreed to let her come over to my
house. We're having a matekap — a sleepover.

Just before we went to bed tonight, Mom
made an announcement. She's decided to have
a special Martian commemoration day for
Thea tomorrow. It's a custom here, where they
celebrate a baby's third month of life. Mom's
invited all the neighbors to come.

Unfortunately, that means Ava will be
coming too.

CHAPTER 43
FRIENDS OLD AND NEW

The next morning, Belle and Ta'al were put to work. They had to clean the Songs' house, and then help Zara make decorations for the party. They cut out tiny stars from old packing boxes, painted them, and strung them together.

"This would be so much easier if we used a 3D printer," Belle complained. Her hands were sore from cutting all the stars.

"I used to do this as a child with my friends," Zara said. "It's nice to use your hands once in a while."

"I'm actually enjoying this," Ta'al said. She was good at saying things that made parents like her. But Belle didn't mind. She was just happy to have Ta'al there.

After finishing the decorations, Belle worked on doing her chores while Ta'al followed, holding Thea in her arms. When they introduced the baby to the turkens, she squealed with delight. In Loki's stall, Thea stared wide-eyed at the giant creature. Belle wasn't sure if her baby sister should be near the huge horsel. But Loki was so gentle that Belle was quite surprised.

"He wasn't that nice to me when we first met," she said.

However, Raider turned out to be Thea's favorite. Belle held Thea up as she rode on the wolf-dog's back. Raider didn't seem to mind. He walked slowly and carefully around the yard, as if he understood that Thea was just a baby. She giggled and made all kinds of funny noises.

People began to arrive for the party exactly at teatime. The Walkers came first. They brought a huge gift-wrapped present for Thea. It had pretty bows on it and colorful hand-drawn designs all over the wrapping.

"It's my own artwork," Myra said proudly. "Even though the paper is the artificial stuff."

"We'll have to be extra careful when we open it then," Zara said. "I want to keep your lovely work."

Lucas volunteered to carry Thea for a while. He was surprisingly good at it.

"Maybe you should have a baby sister too," Belle said jokingly.

"It would be fun to have a sister — or a brother," he replied.

Thea rubbed his face with her tiny hands and laughed. Lucas laughed and didn't seem to mind. Thea did it for a whole ten minutes, until Ta'al's parents arrived.

"You'll be pleased to hear that a new organization has been formed," So'ark told everyone. "Terran, Martian, Sulux, and

Nabian representatives will meet regularly to work through the difficulties we've had in the past. We will 'put it all on the table,' as the Terran expression goes."

"That sounds like a step in the right direction," Yun said. "There are a lot of questions to answer, especially for the human authorities. But I'm hopeful that all the races can leave the past behind and work together for a bright future here on Mars."

"How do you feel about it?" Zara asked Ta'al's parents, serving them a cup of Martian tea.

"Being adversaries with one's neighbors is taxing on the spirit," He'ern said. "I, for one, am open to this change."

Belle frowned and looked to Ta'al. She always had trouble understanding Ta'al's dad. He used such big words.

"He means, it's tiresome to be angry at your neighbors all the time," Ta'al whispered.

"You are so right," Myra said, smiling at Ta'al. "It's time we learned to live together in peace. Our own children have already shown us how."

Lucas came into the room with Thea in his arms. "Look what I taught her to do." He showed the baby his palm, and she met it with hers. "She high-fived me!"

That broke the serious atmosphere in the room. Everyone laughed. Lucas and Thea repeated their trick over and over to everyone's delight.

A few minutes later the main door swished open as the Senn family walked in.

Alex and Aiden came into the house first. They brought a small box with them and showed the contents to Lucas, Belle, and

Ta'al. Lucas and Ta'al were fascinated by their collection of colorful insects. Belle only pretended to be interested in the bugs.

"We found these all around our farm," Aiden said.

"Do you know where all these bugs came from?" Alex added. "Can you believe they were accidentally brought from Earth in grain bags?"

Belle looked at Lucas and laughed. He'd told her the very same thing shortly after they had met.

Ava came in last, behind her parents.

"I don't want to go anywhere near those disgusting creatures," she said. "They're almost as bad as that horrid lizard Aiden caught in the cave."

She waved hello to Belle's and Lucas' parents, but completely ignored Ta'al and her family. Mr. and Mrs. Senn, though, seemed quite happy to talk to everyone.

Ava slipped her arm through Belle's, pulling her away from Ta'al. "Show me around your house, bestie! I want to see everything, especially your room."

Belle looked over at Ta'al, who shrugged. Gently, Belle peeled Ava off of her and looked her straight in the eye. Her heart beat hard against her chest. This could go really badly, but it was time to be brave and stand up for her friend.

"Ava," Belle began quietly. "I'm really glad you've moved here to Sun City, and I like you." She didn't add 'some of the time' like she wanted to. That would've been rude. "But Ta'al is my best friend. If you don't like her, that'll make it hard for all of us to be friends."

Ava frowned and bit her lower lip. She glanced at Ta'al, then Lucas, and finally Belle. Ta'al came closer and offered her hand.

"I don't think we've spoken at all since you arrived," Ta'al said. "We can start again, if you want."

Ava pursed her lips. "It's just that . . . it's really hard to get used to how you look."

"*What?*" Ta'al and Belle said at the same time.

"I mean, your nose is on top of your face!" Ava exclaimed.

"Ava, that's rude!" Alex walked over to Ta'al's side. "You should apologize immediately."

Ta'al shook her head. "At least she's honest."

Belle wasn't so sure this was the right response to Ava's outburst.

Ta'al stepped closer. "Not all Terrans have spent time with aliens, Nabian or otherwise," she said. "And we do take some getting used to."

"I didn't," Belle protested. "I liked you right away."

Ta'al smiled at her. "Be honest," she said. "My appearance did alarm you at first, though you hid it well."

Belle blushed. "Well, maybe just a little. And only for a very short time."

Ta'al turned to Ava. "Can you imagine how we Nabians felt when we first encountered humans? You look as strange to us as we do to you."

The crease between Ava's eyebrows deepened. She was silent for a long while. Then her frown broke into a smile.

"Oh my gosh! You're right!" She spoke so loudly, even the adults turned around to see what was going on. "I just realized it. To you, I'm an alien!" She threw her head back and laughed. Belle thought it was a bit too dramatic.

Ta'al's eyes, which usually reflected the colors of her surroundings, turned a bright blue and pink, the color of Ava's clothes. She burst into laughter too. Together, they were so loud that Belle was stunned for a second.

"It's true," Ta'al said, with tears of laughter in her eyes. "We're all aliens to each other . . . until we become friends."

Belle hugged her best friend. She sounded so wise when she said things like that.

As more guests arrived, Belle and Ta'al helped Melody serve drinks and food.

"Can I help too?" Ava asked. "The boys are racing their bugs, and they make me squirm."

Belle and Ta'al were happy to let Ava join them. They cut up the giant cake that Melody had made, and served each guest a slice.

"Oh, my. Is this cake made from mealworm flour?" Myra Walker asked.

"It is," Melody replied. "I made a small change to your recipe. Is it acceptable?"

"Oh, it's delicious," Myra said. "I didn't know mealworm flour could have such a smooth texture. You must tell me what you did." She followed Melody into the kitchen where the android showed her how to change the recipe.

"Melody is a wonderful addition to your family," Myra said, emerging from the kitchen a few minutes later. "I don't know why we were afraid of her when we first met."

"It just goes to show," Belle whispered to her friends, "that sometimes first impressions can be wrong." She was so glad her neighbors were warming to her android. Melody was her oldest friend and would never hurt anyone.

"All it takes is getting to know someone better," Ava added, glancing at Ta'al. "New friends can bring great rewards."

"Well, I suppose everyone can learn to be more open about new friends," Ta'al said. Then she looked over at Raider, who was munching on a bone in the corner. She walked over to him and scratched him behind his chewed-up ear. "So, I suppose I can at least try to be less afraid of the dog."

Laughter filled the Song house. Even Thea giggled at every new stranger she met that day. Belle couldn't have been happier.

It had taken a whole cycle to get used to life on Mars, but Belle finally felt like this was truly home.

She couldn't wait to discover more adventures on the red planet. It could be dangerous, and she might get into trouble again. But with her android, her dog, and her growing group of friends, she knew she could handle whatever the future had in store.

Sol 102/Summer, Mars Cycle 106

This was the best day ever! The party went on all afternoon. We played games, and Lucas even helped Thea ride on Raider. She really seems to love pretending that our dog is a horse!

In the evening, we went upstairs to watch the stars come out. We brought chairs and picnic blankets and kept our eyes on the heavens. What a show it gave us! We spotted all kinds of constellations.

Then Dad introduced us to an old game that his dad had taught him as a kid. It's called hide-and-seek. I found the best place to hide, under a pile of hay in Loki's stables. No one found me, so I won the game. I think.

Thea surprised everyone by sitting up on the blanket all by herself. She's a fast learner, that one. I bet when she's old enough, we'll be going on adventures together. I wonder if she'll be as good at breaking rules as I am?

MARTIAN WORDS AND TERMS

deng yav (DENG YAHV)—Sulux words meaning "upstairs"

elixian (ee-LICKS-ee-uhn)—Nabian word meaning "equal partner"

gyrvel (guhr-VEL)—Nabian word meaning "welcome"

ivusyxd (ih-VOO-sicksd)—Nabian word meaning "accident"

korDar (kohr-DAHR)—Sulux word meaning "family"

Mars Cycle (MARS SY-kuhl)—the Martian year, equal to 687 Earth days, or 1.9 Earth years

matekap (MAH-teh-kap)—Nabian word meaning "sleepover"

Nabian (NAY-bee-uhn)—an advanced alien race with nose ridges and plastic-like hair; their eye color reflects their surroundings

para-ta-num-peia (PAIR-uh-tah-noom-PAY-uh)—Nabian phrase meaning "no-man's land"

sia-mi (SEE-ah-MEE)—Nabian word meaning "thank you"

Sol (SOHL)—the name for the Martian day

Sulux (SUH-lux)—an alien race with purple skin and arm and neck ridges

Terran (TAIR-uhn)—a person or thing that is originally from Earth

teyqarro (tay-KAR-oh)—Nabian word meaning "me too"

Veth yln (VETH iln)—Sulux saying meaning "That's life."

ABOUT THE AUTHOR

A.L. Collins was born in England and has lived all over the world. She has a law degree from Singapore, Montessori teaching credentials from the United Kingdom and United States, and an MFA in writing for children from Hamline University. She has always loved science fiction. She enjoys creating new worlds, and wondering what the future will be like. While writing *Redworld*, she collected a map and a rotating model of Mars, which helped inspire her stories about Belle Song's adventures on the red planet. When not writing, Collins is out training her four dogs for rally, obedience, and agility events. She also enjoys reading at her home in Seattle, Washington, often reading several books at once.

• • • ● ● ● •

ABOUT THE ILLUSTRATOR

Tomislav Tikulin was born in Zagreb, Croatia. Tikulin has extensive experience creating digital artwork for book covers, posters, DVD jackets, and production illustrations. Tomislav especially enjoys illustrating tales of science fiction, fantasy, and scary stories. His work has also appeared in magazines such as *Fantasy & Science Fiction*, *Asimov's Science Fiction*, *Orson Scott Card's Intergalactic Medicine Show*, and *Analog Science Fiction & Fact*. Tomislav is also proud to say that his artwork has graced the covers of many books including Larry Niven's *The Ringworld Engineers*, Arthur C. Clarke's *Rendezvous With Rama*, and Ray Bradbury's *Dandelion Wine* (50th anniversary edition).

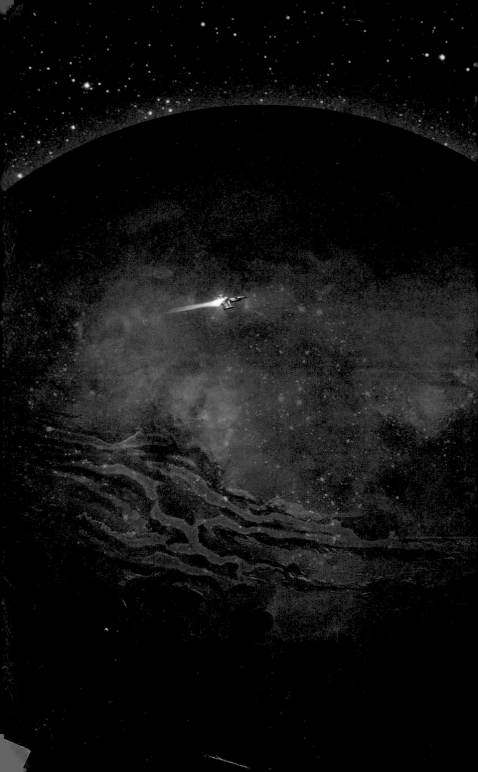